# The Pickup Artist

Terri Benson

Literary Wanderlust | Denver, Colorado

# Dedication

This book is dedicated to all the people who share my love of classic cars, especially those pre-1950 (cars, mostly, but also people). As well as to my husband, Rick, who gave me a classic Triumph Spitfire-in-a-Box for a Christmas present and future build project, and his brother Ed, who has returned several classics to life.

# Prologue

His eyes fixed on her the moment she walked in. Beautiful. Blonde. Perfect. He wedged into an unoccupied corner next to the swinging restroom door to consider whether he should take the risk so close to home. Occasionally the door hit him in the shoulder, and some busybody asked if he wanted to shift over. He shook his head and murmured about waiting for someone. The beer in his hand grew warm and flat, but faking a sip now and then, combined with carefully timed interest in an NCAA game on the silent big screen, sent the circulating waitress away.

Years of avoiding the attention of his father, teachers, jealous jocks, and later, girls who wouldn't take a hint, paid off in the crowded bar, as they always did when he hunted. He was the invisible man in a plain ball cap, tan T-shirt, and baggy jeans. The thick-framed glasses and neatly trimmed beard would be gone tomorrow. *No one suspects me. She's the most perfect one yet. Timing's right. It's karma.* He let out a soft snort of amusement.

His prey started for the exit just after ten. He slithered

through the crowd, careful not to jostle anyone, and slipped out ahead of her. An overgrown juniper gave him a place to loiter, unseen, as he watched and waited. The muscle-bound bouncer helped her with a puffy coat, then leaned over her shoulder and said, "Let me take you away from all this, gorgeous."

The blonde turned and gave him a quick peck on the cheek. "Maybe later, Deano."

The bouncer returned inside, and she walked past, head tipped back as she smiled at the yolk-yellow full moon hovering over the western horizon.

She picked her way over the uneven surface, stilettos clicking on loose stones, and headed around the side of the old building. Tennis shoes silent, he padded across the unpaved lot behind her. She made a beeline toward the shadow of an immense leafless cottonwood tree and a glow-in-the-dark chartreuse car that shone in the dappled moonlight beneath. They were at the back of the building, far from the rowdy patrons on the patio and busy parking lot. Excellent.

She stopped next to the car and fumbled in her purse. He palmed a black plastic electronic from his pocket.

"Excuse me," he said in a soft, unassuming voice. His words came out with puffs of vapor in the frigid air. "I think you dropped this."

Startled, she looked over her shoulder. He held out his leather-gloved hand, revealing a small portion of the phone-sized item. She patted an outside pocket on her purse.

"It's not mine, but thanks for checking."

"Are you sure? I could have sworn it fell as you walked by." He took a step closer.

Keys in hand, she smiled, shook her head, and turned away.

He glanced around to ensure they were still alone and then touched the stun gun to her neck, pressing the red button as he counted to five. Dispassionately, he observed her body jerk and knees give out. She sprawled at his feet, chest heaving with erratic breaths. Wide gray eyes stared up at him, a frozen grimace on glossy scarlet lips.

Experience allowed him to efficiently zip tie her wrists and ankles before picking her up, tossing her over his shoulder, and slipping between a pair of foul-smelling dumpsters to where his truck waited. She was tall, taller than the rest. By the time he tucked her onto the passenger-side floorboards, his breath was coming hard and fast. He shut the door against her back before she could fall and then went around to the driver's side, glancing at his watch.

Plenty of time.

# Chapter One

Renni practically skipped down the concrete apron, Buster bounding along beside her, his tongue lolling. She skidded to a halt and hip-checked her shop manager, Luke, as he climbed down from the tall Dodge D350 dually's cab.

"Took you long enough," she said, mock-frowning.

"Hey, I can't help running into a dust storm out in HellandGone, Utah." He hooked an elbow around her neck and gave her a very un-employee-like nuggie.

Renni ducked under his arm and jumped onto the trailer hitched to the Dodge. "You'd conjure up a sandstorm just to be contrary and you know it."

She surveyed the monstrous hulk chained to the trailer. The old Ford pickup's sixty-plus years of age were betrayed by scrapes, rusted scabs, and a dented grille. Those badges of honor indicated it had led a rough life since starting out as a 1952 chassis, modified to all-wheel drive by the Marmon Herrington Motor Company. In her mind's eye, she already saw it in a deep copper metallic flake with high gloss black trim. Oversized tires. A nice lift. Stake bed in dark oak, or maybe walnut. It would be a sweet ride—one she'd dreamed of building ever since she spied a Marmon with its gigantic grinning mouth of chrome at a track outside Kansas City a decade or more ago.

She edged along the trailer, stepping over chains and boomers that held the pickup in place, grabbing the side mirror to steady herself.

In the split second it took to register the familiar—and dreaded—frisson flashing through her body, she saw women's faces. Faces etched with indescribable agony. Faces she didn't recognize. And one she did.

Then everything faded to black.

The next thing she knew, someone shook her, hard. She opened her eyes.

"Renni!" Luke knelt next to her, his face ashen.

She blinked. Cottonwood fluff swirled around her head. She was on her side on the concrete, her view filled with the underside of the trailer. Propping herself up on her elbows, Renni winced from pulled muscles in her back and neck. *Damn, it's been a long time since that happened.* Long enough to take her completely by surprise, but definitely *not* long enough.

"Don't move. You might have broken something."

Buster lunged to lick Renni's face, and Luke yanked on his collar. "Get back, you stupid dog," he snapped, anxiety revealed by uncharacteristic harshness.

Renni stumbled to her feet and over to the Dodge's fender. She leaned on it, shaking, and took deep breaths. "Give me a minute. And don't yell at Buster. He's sensitive and you'll hurt his feelings." She slid down until she was sitting, her back against the smooth hubcap, legs stretched out. Buster pulled away from Luke and plopped down beside her, chin on her lap, whiskey-colored eyes darting between her and Luke. She pulled the spaniel's ears gently to calm him. "I'll be fine," she said, as much to reassure herself as the dog. And Luke.

"Hell you will! You flew off that trailer like a Hollywood stuntwoman."

She scrubbed fingers through her short spiky hair, ignoring him as she stared over at the Marmon. *What am I supposed to do now?*

"Renni?" He frowned, but then his face cleared. "You felt something, didn't you?"

"Yeah, I think maybe a wrecking ball." She shivered like it was mid-winter instead of a hundred-degree August day and swallowed down bile.

"What was it this time? A crash?"

Renni paused for a moment, deciding how much to tell him. As far as Luke knew, her visions only exposed little tidbits about a vehicle's history. Interesting maybe, but not significant. This was something altogether different. Something frightening. How could she explain something she didn't understand?

"Hell if I know, but it was bad. I saw Lauren's face and a bunch of other women too." The split-second vision of her best friend—her dead best friend—was seared onto the back of her eyelids. She had only to blink to see Lauren's tear-filled gray eyes and model-perfect face creased with lines of pain and terror. The other women wore similar expressions of horror.

"Lauren?" Luke's forehead puckered and he cocked his head.

"They were totally freaked. I mean serious panic. And confused. I think they were all inside that damn truck, but at different times." Renni rubbed at the piercing pain in her temples as she glared at the Marmon, her earlier elation replaced by gut-churning loathing.

"Come on. You need a drink." Luke helped her to her feet and kept one arm around her waist as he guided her up the gravel drive to the front door of Delacroix Restorations, his uneven gait keeping her slightly off-balance. A chime sounded as he pushed inside, alerting Maisie, Renni's office manager, who looked up from her desk. Buster slunk between their feet, nearly tripping them as he ran to Maisie and impatiently nosed at the treat drawer.

"Get me some water, Maze," Luke called as he helped Renni

into her office and sat her on the antique mohair sofa in the corner. Buster, treat sticking out of his mouth like a lollipop, trotted in, hopped up, and plopped down beside her. He burrowed insistently under her arm until she laid her hand on his head. Maisie hurried in and handed Luke a glass of ice water.

"Here, Ren," he said, trying to tip the glass to her lips. He succeeded only in drenching her, and Renni tugged the damp fabric away from her chest.

She regarded him wryly. "Real smooth, nimrod. Please don't try to help me anymore. I'm not sure I'll survive." She took the glass with a still-shaking hand and sipped, then rolled it across her forehead, eyes closed.

Maisie's intent gaze flicked between them. "What the hell's going on? Are you sick?"

Instead of answering, Luke went to the restored Crosley Shelvador refrigerator, opened it, tipped down the freezer door, and removed a bottle of Fireball. He took Renni's glass and dumped the last of the water on a tall Ficus tree in the corner, then filled the glass half full of ice-cold whiskey.

"You know it's a fake tree, right?" Renni grumbled.

"Shut up and drink."

She shot him a dirty look. "You been taking bossy lessons from Maisie? You're worse than she is." But she took a gulp, choking as the cinnamon liquor burned all the way to her stomach. As soon as she quit coughing, she took another, smaller, swallow. "Thanks," she croaked, and sipped slower, giving herself time to think. She struggled to act normal on the outside and hide her shock, remembering other times she'd connected to a car. This was the worst ever. Worse even than when she'd touched the car that killed her parents. She hadn't seen *them,* thankfully, just the kid driving the other vehicle. But this time . . .

Luke rolled the desk chair over and sat down, his knees touching Renni's. Maisie wriggled onto the prickly sofa and attempted to shove Buster over to make room for her oversized behind. He shoved back just as hard with his hind legs. She glared at him, then focused her gaze on Luke and Renni.

"Are you going to tell me what the hell is going on?"

"She got something from the old truck I brought back," Luke said before turning back to Renni. "What was it, Ren?"

Renni shook her head. "Christ, I'm not sure what I saw. Flashes of faces. The only one I recognized was Lauren." The sob she tried to force down came out as a loud hiccup. "Her heart was pounding, and she couldn't breathe. Someone else was in the truck, but I couldn't see them. I felt a . . . a presence. It was cold. Evil."

Understanding washed over Maisie's wrinkled face. She got up and grabbed the Fireball, poured more in Renni's glass, then fetched two Styrofoam cups from the breakroom across the hall. She filled them three-quarters of the way up and passed one to Luke. They sipped, watching Renni.

"So, what do we do about it?" Maisie asked after a few moments of silence.

Luke pulled out his phone. "Siri, call Matt Brody." He stood and limped to the other side of the room, where he spoke too quietly for Renni to hear the conversation. A few minutes later, he hung up and turned back to them.

"Who's Brody?" Renni asked.

"A friend of mine. A cop. We went to the same school here and enlisted together after we graduated." He rubbed his thigh, probably not even realizing he did it. "He moved back and joined the police force a few months ago."

Renni slammed her fists onto her knees, startling Buster into a yelp. "God damn it, Luke! Jesus, you have no idea how people act when they find out about me. Why do you think I keep it quiet? I only told you guys because you've seen me react and I had no choice." She dropped her chin to her chest and ground white-knuckled fists harder into her skin. "It'll be just like before. There'll be a story in the papers about how I'm a wacko who thinks she can talk to cars. Everyone will stare at me when I go to the grocery store. No one will ever bring work to the shop—"

She squeezed her eyes shut hard enough to see stars as she remembered those incredulous stares. Heard again the cruel words that followed her as she grew up, all of it worsening as she got older and understood more, noticed more. Felt again the pain of people she'd considered friends turning their backs when she came into a room. Only in the last few years, after moving to a new state and keeping her visions to herself, had the whispers stopped.

"Brody's cool." Luke punched her shoulder softly. "Besides, I know about you, and I still like you."

She shook her head in resignation, slugged him back a bit harder, and let her lips curve up at his attempt to lighten her mood. Just because experience told her how bad it would be didn't mean she should blame him.

"We can't pretend it didn't happen," he said. "It's *Lauren*."

"I know," she moaned. And that was the problem. If the person who murdered Lauren six months ago, and maybe several other women, had owned that truck, she had to turn it over to the police even if they pegged her as a nutjob. Still, she needed time to prepare, because once she told the cops how she knew the Marmon fit in, it would begin again. The whispers. The sideways glances. The snorts of disbelieving laughter. Not even the growing whiskey-warmth in her belly dulled those memories.

Renni sighed and stood, shoulders drooping, and stepped to the bank of windows overlooking the shop on the level below. Cast-iron peach packing equipment once filled the cavernous two-story space but had been scrapped decades ago. Now the clean, brightly lit work area contained tidy workstations and classic vehicles in various stages of dismantlement or restoration. Shiny red and silver toolboxes, all neatly squared away, shared space with large pieces of equipment like the rotisserie, metal brake, hydraulic press, lifts, and bins of odd-shaped dollies, most of whose use and operation were known only to the select few initiates who devoted their lives to bringing old cars back to life.

She bit her lip. Most likely before the end of the year, those cars would be gone, and she'd be planning an auction to dispose of the equipment. She'd learned no one wanted to do business with a crazy woman. That lesson hadn't come from high school auto class or Penn Tech's Classic Car Restoration Program. Renni had made the mistake of trying to explain what she saw a few times, thinking the other students and teachers would share her interest in the peculiar knowledge. She'd been a slow learner but eventually figured out she'd better keep quiet.

This time she couldn't. Not if it would help find Lauren's killer.

# Chapter Two

Renni paced the office until the door chimed less than ten minutes later. Luke went to the lobby and she watched in the reflective glass as he ushered in a tall raven-haired man. No paunchy, clichéd TV cop, Brody was tall and lean. Instead of a uniform, he wore a black T-shirt stretched tight over a broad chest, and his well-muscled arms were just shy of the awkward ape-like swing of a weightlifter. Worn, low-slung black jeans and work boots made it clear he wasn't a skinny jean, penny loafer kind of guy either.

Luke waved around the room. "Detective Matt Brody, Renni Delacroix, and Maisie Fletcher." He jerked his head toward the attentive spaniel. "And Buster."

"Nice to meet you, Detective Brody," Maisie said politely from the sofa.

Renni turned from the window and eyed the cop. He stared back, expressionless. *Hell of a poker face.* She gave a brief nod. "Detective."

Luke took Renni by the arm and steered her back to the sofa, then addressed Brody. "What we need to talk to you about is going to sound pretty weird. You need to keep an open mind, okay? A seriously open mind." He nodded Brody into the wheeled desk chair and snagged a side chair for himself. Brody sat heavily, studying each of them in turn. Straddling his chair backward, Luke jerked his chin at Renni, encouraging her with a smile. "Tell him."

She took a deep breath and let it out. "I, um, restore old cars."

Brody nodded and swirled his index finger impatiently.

"Well, sometimes, when I get a project in, and I touch it, I see—"

"Dead people?" Brody asked. Sarcasm, viscous as motor oil, dripped from his words.

She screwed her eyes shut, hands fisted. "No," she snapped. Then her shoulders slumped. "Well, not exactly."

Brody stood up so fast the chair careened backward several feet. "I don't have time for this shit, Luke. We've got a lot going on down at the station."

"Yeah, I heard a cat was up a tree. Funny, though, seems like if you're so busy, you wouldn't have been able to drop everything and run over here as soon as I called about a potential killer on the loose." At the annoyed glance the cop gave him, Luke said, "How long have you known me, Bro? Since we were in middle school, right? The only game I ever played with you was football. We're not messing around." He rolled the chair back into place. "Now sit down, shut up, and listen."

Renni choked back a laugh at the shock on Brody's face. Only the fact that he already looked pissed enough to walk out restrained her.

Crossing his arms, he plopped into the chair and leaned back. "All right. So let's get on with this fairy tale."

Even without the scathing words, his body language made it clear he'd already dismissed her. Before she lost her nerve, Renni blurted, "I've had this thing, an ability, since I was a kid. When I touch old cars, I . . . I get a flash of their past." She shrugged. "Usually, it's something simple. Families going on a picnic, guys going to work, women looking in the mirror and putting on lipstick. Stuff like that. Sometimes I get a bad feeling or smell. It's been lots of different things."

Brody opened his mouth, a frown creasing his forehead, but Luke elbowed him and shook his head.

Renni ran the fingers of both hands from the base of her neck up through her hair, leaving the short blonde strands standing on end, then scrubbed her palms down her face. "Sometimes it's a temperature like it's warm and I know the people who owned the car were happy, or it's cold and I know something bad happened, like a crash."

The cop rolled his eyes, lips compressed, and turned down at the corners. It was a look she'd seen too many times before.

"Go on, Ren," Luke urged, flashing Brody a warning glare.

She took another deep breath and closed her eyes. "I bought a truck in Blanding, Utah, from an online auction. Luke drove over early this morning and picked it up. When I touched it, I saw brief visions of women. Something horrible happened to them. My friend . . ." Head tipped against the sofa, she struggled to hold back tears and regain her composure. The thought of Lauren being hurt, being tortured, brought bile to her throat for the second time. "My friend Lauren Cooper was one of them."

Brody's eyes narrowed. "Lauren Cooper?"

"Yeah," Luke said. "Figured you'd remember her. It's not like we have murders in little old Rampart every day."

Brody leaned in, elbows on knees. "Are you trying to tell me you saw Lauren Cooper's murder?"

"I didn't see much. I just felt—" She caught herself before she ruffled her hair again, stuffing her hands under her thighs to keep them still. "It's not something I can explain. But what I got tells me whatever happened to Lauren started in the truck. And what happened to the other women did too." She swallowed hard. "I'll be able to fill in some blanks later."

"Why don't you fill in those blanks right now?" His tone

made it clear he was at the end of his patience.

She bit back a snarky comment, reminding herself he didn't know about her *thing* and sighed. "Because that's not how it works. The truck's story will play out like a movie in my dreams. I won't know more until I get all the awful, gory details in my nightmares and I know whatever it is it wants me to know." Her stomach churned, already anticipating the horrors that would visit her in the deepest, darkest part of the night. Wondering what scars Lauren's experience would leave on her mind.

Sitting quietly until now, Maisie jumped up and took a protective stance in front of Renni. "She's telling you the truth, Detective. Lauren Cooper was her best friend. If you knew Renni, you'd know Lauren's death devastated her."

Brody shook his head, puffed his cheeks, and blew the air out. His gaze slid over each of them, lingering on Renni. "You all better not be screwing with me, because if you are . . ." He glowered at Luke. "Friendship or not, I'll bust you for filing a false report and anything else I can slap on you." His eyes flicked over the two women. "All of you."

Luke opened his mouth, but before he could say anything, Renni stood and stepped around Maisie. "How many other women are dead?"

"What?" Luke and Maisie blurted in tandem.

Frowning, Brody considered Renni for several moments. "What do you know about other women?" he asked.

"I told you. I saw other women." She closed her eyes and concentrated. "Six. No, wait. Seven, including Lauren."

The poker face returned. "Can you describe them?"

Weary, she shook her head. "Not now. I'll sit down later and write out everything I can remember. But not now. I can't."

"I think you should come to the station and go over some photos now, while it's fresh."

Luke put his arm around Renni's shoulder. "Later, okay?"

Renni shrugged him off with a sad smile and squared her shoulders. "It's all right. Let's just go." She grabbed her ratty leather backpack from the floor by her desk and led the way down to the shop floor. They passed two nearly identical unrestored '38 Packard Eight Series 902 Coupes, a gleaming resto-mod, and a beat-up WWII motorcycle, before stepping through the man door next to the overheads. Outside, the concrete apron led to a gravel driveway that swung up a broad curve to the lobby and street level. Luke followed Renni into the broiling heat, as she headed for a vintage, cherry-red Triumph Spitfire.

Maisie halted outside the door and hollered, "I'll keep Buster here until you get back. Call me and let me know what's happening." She held her fist to her ear, thumb, and pinky finger extended.

The Spitz's top was lowered, and the red and tan leather radiated heat like lava. Renni unfolded a towel on the driver's seat and eased down, feeling the burn through her jeans. She gave Luke a sympathetic shrug. "I only have one."

He slid into the bucket seat but immediately levered himself up with his arm on the edge of the door. "Holy shit, that's hot," he exclaimed, before gingerly settling back down.

Renni bit back a grin as she turned the key and the convertible started with a throaty roar. She wheeled it around the trailered Marmon and Dodge. The car's steering wheel was as hot as the seats, and she drove with fingertips fluttering like Mozart's on the piano as she accelerated past Brody in his black and white Explorer. Luke waved as they sped up to the main road.

# Chapter Three

At the station, Brody used his key card to get them past the lobby, taking them down a series of hallways before showing them into a small conference room.

"Have a seat," he said brusquely. "I'll be right back." He left, shutting the door behind him.

Renni bit her lip, glancing at the table to make sure there weren't any metal brackets he could handcuff her to. She thought about trying the door handle to see if they were locked in, but Luke seemed oblivious to any such concern, relaxing back in a plastic chair. She pulled out the chair next to him and sat. Her knee bounced, and she sat on her hands again to keep from running her fingers through her tangled mop of hair.

The cop returned shortly with a thick folder. He sat across the table from them, opening the file and taking out a couple dozen 8x10 color photos, all blondes of a similar age. He laid them in two rows down the table. "I'd like you to check if any of the women you . . . saw . . . are here."

Renni couldn't decide if the pause indicated Brody thought the whole thing was a waste of time or if he was struggling to accept what she'd told him. It didn't matter—nothing but finding Lauren's killer mattered.

She stood to view the photos clearly and forced herself to scrutinize each one. They were obviously morgue shots. Eyes closed, hair matted and wet-looking. Some had swelling on their pale blue-gray waxy faces, but not so much she couldn't recognize the ones she'd seen in her vision. One by one, she selected four photos and placed them in their own row. "These and . . ."

Her hand shook as it hovered over the last photograph.

Lauren.

The ghostly face wasn't the same laughing, vibrant woman Renni met the first day she arrived in Rampart. Nor the joke-telling, world-traveling professional photographer. Or the mischievous prankster who got Luke's wife, Vicki, drunk enough at her bachelorette party to get a tattoo of Rat Fink, Luke's favorite cartoon figure, on her butt. Tears dripped onto the glossy surface as Renni picked up the photo and laid the image of her dead friend next to the others.

She raised her eyes to Brody's face and for the first time saw something less business-like in his expression. It could have been pity, or maybe understanding. The room was silent except for the creak of leather as he shifted in his seat to get a better view of the five photos she'd selected. Brody stood and brushed his hand over the others, gathering them up and taking an inordinate amount of time tapping them into a neat pile. He put them back in the file. When he turned to her again, whatever expression she'd glimpsed earlier was replaced by something resembling indecision.

"What now?" she asked.

"I need you to wait a few more minutes." He started out of the room, then paused and contemplated the two of them. "Would you like some coffee or a soft drink?" His tone was courteous, almost friendly. At their negative responses, he hurried down the hall and out of sight, this time leaving the door ajar.

While they waited, Luke played Angry Birds on his phone and Renni checked her business emails. There weren't any personal ones—there rarely were, unless Uncle Oscar or Cousin Bubber thought to check in between racetracks. Once she'd responded to the important messages, she sat staring at the screen for several minutes. Then she opened a new email, addressed to Lauren. She described how lonely she was now that Lauren wasn't around to goad her into getting out and meeting people. Recalled every blind date, and how they'd laugh together over the post-date blow-by-blow. Reminisced about their Full Moon Fridays, girls' spa days with Vicki, trips to the Glenwood Hot Springs. Promised Lauren she'd find her killer.

Then dug through her pack for a Kleenex.

Luke glanced over at her. "You okay?"

"Yeah. Allergies."

After years of hiding her emotions, self-preservation made it easy to pretend everything was okay—even though of anyone in Rampart, Luke would understand. Everyone who knew Lauren missed her. The local girl who'd made it big as a world-famous photographer but stayed close to her friends. True to her roots. She was Luke's cousin, and his wife, Vicki, was Lauren's oldest friend. But Renni and Lauren had a unique kinship, a friendship that few ever found. And someone had destroyed it. Deliberately. Horribly.

Renni stared at what she'd typed on the screen, wishing more than anything she could hit send and know Lauren would receive the email. Instead, she sent it to herself.

She'd keep it until she fulfilled her promise.

Almost an hour passed before Brody came back, and by then Renni had a throbbing headache. He paused in the doorway, peering up and down the hall, then came in and shut the door.

"I'm going so far out on a limb here . . ." He shook his head. "If you two are shittin' me, I'll be out of a job. But I guarantee you'll both find out what the inside of a cell looks like before then. If this is a stupid joke, tell me now. If it comes out later, it'll be way too late for all of us." He stared hard at both of them in turn.

"Detective Brody," Renni said, "I've never personally seen or met any of the women in my vision except Lauren. She was my best friend. If I could tell you what happened to her, I would." She cocked her head. "You know more about this than you're telling us. You *knew* other women were killed like Lauren."

Instead of elaborating, he asked, "How do you explain choosing those specific photographs?"

"I can't explain it. Those are the faces I saw. Are they all victims?"

He didn't answer.

Renni persisted. "Two of the women in my visions weren't in your photos. Why?" Her eyes slitted. "It was a test, wasn't it?" She stood up, shaking her head in disgust at his transparent attempt to discredit her. "Unless you decide to charge me with something, like trying to help the police, I'm leaving now. I've got the mother of all headaches."

Luke stood beside her.

Brody rubbed his hand over his mouth and chin. "There's one more thing. I need permission to have the crime scene techs inspect the truck somewhere clean and private. I can't go through the normal channels. Not yet. If I tried to get a search warrant, the chief would ask me where I got my info, and there's no way I'm telling him some chick . . ." He had the grace to look embarrassed. " . . . I mean citizen . . . has visions. Not only will I probably get fired, but you and I would be the laughingstock of Rampart by morning."

A cross between a growl and a moan erupted from Renni's throat. *And so it begins.*

Luke grabbed her by the shoulder and looked her in the eye. "Not going to happen." He turned to Brody. "We want to find out what happened, and this is the best shot we've got. You can put the truck in the shop."

"Did either of you touch it?"

Luke shook his head. "The auction crew drove it onto the trailer, then I boomered it and towed it home. I have no idea who messed with it before then."

"I touched the driver's side mirror, but that's it," Renni said.

"Good. Leave it alone until I arrive. I'll get a couple techs to meet us there when they get off shift. Make sure your shop floor is really clean. And cover the other stuff in there with drop cloths or something." Brody fished a folded piece of paper from his pocket. "I need you to sign this authorization so I can search the truck. If we find anything, I'll need it to keep me from getting fired."

Biting her tongue to keep from informing him her shop was always clean, Renni pulled a pen out of her pack and signed where he indicated. "Of course, Detective Brody. We all realize your job is far more important than my business."

His face flushed, either from embarrassment or annoyance, but she was past caring.

"And now, if it's not too much to ask, I'll get back to what's left of my business." Head pounding, Renni grabbed her backpack and headed for the door, pushing through before Brody could open it.

"I'll be right there, Ren," Luke called after her.

She paused, struck by the sudden fear that Luke might be having second thoughts about believing her. The idea was like being hit in the chest by a medicine ball. She held her breath and pressed against the wall as she eavesdropped.

"She's the real deal, Bro. It's happened more than a few times. Nothing like a murder or anything, but she knows shit we've been able to confirm later. Weird stuff about the people who owned the cars, fifty, sixty years ago. Clear across the country. She's not faking."

"I'm bringing out crime scene people, Luke. We'll know something pretty damn quick. After that, we'll see."

She saw the door start to move and hurried down the hall.

# Chapter Four

Brody went back to his desk after Luke left, then put in a call to two of the forensics crew who would trust his judgment, or at least withhold their own. After swearing them to silence until they either found something or didn't, he asked them to meet him at Delacroix Restorations after shift change.

With a few keystrokes, he pulled up Lauren Cooper's case file, reading through it to refresh his memory. The Federal Bureau of Investigation had designated the unsub as the Rocky Mountain High Killer, or RMHK. The killer had been active for more than ten years, based on a distinctive MO of death by suffocation and shallow burial in highly visible areas along a section of Interstate 70 in western Colorado. When Brody finished reading, he made a note of the FBI case number referenced in the Cooper file.

There were seven victims on record, and Renni said she'd seen seven but only picked out five photos. *Why couldn't she pick out all seven?* He twirled a pen between his fingers like a baton, then suddenly sat up straight. *Unless she knew about two they didn't, and they knew about two she didn't?* The possibility of more victims caused acid to roil in his stomach. It occurred to him that the reason Renni might not have intel on all the murders was because some of them weren't related to the truck. But that supposed she *did* have a psychic ability.

*Yeah, right.* Either she knew more than she let on or she'd turn out to be a grandstander, he'd bet his badge on it, no matter what Luke said.

"Hey, Bro, you want more coffee before I turn it off and wash up?" Detective Westphall asked from right behind Brody, startling him.

He looked around and realized the other officers were shutting down their computers. He'd spent a lot more time perusing the file than planned and would be hard-pressed to beat Crime Scene Investigators Olivia "Liv" Rivera and Pete Patterson to the truck.

—

At the crunch of gravel outside the shop, Renni opened the man door and peered out to the parking apron. Brody wheeled his black and white into the parking area, followed closely by a Kia Soul, and climbed out. He waited until a man and a woman from the other car joined him, then all three walked toward her.

Nodding a hello, Brody said, "This is Olivia Rivera and Pete Patterson. They're the CSIs who will be going over the truck." He gazed at the big Marmon and then back to Renni, looking her up and down. His droll expression made it clear he couldn't envision her being able to climb into the massive pickup, let alone being able to see over the hood. "Keys?" he asked, holding out his hand.

Renni silently dug into her pocket and pulled out a replica Dodge Brothers silver radiator badge keychain. As she handed it over, Luke sauntered up beside her and hit a big green button on the wall inside the shop, running the overhead door up.

Brody took the keys and eyed the open space inside the shop, then turned to the CSIs. "We'll put the truck inside. There's plenty of room and it's supposed to be clean. Pete, you have groundsheets?"

"Yep," Pete said. "Liv, why don't you go ahead and suit up. I'll set up, then Brody can guide you to back the trailer in."

Renni watched with narrow eyes as Pete hefted a large duffel into the shop. He pulled out bundles of white fabric, which he laid out on the floor she knew was clean enough to eat off of. Outside, the female CSI—clad in a white, full body suit with booties, gloves, and a snug-fitting hood—climbed into the pickup and backed it slowly into the shop.

Still pissed that they'd wasted most of the day cleaning, as per Brody's orders, Renni spun and stomped up the stairs. Luke joined her on the landing. They watched from their vantage point as the trailer was unhitched, leaving it and the Marmon centered on the sheets. Pete came back in, wearing the same kind of protective suit as his partner and lugging two heavy cases. The CSIs donned safety glasses, opened the cases, and began setting out plastic envelopes, small bottles, and other paraphernalia.

Brody strode over to the bottom of the steps and looked up, waving impatiently. Luke took one look at Renni's stiff jaw and thin lips and hurried down. He and Brody huddled in conversation. Suddenly the cop looked up, and Renni's face flushed at being caught glaring. She whirled and headed to her office. Plopping into her desk chair, she swiveled side to side, musing about the mess the Marmon had created.

Going to the police was the only way to find Lauren's killer, but—damn it—she'd put so much work into her shop! Years of school, constantly dealing with sexist teachers. Being the butt of all kinds of pranks, some not so innocent, perpetrated by the male students. Having to work twice as hard to convince potential clients she could compete in the male-dominated industry.

And she wasn't the only one who would suffer if her "gift" became known and her business went down the tubes as a result. Both Luke and Maisie would be out of a job as well.

Maisie, a widow, needed the income, and with no other high-end restoration shops within a two-hundred-fifty-mile radius, Luke would have to take a job at some crappy body shop doing insurance work. Or he'd have to move to Denver or Salt Lake to find a comparable-paying job. He'd be forced to sell the house he and Vicki spent so much time and effort on and uproot Vicki from her established job as a speech therapist.

A few minutes later, Luke came in and went straight to the Crosley. He pulled out a pair of Apricot Blonde ales and popped the caps, then walked over and leaned his hip on her desk. Setting one of the bottles down beside her, he took a slug off the other.

"Brody asked if you planned to leave town any time soon."

Renni froze in the process of reaching for the beer and closed her eyes, teeth clenched.

Luke continued in a conversational tone like he was explaining the weather. "I told him you thought about going to that show in Santa Fe next week but decided to stick around instead, and you didn't have anything else coming up."

Renni leaned back and gave him her best Boss Stare. He grinned at her, unrepentant. Okay, so maybe not her *best* Boss Stare.

"Since when are you my social secretary? Maybe I do have plans for a trip somewhere this weekend."

"You do?" His voice held more than a hint of surprise.

"Damn it, that's not the point." It chapped her butt, and totally trashed her superior attitude, that he was so sure she would be around. It chapped even more that she *would* be. As usual. With the hours she put in, a real life was hard to come by. Lauren was once the master of making her take the time, but it had seemed like too much effort the last six months.

Curiosity got the better of her, and she jerked her chin toward the window. "What's going on down there?"

"They're doing our job for us. Took out the seat first thing, and they've probably got the whole interior stripped by now."

When she sat up straight and grabbed the arms of her chair, he said, "Don't worry, they're being real careful, probably more than I would be. Brody said they'd disassemble the door panels and take the flooring up. It's so cool. Like that TV show *CSI*. You know, checking everywhere something might fall into."

Renni stretched and rolled her neck, then grabbed the beer. Resigned, she leaned back and took a long drink. She put her feet up on the corner of the desk and cradled the beer on crossed palms in her lap. "Why don't you go home?" She squinted at him. "Isn't this date night? Vicki'll be pissed."

A mischievous grin split his face. "Naw, she already called. Her sister, Leslie, is in town and they're going to a movie. Leslie doesn't much care for me. I can't understand it. I mean, I'm a great guy, right?"

Renni laughed. "Well, you are a guy. And you have a great amount of conceit, so you covered a couple of the bases, anyway."

"Harsh, Ren. Real harsh." He hauled one of the client chairs over to the window and positioned it to peer down into the shop, then returned, knocked her feet off the desk, and pushed the chair, and Renni, over. He sat beside her, shoved open the window, and rested his forearms on the sill. "I ordered pizza. Cheaper than the movies and could be pretty damn interesting, right?"

She took another slug of beer. "Leave it to you to make this mess into entertainment."

The door chimed.

"Stay put," Luke said and limped out to get the pizza. Renni wondered how much his leg bothered him and if it would get any better. It was nearly three years now since he came back from the hospital in Landstuhl, Germany. She made a mental note to ask Vicki the next time she saw her. The old peach packing plant made a great shop, but having to traverse the steep flight of steps multiple times a day must be painfully hard on his war injury.

Luke brought in slices of pizza on paper plates, along with

paper towels for napkins. Renni fetched another round of beers, and they munched on Red Hot Tomato's thick crust pizza with bacon, chicken, capers, and white sauce as they watched the two white-suited techs crawl over the pickup twenty feet below. Brody stood off to the side with a tablet computer.

By 9 p.m. the novelty wore off, and Renni convinced Luke to go home. "I'll stay until they leave and lock up. See you in the morning." She hugged him, ducking under his intended nuggie, and sent him on his way.

For a while, she tried to focus on billing paperwork. After adding a stack of invoices three times and getting three different answers, she gave up and wandered back to the window. The two techs and Brody were deep in an animated conversation over a pile of bags and envelopes. It ended with Brody nodding and heading toward the stairs.

*I don't like the looks of this.* She started for the lobby. Buster, who'd spent most of the evening snoozing on the sofa, trailed after her. She stepped out onto the upper landing.

"Well?" she asked.

Brody stopped two treads below her, which put them at eye level, and pursed his lips, arms crossed over his broad chest. "Your shop is now a crime scene. There'll be a black and white here shortly to make sure no one disturbs the evidence."

"Wait . . . What? You're telling me I can't work in my own damn shop?"

He ignored her dismay and said coolly, "We should be able to move the truck tomorrow. Once it's gone, we'll take down the tape. But I'm going to need you to come back into the station."

"Why? What'd you find?" She peered down into the shop. The techs were reeling out crime scene tape and tying it to anything handy, from the base of the staircase to the doors and pretty much everywhere else.

"You're absolutely sure you never got in the truck?"

Renni frowned. "Yes. I told you, I just touched it. Luke was there. Ask him." She put her hands on her hips, her jaw tight.

"Unless, of course, you think he'd lie to you."

He stared at her, his expression blank. "We're not interested in Luke right now. Plan on being asked for a whole lot more details on the truck. And not just by me. My boss, the CBI, and probably the FBI will want to talk to you too."

"I told you everything, Detective." She ran her fingers through her disheveled hair. "Jesus, I should have sent the damn truck to the crusher," she mumbled, though she knew in her heart if it provided the answers to Lauren's death, it would be worth it. No matter how bad *it* turned out to be.

Without another word, she whirled and went to her office, grabbing her bag. He watched from the stairs as she stomped out the lobby door, locked up, and headed for her car, Buster at her heels.

# Chapter Five

Even at 10 p.m., the night air was sweltering, especially when added to the hot fury that overcame Renni every time she thought of the cop's dictatorial, dismissive attitude. It didn't matter to him that being locked out of her shop could mean missed deadlines. Critical ones. Or that badgering her about answers she didn't have couldn't magically make those answers appear. She chewed her lip. Besides, he didn't believe anything she told him—he'd made that abundantly clear, both by his words and by his attitude.

"He better not go after Luke," she muttered, feeling a pang of concern the cop might, friendship or not.

Renni fumed as she turned onto Red Haven Street, her short hair fluttering in the wind. The Spitz growled its way through the small town of Rampart, which, after 8 p.m. on a weeknight, was pretty much shut down. After a few minutes, aromas from the fields and orchards invisible in the dark began to penetrate her anger. The scent of ripening peaches, muddy ditch banks and warm mulch wafted over her. Her white-knuckled grip on the wheel relaxed. Buster stood with his front paws on the armrest and snuffled, ears flapping in the breeze, which further calmed her ire.

After crossing the river, she down-shifted and took the switchbacks up to the mesa where her old farmhouse squatted, surrounded by the remnants of an ancient orchard. As she gained elevation, the fragrances of sagebrush and alfalfa in bloom joined the earthy odor of orchards and vineyards.

She tucked the Spitz in the garage next to her snub-nosed Divco van and matching teardrop travel trailer. With Buster scampering along beside her, she trudged through the unlocked front door. Her purse landed with a plunk on the old highboy, and she heaved an exhausted sigh as she headed to the kitchen. Grabbing a pint canning jar off a shelf, she filled it with ice and added gin, tonic, and a chunk of lime. Drink in hand, she stepped out the back door to be greeted with the sound of crickets chirping from under every rock and hidden place, and frogs croaking and screaming mating calls along the ditch bank. The sounds were familiar, soothing. Tension seeped from her shoulders.

Even though it was still at least eighty degrees, she went to the iron fire ring and tossed in kindling and pieces of split cedar, managing to light the fire with one match. Once the small blaze crackled and snapped satisfactorily, she plopped down in an old wicker rocker positioned well back from the heat. The fire cast dancing shadows in the dark, allowing memories she'd suppressed these past six months to blossom behind her closed eyelids—petal by petal, like a rose unfurling.

Lauren arriving in a plume of dust at Hollister's fruit stand, grinning from the window of a neon-bright chartreuse '68 Nova Luke had restored for her, Buster's chocolate-brown head poking out over her shoulder.

That last Full Moon Friday at Rampart Brewery. Dancing with dozens of friends and laughing at Lauren's stories about the ridiculously expensive wedding she'd photographed for an Indian maharaja and his bride, who had been so heavily laden with gold jewelry she collapsed on her way to the altar.

Seeing a TV headline about a body discovered in a shallow grave near the Kokopelli bike trail. That same soul-crushing headline plastered on every newscast and in Rampart's weekly newspaper, announcing the body was Lauren's.

Listening over and over to hyped-up rehashes of the few details released by the police. Speculation on whether it might have been a romance gone south, or a robbery, or a random act of violence. Ad nauseam.

Smelling freshly mown grass from the yard across the street the day she'd gone to Lauren's silent, empty house to box up her things to send to her folks. A scent Renni now hated.

Standing on the sidewalk and staring at the pretty little gingerbread-bedecked cottage she'd helped paint in a color scheme ranging from the palest aqua to deep teal.

Her discovery of a half-starved Buster, restlessly pacing around the house, searching for Lauren. Renni had taken him home, and the two slowly helped each other overcome their loneliness, day by day until they began to function normally again.

Tears dripped off her cheeks and fell into her lap as the fire burned down to flickering orange coals. Buster lay next to her chair, his chin on her foot, awake but silent, as if sharing her sadness. She took out her phone again and sent a text, one she knew would never be delivered.

*We all miss you.*

# Chapter Six

He watched her across the room. She sat in profile, the reading lamp that shone on the back of her white-blonde head making a halo. A perfect angel.

Sensing his attention, she turned her head slightly toward him. Enough for him to see the way her lip thickened and twisted on the other side of her face.

"Wassrong?" she asked in the lisping voice that grated on his nerves. It was all he could do not to turn away from what she'd become. What dear old Pop made her into.

"Nothing, K-1." The pet name never failed to turn the undamaged side of Karen's mouth up in a smile, ever since the two of them received Dr. Seuss's *The Cat in the Hat* on their fifth birthday. Back when they'd been inseparable and almost impossible to tell apart. Before Pop brought the jar home.

His gaze flicked to the two photographs on the wall behind her. One of Karen, full face. Smiling. Beautiful. She wore her cheerleader uniform—short skirt, bare midriff. One leg was kicked up so high her foot was even with her head. All the guys wanted to date her back then like all the girls wanted to date him.

As if he was interested in their vapid conversation or considered them pretty with their masses of makeup and silly hairstyles. He turned to the other photo, of him kneeling in his football jersey and pads, helmet on knee. Not only was he damn good-looking, he was way more of an athlete than anyone else on the team. Even the coach and those stupid jocks who were all muscle and no brains knew as much, though they'd never have admitted it.

Their photos showed that he and Karen shared the same smile. The same perfect features and blond hair.

Ma had gotten the photos taken and then framed, proudly hanging them side by side. But when Pop found out how much she'd spent, he was furious. Said anything to do with sports was a waste of time; the only thing worth celebrating was hard work. Work that meant something and showed how smart you were, not standing around letting everyone stare at your body, or throwing a ball to other stupid, ignorant kids.

Pop told Ma to throw the pictures away, but Karen hid them in the laundry room behind some boxes. After Pop died, she'd dug them out and put them back where they belonged, back where everyone could see how perfect they were.

His jaw flexed as he silently gritted his teeth. How perfect she *was*.

# Chapter Seven

After ensuring Liv and Pete logged in the evidence, Brody went to his office and reread the files. All seven of them. Wondered again what Renni Delacroix knew and how she'd learned it. Luke was his best friend, but clearly he'd been taken in by the petite blonde. Unless she'd seen something that night that she wasn't telling, there was no way she could know the Cooper woman or any of the others were in the truck. He tapped his lips with the end of a pen and amended his thoughts. Someone in Rampart's police department or the Colorado Bureau of Investigation could have leaked the details, giving her inside information. *Hell, it could have been the FBI.*

Was her intent to get publicity for her company or something else? Odd she only picked out five. But maybe she planned on making a public reveal of the other two, waiting for the right time, right place.

Brody forced himself to keep reading. Delacroix was interviewed in the first days after Lauren Cooper's murder, along with more than a hundred others, but not by him. He'd joined Rampart's force a couple months later after the investigation stuttered to a halt from lack of evidence.

The interviewing detective's report noted she didn't have an alibi. She'd left the brewery by herself near the time the coroner estimated Cooper died. But all the other interviewees were solid in their opinion that the two women were best friends. Investigators hadn't uncovered any motive for Delacroix to want Cooper dead, and as her murder was clearly linked to the other RMHK cases, the Fibbies had also traced Delacroix's history for other RMHK kills. They found solid alibis for a couple, including being in a classroom several states away with ten other students and a professor when one abduction occurred.

Besides, there was the difference in size. Cooper was nearly six feet tall and in excellent physical condition, according to the report, regularly taking spin and aerobic classes. Delacroix was five foot four at best and might have weighed a hundred ten soaking wet. Not likely she could've overpowered the other woman, even though she *was* in good shape. He grinned. *Had* a damn good shape. He shook his head to purge it of images of the petite woman in her snug jeans and tight-fitting T-shirt. That kind of thinking would only lead to trouble.

The file summarized their exclusion of Delacroix as a suspect by stating that, while she could have approached Cooper outside the distillery, Delacroix wouldn't have been able to force the larger woman to do anything against her will. Brody remembered watching Luke, at about five foot nine, fold himself into the Spitz's bucket seat. It was pretty hard to envision someone of Delacroix's size forcing the much taller and heavier woman into the car, and the minuscule trunk wouldn't even hold Delacroix's dog.

He gave an involuntary snort when he thought how well-matched a Spitfire was to Delacroix's fiery temperament. If she were a redhead like Luke, instead of a cropped blonde, it would be even more perfect. To be fair, what she was going through with her shop being locked up probably didn't help her attitude. And it was likely to get a whole lot worse.

Brody sighed and leaned back in his chair. He kinked his neck left and right, getting a tension-relieving pop each way. A glance at his watch told him it was nearly midnight. Time to go home. Tomorrow would be a bitch.

—

Too keyed up to sleep, Brody climbed into his hot tub an hour later with a tumbler of Dickels. He leaned his head against the cushion and let the hot water soak away tension gripping his neck and shoulders. Tired of having bubbles bursting in his face, he turned off the jets and savored the instant peace and quiet after a long, busy day. A full moon lit the lawn, but the yard's perimeter was deep in shadow from towering cottonwoods at the corners. He closed his eyes.

His mind immediately conjured the image of angry green ones glaring back at him. Renni Delacroix was as pissed as he'd ever seen a woman when she stalked out of her shop earlier that evening.

By the end of tomorrow, she would probably break that record at least once.

Luke had done his best to convince Brody she was the real deal. That she really could "read" a car's memory. But it didn't matter if he believed it or not, Chief Wilcox wouldn't, let alone the FBI guys. No way. Before the investigation finished, Delacroix's entire life would be under a microscope. Every detail stripped bare, going back to day one if necessary.

Brody was good at reading people, the precinct's go-to guy for interviews. Not only because he generated trust with suspects, but because rarely could someone pull off a lie without him ferreting out their tells. Little Miss Delacroix could bluff with the best of them. *If* she was bluffing. He shook his head at the thought Luke would—could—deliberately lie to him. They'd known each other since they were kids. Played football together, Luke's receiver to Brody's quarterback, in high school and college, until they enlisted and went off to serve multiple tours in the Middle East. Brody would trust him with his life. *Had* trusted him with his life, and Luke had the scars to show for it. But the car thing . . . it was just too damn crazy.

# Chapter Eight

Country music from scratchy, blown speakers echoed next to her ear, and cold metal bit into her back. She was crammed in a tight space, her knees right in front of her face. Her mouth wouldn't open. She couldn't scream. Couldn't ask what was happening. Couldn't ask *why*. Wheezing breaths sucked in and blew out through her nose like a whistling tea kettle. Her shoulders burned from her arms stretched behind her back, immovable from elbows to wrists. Her calves alternated between complete numbness and excruciating needles of pain. Low wavering moans reverberated in her head.

—

Buster's frantic barking brought her to full awareness. Renni realized her own moans echoed from the nightmare. She struggled to sit up.

Her body was slick with sweat, and damp sheets tangled around her like a boa constrictor. She shoved the linens away and wriggled out of bed, stripping off a "Lord, give me strength. Or wine. Either is fine." T-shirt and lacy underwear and stumbling to an enormous clawfoot tub. Hundred-year-old exposed piping ran up the wall, branching off to the faucet and handles, and continuing up to a broad rainfall showerhead, considerably newer than the rest of the bathroom fixtures.

*Please, please let that be the end of this,* Renni prayed as she stepped in and turned the tap on full, pulling the shower curtain around the circular rod. She stayed under the torrent of spray for much longer than usual to quell racking shivers that came and went at irregular intervals.

With no appetite, she jerked on a pair of jeans faded from years of washing rather than chemicals, a tank top, and flip-flops, footwear that didn't belong in her shop. "I'll just do paperwork today," she said, then remembered she didn't have a choice as long as the Marmon was on-site. "Come on, Butter Butts, let's go to work." Already as tired as if she'd put in a full day in the shop, she slogged along behind Buster, who bounced on his hind legs—always happy to go on a road trip—but darted glances at her as if sensing her unsettled mood.

Once in her car, Renni called Luke on her cell and told him not to bother coming in, but when she tried to catch Maisie, she didn't get an answer.

Instead of parking down below like usual, she pulled into the upper lot next to Maisie's hot pink VW Bug. Renni hesitated, steeling herself for the Maze Mugging bound to hit as soon as her office manager caught sight of her. With a deep breath, she pushed through the door and made a beeline for her office.

But Maisie, positioned inside the office doorway, had laid the perfect sneak attack. She pounced as Renni set foot over the threshold.

"Oh, my gawd! What's going on? They won't even let me go down the stairs." Maisie threw her arms around Renni's neck in a chokehold, and it took all her strength and balance not to go over backward. The rotund Maisie would flatten her like a pancake. Black spots were beginning to dance in front of Renni's eyes when the phone rang, and the bottle-born redhead let go to answer it in the lobby.

Gasping, Renni locked her door and staggered to the far wall. She peered down into the shop. There were four suited techs this morning, and two uniformed police officers loitering by the closed overhead doors. The cab of the truck was dismantled, its parts scattered on the sheeting. What appeared to be a small shop vacuum sat next to the driver's side of the truck. She turned away and melted onto her chair.

There came a banging on the door, Maisie hollering that she needed to talk.

Renni sighed, hoisted herself back up, and unlocked the door. As she flung it open, she immediately sidestepped, barely avoiding Maisie's grab for her.

"What?" she snapped. *Please let it be something simple like a backed-up toilet.*

"That hunky detective called. He said they'd get the shop released as soon as everything is documented. What's going on? Are you in trouble?"

"If you'll calm down and shut up a second, I'll explain as much as I can." She led the way into the lobby, skirting a coffee table covered with glossy car magazines, and collapsed onto one of the worn leather club chairs. Maisie sat in the other, hands clutched in her lap, eager expectation on her face. She scooted right to the edge of her seat.

"Detective Brody brought crime scene techs here last night, and I guess they must have found something in the Marmon. Dudley Do-Right—surprise!—doesn't believe I could know anything about the truck unless I'm involved. He's convinced I'm not telling him all the gory details." She flopped one leg over the chair arm. "He'd probably like nothing better than to strap me to a metal chair with a spotlight in my face while he grills me about what I had to do with Lauren's death. Oh, and since at least some of the other women I saw in the vision are dead too, I'm a serial killer."

Maisie's mouth was slack, her eyes wide, and Renni

recognized the warm-up to a girly hug-fest. She thought fast.

"Maisie, do you still have any contacts at the DMV?" She already knew the answer. Her office manager frequently mentioned her tenure as a part-time clerk at the Department of Motor Vehicles. While she appeared to hate the actual job, she'd made friends in DMV offices all over Colorado as well as the other Four Corners states, plus Wyoming and Kansas. These contacts had helped a few times when Renni was trying to verify provenance of old cars she'd acquired. It was time to put Maisie's skills to work.

"Well, yeah. Of course I do. Last week I was chatting with—"

"Good. Great. I need you to research the Marmon's VINs."

"VINs? As in, plural?"

"Yes. The auctioneer told me over the phone that they'd found a bunch of different VINs on different parts they checked. I'll email you the list he gave me. It's a Frankenstein, but since I planned on doing the build for myself, I didn't care. Anyway, see if you can find out who all owned the truck or trucks. Go back as far as you can, will you?"

"You bet," Maisie said, her eyes bright with excitement as she rubbed her hands together.

"Like now, Maze."

"Oh, sure. I'll get right on it." She stood and walked to her desk, booting up the computer and picking up the phone at the same time.

"Just send me an email with the info, okay?"

At Maisie's enthusiastic nod, Renni went back to her office. She hoped the cops would stay down in the shop—it was highly likely what Maisie was doing was a tad against the rules, and she didn't want the old woman to get in trouble for doing what her boss told her. Renni checked her fitness band. It was 8:30. Time to get some work done.

# Chapter Nine

The long table in the conference room was covered with Brody's carefully curated materials. He scanned the CSI's evidence bags, dozens of photographs, and copies of specific pages out of the RMHK's murder book. After rearranging a couple pieces, he confirmed his laptop was synced to the jumbo-sized monitor on the end wall, then nervously tapped the double-spaced outline of his presentation into a perfect stack. *It's as good as it's gonna get. I'll either walk out of here assigned to the case, or . . .* He grimaced. *Or be hunting for a new job.* He knew he had some solid information, but it was too early for DNA results, so he was still on thin ice.

Ten long minutes later, Chief of Police Wilcox arrived, along with Detective Wagner and Captain Hatten, Brody's superior.

As he kicked the door shut behind the group, Chief Wilcox snapped, "So, what the hell is this all about, Brody?"

"If you'll all have a seat, sir, I'll explain." After they arranged themselves around the table and were facing the big monitor, Brody took a deep breath and clicked the mouse to start his presentation. He walked them through the evidence step-by-step, referring to his detailed notes as he navigated the slide show.

"The truck was initially impounded outside Spanish Fork, Utah, as an abandoned vehicle, and it went to auction about four months ago when no one claimed it. The tow company that brought it in won the bid. They turned around and sold it online to Delacroix Restorations, aka Renni Delacroix."

From there, it took more than two hours to review everything collected and identified so far. He led with a report on a tiny smudge of blood from the bottom of the passenger dash, which was consistent to known victim Diane Anderson, who had rare AB-negative blood, then moved on to an evidence bag containing an as-yet-to-be-identified hair sample sporting a follicular tag from the passenger door hinge. He knew without definitive DNA, everything he was going over was circumstantial.

"Multiple bodily fluids were collected from the passenger floorboard, and Liv and Pete are running ELISA and immunochromatographic mRNA tests." At Hatten's raised eyebrows, he added, "No semen present, which fits with the profile—none of the RMHK's victims have been raped. The DNA results are pending with CBI, but they've fast-tracked them and we should have them first thing in the morning. There were also some hair samples Liv thought might be animal fur."

Something niggled in his brain, but he didn't have time to think it through. He kept moving through his presentation. When he finished, he could see the three of them were definitely interested, if not altogether hooked.

Captain Hatten was the first to bring up the critical point. "What made you check that truck? I hadn't heard of any new leads from the FBI."

"Yeah." Wilcox frowned. "I wondered that myself."

Brody took a deep breath. "The tip came from a friend of mine. A local guy who works at Delacroix Restorations. After his boss bought the truck, she sent him to Utah to get it. When he brought it in, she, um, thought there was something hinky about it." He rubbed his chin. "I called Liv and asked if she and Pete could stop by and give the truck a once-over. The owner gave permission, so I didn't need a warrant." He saw the chief's face redden and hastened to add, "I have the authorization form duly signed, and solid chain of custody."

"Damn it, Brody, that's not how it's done. You should have come to me instead of pulling this hot-shot crap. I know you put in for SWAT and you probably figure you can game the system and ignore protocol because you came from them fancy military cops and us poor little country folk don't know our hats from our asses. But if you compromised evidence or did anything else to screw up this case, I'll make sure your next job is as a Walmart security guard."

Wilcox was pissed, but Brody had expected that. The chief had a reputation for disliking anything that might reflect poorly on him. This being an election year, he was even more averse to thinking outside the box.

"Sir, the CSIs followed proper procedures. The scene was under oversight the entire time. It's clean evidence."

"We'll see what the Feds think, won't we? Jesus, Brody. I ought to fire your ass right now, and Patterson and Rivera too."

Brody winced at the threat against the two CSIs. Then he realized, *He said "ought!" Good sign.* He bit back a grin. The chief's face told Brody he was already scheming a way to spin the RMHK case in his favor to whomever was elected to City Council in a few months.

"If this even hints at going south, you'll be in for a fitness for duty eval. You understand? No more Lone Ranger crap." Wilcox turned to the captain. "Hatten, you take Wagner—"

"Sir," Brody interrupted, "I'd like to—"

"I don't give a rat's ass what the hell you'd like. The only reason I don't suspend you right now is you're gonna be the one doing a dog and pony show for the Fibbies." To Hatten he said, "Head over to that car shop and talk to everyone there. Let me know what you think when you get back." With a glare at Brody, he pulled out his phone, poked at the buttons, then stood and stepped into the hallway.

Hatten turned to the detective. "Wagner, pull the full jacket on the Cooper murder. I'll meet you in the bullpen in a few minutes." It was clear even to Wagner, who no one considered the sharpest tool in the shed, that he'd been dismissed. When the door swung shut, Hatten shook his head. "You stepped into it this time, Bro." Then he cocked his head and raised an eyebrow. "What are you leaving out?"

Brody snorted. "Who, me?" He waved his hand across the table. "I got all this evidence. Isn't that enough?"

"Yeah, you. There's something you didn't tell The Man. Spill." He fixed Brody with a hard stare. "I can't help you if you don't come clean."

As quickly as possible, Brody gave Hatten a recap of why he'd decided to have the truck checked.

Hatten shook his head again. "Man, you are so screwed. You'll be lucky if you get off with an FFDE. Chief finds out about this, he'll have you committed."

Brody cringed. He knew a couple officers who'd had to take fitness for duty evaluations. It wasn't something he ever wanted to go through. Should have expected it, though.

"I've heard Wilcox loves to use FFDEs on officers he's pissed at," Brody said, adding, "and I bet I'm—"

Hatten held his index finger to his lips and sat up in his chair, giving Brody a hard stare. Before he could ask what was up, Wilcox shoved the door open.

"What are you still doing here, Hatten?"

"On my way, sir."

—

Brody let out a deep breath and resisted the urge to lay his forehead on the table. His briefing with the FBI investigator and forensics specialist had lasted over four hours, on top of the lengthy interview earlier in the day with the chief. The only reason they'd bothered to listen once Wilcox forced him to reveal his source, and the specifics about Renni Delacroix's supposed psychic ability, was that FBI Agent in Charge Darren Tanner had been a junior investigator on a case where the Fibbies used information from a psychic to find a missing mother and child, and he didn't seem to have an issue with someone's "visions."

Brody cracked a smile. Wilcox's face when the AIC asked for details on Renni's background instead of laughing Brody out of the room almost made up for the misery of the rest of the interview.

But not quite.

He'd managed to get assigned to the RMHK task force, but once it was over, he'd be lucky to keep his job. No doubt Wilcox was already devising an excuse to can him. But that was a concern for later. He put all his case files and related materials in a box and carried it to the RMHK task force's newly designated office. Techs were already there setting up monitors, desks with laptops, printers, copiers, and, surprisingly, a shiny new Keurig coffee maker.

"Those FBI guys know how to live," he said to himself. He snagged a desk close to the A/C vent and set his box on top to claim it.

"Hey, Brody, what'd you do to get stuck babysitting the Fibbies? You tick the chief off?" one of the techs asked.

"Job security, man. Job security." Pretending it was bureaucratic bullshit was easier than trying to explain he would have given his right testicle to be in on this investigation. "Thanks, guys. It's lookin' good in here."

He waved and started home. It was already dark, but tomorrow couldn't come soon enough.

# Chapter Ten

After shoving papers around on her desk for hours, Renni gave up. The shop was still a beehive of cop activity with no end in sight. As she made her way through the lobby, she spotted a couple outgoing checks for parts in Maisie's outbox, apparently forgotten when Renni sent her office manager home at lunchtime to get some relief from the constant barrage of questions and dire predictions.

"I'll take care of them on my way home after I drop off the paint chips. There isn't anything else I can, or want to, do here," Renni said to Buster, who seemed very interested in her plans. There was a ton of stuff that needed doing in the shop, but none of it was going to get done any time soon. Fretting at home would be even less productive.

She scooped the envelopes out of the basket, almost wishing Maisie were still around to run the errands instead. Errands meant making small talk with people, not something Renni liked or was good at. She usually ended up feeling like she'd offended someone by not chatting about all kinds of personal things, or leaving with way too much information about people she barely knew.

With Buster as co-pilot, she headed out into the sweltering afternoon. Her first stop was at a large cinder block building in a run-down part of town next to the railroad tracks. Several vehicles were parked inside the ten-foot-tall chain-link fence enclosing the dirt parking lot at Sion and Son Painting. As she got out of the car, the owner ambled over, dressed in paint-stained coveralls, a skull-bedecked do-rag, and a pair of goggles around his neck.

He jerked his head in greeting. "Nice to see you, Miss Delacroix. What can I do you for today?"

She handed over a sheet of paper with a Vermillion Red paint chip attached, a duplicate of two identical sets back at the office—one for her file, and one for her client, Ed Benson.

"Hey, Mr. Cavanaugh." They shook hands. "This is the selection for the Caddy. We'll bring it over as soon as you're ready for it. I appreciate you working me into your schedule so fast." She motioned to all the hulks scattered around the yard, waiting their turn in the paint shop. "Appears you've got plenty of work."

"No sweat. You're my favorite client 'cause you always pay on time." He smiled, showing slightly yellowed, even teeth. "I'll have the Caddy ready in a week. No problem."

"If it's as good as the job you did on the Chevy, I'll be in heaven and so will the owner."

"'Preciate it." He waved as she got back in the Spitz.

Renni headed to the post office to mail the payments and pick up some stamps for the few personal bills she still sent out via snail mail. As she put her hand on the door to push it open, she realized who was manning the service counter. *Damn it.* The clerk, a distant cousin or something to Maisie, grinned broadly when he saw her. He gave the impression of an aging rocker from the big-hair-band days, sporting a polyester shirt in the latest retro style, but which likely came from his thirty-year-old wardrobe. The shirt had too many buttons left undone, exposing a werewolf-approved mat of chest hair with several gold necklaces tangled in it. His head was not as well endowed, a monk's tonsure of hair rimming his head and dropping to shoulder length, either naturally frizzy or badly permed. The top of his head gleamed in the fluorescent light.

It was too late to turn back, so she plastered on a polite expression and gave him a wave as she stepped up to the counter. "Hey, um . . ."

"Well, hello, Renni. It's Kevin. Kevin Green. How've you been? I haven't seen you in here for a long time. I missed you."

She gave a tight smile and handed him her envelopes. "And give me a couple sheets of stamps, please." Renni rummaged in her backpack for her wallet. *Please just give me my friggin' stamps so I can get out of here.*

But of course he didn't. He asked how business was. Commented on the weather. Told her about his sister's ongoing bout of hay fever. Gave a blow-by-blow recap of the local high school team's football season.

"I bet you were a cheerleader when you were in school, right?" he asked, his eyes fixing—and lingering—on the neckline of her tank top.

"Um, no. I spent my time outside of school helping my uncle and cousin with their race cars."

His eyebrows raised at the whole new line of conversation this presented. As he opened his mouth, she said, "It's been great to catch up with you, Kev, but I really need to move along. Busy day, you know."

His head bobbed. "Yeah, sure. Sorry to keep you." He pulled a box out from under the counter. "I got a lot of new stamps in. How about these Wonder Woman ones? They'd be perfect for you because—"

"I'll go with the 'Healing PTSD' stamps," Renni quickly said, handing over a twenty.

He dug through the box and pulled out the stamps. "You know these cost a little more, right?"

She nodded and forced a smile as he hemmed and hawed while making her change, doing his best to keep her there—or at least that's how it seemed.

As she put her hand on the door handle, he blurted, "Are you dating anyone these days, Renni? A pretty girl like you ought not be all alone. I got some tickets for the next Denver Bronco game. We could—"

"Um, thanks, Kevin. Er, Mr. Green. That's sweet. I'm real busy, though, and probably won't have time for anything outside of work in the foreseeable future." She waggled her fingers over her shoulder and made her escape. As the door wheezed shut behind her, she let out a long, slow breath and shook her head. Maisie was stuck with stamp runs forever, or at least until Kevin retired.

As she drove off, it occurred to her she'd pretty much isolated herself from the world over the past six months. Even in the course of business, she did as much as possible via email or phone. Painful and awkward as it might be, it was probably time to start getting out in the world again, unless she wanted to become a hermit.

Then she remembered the situation with the Marmon. There was a good chance she would either be forced to become a hermit when she lost all her friends and customers, or she'd have to put herself out in public, going to interviews and praying someone would hire her. Neither was something she wanted to contemplate.

Back at the shop, Renni struggled to get through the door as Buster strained at his leash and wriggled through ahead of her, desperate to get to the treat drawer in Maisie's desk. Unwrapping the leash from her wrist, she dropped it so she could pull her key from the door. She shook her head as Buster nosed the drawer open and poked his head into the open treat box, then turned back to lock the door from the inside.

Two men were coming up the walk, intent expressions on their faces.

She took in the dark suits and poker faces. A flashing neon sign that said "cops" couldn't have been more obvious. *Shit. This day is going to hell in a handbasket faster by the minute.* With a deep breath, Renni pulled the door open and said, "Gentlemen. How can I help you?"

"Miss Delacroix?"

"Yep, that's me."

"We need to talk. Is there somewhere we can go?"

—

Three hours later she watched the lobby door swing closed behind Detectives Hatten and Wagner. Shoulders slumped, Renni went into her office and shut the door, then leaned her forehead against it. She took a deep breath, padded over to retrieve a beer from the fridge, and collapsed on the sofa. Patting the seat next to her, she said, "I need some lovin', Busty."

After being cooped up in the office during the interview, the spaniel was happy to comply. He jumped up and made a few turns to get comfortable. She ran her fingers through his soft fur, receiving a thank-you lick in return. He snuggled up, chin on her thigh.

Eyes closed, Renni recalled the glowers of combined suspicion and total disbelief on both men's faces almost from the moment they sat down, and which were pretty much unchanged when they left. Of course they didn't believe her. They'd kept hammering at her to tell the truth about how she knew the truck belonged to a killer. She explained every way from Sunday, but they weren't buying it. The worst part of all was this was only the beginning.

She finished the last swallow of beer and stood to toss it in the recycle bin, gazing down into the shop as she neared the windows. Surprised, she watched as the crime scene techs wadded up ribbons of yellow tape and stuffed them into heavy-duty trash bags. The trailer with the Marmon was gone. Renni pushed through the door and went down the stairs, stopping several steps from the bottom. "Excuse me!"

It took more yells and some arm-waving before one of them saw her and came forward. "Yes?"

"Are you releasing the shop?"

"Yeah. We'll be out of your hair shortly."

One of the other techs came over with a clipboard. "Please sign for the truck and trailer, ma'am." As Renni scribbled her name, he said, "You can check with the detectives later to find out when you can have them back."

*Yeah, like that'll happen in this decade.* She handed back the clipboard, watching as the man joined the other techs and the quartet trooped outside through the open bay door. With a sigh of relief, she ran the overhead door down and locked it, as well as the other bay and man door.

Hands on hips, Renni surveyed the spacious shop and the mess the CSIs had left. Disposable gloves, plastic packaging material, paper wrapping, and spilled fingerprint powder were strewn around the concrete floor. There would be hours of cleanup and organization before she or Luke could get any serious work done tomorrow. She thought about jumping right in but realized she was too beat to tackle the unpleasant job, and some of the equipment would take two people to move.

A call to Luke confirmed he would be in at 8:00. She'd already told Maisie to take the rest of the week off, assuming the shop would still be off-limits, and it was easier to leave it at that. They'd get more work done without Maisie's overexcited gossiping, anyway. She could put a sign on the door that they were closed and an out-of-office message on the phone. Then the two of them would have time to work undisturbed.

# Chapter Eleven

Beth Ann looked up as Detective Wagner sauntered into her office in the Records Department. He leaned against the doorway and stared at her. Well, ogled was more like it. She quickly turned back to her keyboard and began typing again, anxious to finish so she could get home on time for the first day in weeks and prepare for her date.

"Hey, Beth Ann. How about dinner tonight?"

"Can't," she said, keeping her eyes on the keyboard so he couldn't see her roll them. "Besides, I'm dating Williams from Property."

"Seriously? The guy's a loser. He still lives with his mother."

She swiveled around in her chair. "His mother has Alzheimer's. He's her only family. Of course he lives with her." With a disgusted snort, she spun back to her computer.

"You hear about the new RMHK evidence?" Wagner asked, trying another tack.

Beth Ann frowned and thought a moment, her hands pausing over the keys. "The Rocky Mountain High Killer? I thought it was cold."

"Was. But Brody came up with this chick. Some psychic or something. We might have the guy's truck. The one he hauled the women around in."

"A psychic? Here? In Rampart?"

"Yeah. Name's Delacroix. Randy, I think."

She perked up in surprise. "Renni Delacroix? I know her. She fixes up these cool old cars. I met her at the Humane Society Fundraiser this spring."

Beth Ann realized her mistake as soon as Wagner grinned, opening his mouth to keep the conversation going.

Before he could, Beth Ann's supervisor stepped in from the hall, slightly out of breath. Squeezing past Wagner, she said, "Beth Ann, you have that report yet? Wilcox is on a rampage."

Wagner frowned at the interruption, then turned and headed toward the detective's bullpen. Relief swept through Beth Ann. With a quick assurance to her supervisor, she turned her focus back to the report. Only a few more paragraphs and she'd be home free.

A few minutes later, Information Officer Jill Stiles poked her head in the room. Still typing, Beth Ann spared her a glance, praying this wouldn't mean another late night.

"Hey, Beth Ann, reception told me that reporter, Lassiter, was back here, but I don't see him," Jill said, head gesturing toward the interview room across the hall.

"There was a bald guy in there a few minutes ago. I didn't see him leave."

Jill shrugged and headed back to her office. "Let him try to get an interview on short notice next time."

—

Back at the Daily Watch office, Fred Lassiter sat at his computer, clenching and unclenching his hands to loosen them up for the biggest article of his career. He couldn't believe his luck. What would have been a dry update on the School Resource Officer program turned out to be the scoop of the year, and it all started with a dropped pen in the police station's conference room and a loud-mouthed detective. He gave his knuckles a final crack and started researching "Rocky Mountain High Killer" and "RMHK."

It didn't take long to find articles about several unsolved murders of women in Colorado, dating back several years before he'd moved to this backwater burg after that little plagiarism issue back east. It wasn't until he built a timeline and plotted the locations where the bodies were found that he realized the women had all gone missing from towns in Colorado around the same time of year, but not every year. He tried searching to see if the computer could make any pattern out of the dates but came up empty.

On a hunch, he searched a local murder from the past winter, Lauren Cooper, and confirmed it fit the MO to a T. That fact alone would give him the front-page story for the next week. "The Rocky Mountain High Killer" would make a great headline, and since they'd also given him the cute little cop shop code of RMHK, it indicated they'd pegged him as an actual serial killer.

Lassiter pulled together histories for four of the victims, to give his article the personal touch. His files continued to grow as he ferreted out more and more data, dissecting their lives so he could give the readers all the sad, and gory, details once he'd badgered the families into talking to him.

A couple hours later, he leaned back, a broad smile on his weather-beaten face. He picked up the phone and called his editor.

"You need to hold me the front page, boss. I got a huge one."

# Chapter Twelve

Brody went out to get the paper clad in nothing but a pair of flannel pants, his mug of black coffee in hand. A long, drawn-out wolf whistle pierced the early morning silence. He raised his head, catching sight of the widow Blevans at her gate across the street, grinning at him. He shook his head with a laugh and waved, then padded barefoot into the house where he spread the paper out on the kitchen counter.

And spewed coffee all over the upper cabinet.

Renni's face, blown up to grainy quarter-page size, stared back at him. The bold black headline read *Psychic or Just Sick?*

He read down the half-page spread. Words jumped out at him. *Local body shop owner Renault Landaulette Delacroix . . . Parents killed in an automobile crash when she was nine . . . Raised by an elderly uncle with no fixed home . . . A bid for attention . . . Women snatched from nightspots all along I-70 . . . Local photographer Lauren Cooper, a victim . . . Shallow graves . . .*

The entire article was a quilt of implications stitched together with conjecture and the bare minimum of facts. Brody figured the only way the newspaper's attorney could have approved it was due to the liberal use of "claimed" and "alleged." The article portrayed Renni as an attention-seeking loner with a sketchy past. "Unnamed police sources" were quoted as stating she was a person of interest in the investigation of multiple murders and that she claimed to have previously undisclosed details about the women's deaths. The article stopped short of saying she was accused of anything. Several victims' names were listed along with hometown and limited family details. It also included locations of disappearances and where bodies were found.

As Brody hurried to dress, he considered where the reporter got the information. The tone suggested it hadn't come from Renni unless she liked being portrayed as crazy or as a psychotic killer. He was sure Luke wouldn't have given any reporter that kind of information. He didn't know about the receptionist at Delacroix Restorations, but the old lady had seemed completely loyal to Renni during their conversation. If the info didn't come from the Delacroix group, it had to be staff at the station. Brody locked up and went to the garage, wheeling out his Harley. He straddled the slick leather seat and kicked the '95 Fatboy to life, its throaty roar echoing in the still morning air as he headed for what was likely to be a very unpleasant day.

—

This turned out to be a serious understatement. AIC Darren Tanner called an all-staff meeting in the training room. The room was packed, standing room only. Hatten and Wilcox flanked Tanner at the podium.

The AIC stood tall, his lips thin, almost quivering with fury. "If anyone has any knowledge about how this reporter got the information for this article, I suggest they speak up quickly. This kind of behavior will not be tolerated." His eyes flicked to Brody and held for a few seconds too long.

The group shuffled around, but no one spoke up. After a long few minutes, Wilcox dismissed them, adding his own admonishment for the guilty party to come forward. As Brody headed to the task force office, he primed himself for a confrontation with the AIC. He wasn't going to let them pin the leak on him.

A pretty young woman sidled up and touched his arm.

"Hey, Beth Ann."

"Brody, I need to talk with you, but not here." She hurried down the hall and out to a small, walled garden area—a quiet space for officers and staff to go if they were feeling overwhelmed by their job. He followed, confused by her manner. He'd dated the brunette a few times right after joining the force, but they never clicked and parted friends. It was still easy to exchange cordial greetings when they met in the hallways or parking lot.

"What's up?" he asked as the door shut behind them.

She paced the small space, wringing her hands. "It wasn't my fault."

"What?" Then it dawned on him. "You know how the reporter got the information?"

"Yeah. I think so." She explained about Wagner's flirting and the man who disappeared from the interrogation room.

"Come on. We need to tell the AIC."

Her face went pale.

"Hey, you didn't do anything wrong. Wagner should never have opened his mouth. He's going to have to deal with the fallout. I'll go with you." He took her arm and ushered her back through the door, heading for Wilcox's office.

As expected, the AIC was sitting across from the chief when Brody knocked on the open door's frame.

"Yeah? What is it, Brody? We're busy here," Wilcox snapped.

Brody stepped inside and tugged a reluctant Beth Ann with him, shutting the door behind her. "Sir, Miss Hawkins thinks she knows how the reporter got the story." He nodded to her.

She swallowed hard and repeated what she'd told him. Wilcox's face turned red, and a vein began to pulse in his temple.

"God damn it!" he shouted, pounding the desk. Beth Ann

jumped and let out a frightened squeak.

The AIC stood and put his hand on her shoulder. "Don't worry, Miss Hawkins. You've done the right thing coming forward. We'll have to check out your story, but I'm betting it will hold up." He turned to Brody. "Where's Wagner?"

"Probably in the bullpen, sir. If not, Captain Hatten can track him down."

The two of them were dismissed, Beth Ann to return to her duties, and Brody to round up Wagner and send him to Wilcox's office. He headed for Hatten's desk and whispered in his ear.

"Oh shit," the captain said, gritting his teeth.

Brody couldn't help grinning as Hatten spotted Wagner next to the snack machine, talking to a detective from Auto, and bellowed, "Wagner, get your big ass and bigger mouth over here."

When Hatten turned back, Brody said, "Since the DNA reports haven't come in yet, I'm heading over to the Delacroix shop to ask her a few more questions."

As he turned to leave, his smile faded when he thought of what he'd find when he got to Delacroix Restorations. Then he remembered her full name from the article and the grin returned. *Renault Landaulette Delacroix.* He'd have to find out about that name. It was a doozie.

# Chapter Thirteen

He ripped the newspaper into shreds, swearing. Karen huddled at her desk, shoulders hunched around her ears. She'd been doing her online medical transcription with earbuds in, but it was apparent she'd still heard him and was upset and needed reassurance. He should calm her, and himself, down.

"I'm going out, sis. Don't worry. Everything's okay. I just—there's this stupid article. The reporter got it all wrong. I'll bring you something special for dinner tonight."

She nodded but kept her head turned away.

On his way out to the barn, he dropped the torn shreds of newspaper into the jumbo trash can by the driveway. Once inside his refuge, he slammed the door and locked it securely behind him. He paced the length of the hall that ran down the middle of the building, stirring up dust, filled with fury and needing to burn it off.

*Renni Delacroix is psychic?* It was unbelievable. Other than her looks and killer bod, he never thought there was anything special about her. He'd seen lots of girls as pretty as her. Why did this have to happen now? How much did she know? What could she have told the cops? The article didn't say anything about the killer. It was all about the dead women. Their graves. And Renni.

If the cops knew about him, he realized, they'd have been there already. His agitation lessened. He stretched his neck and rolled his shoulders. He just needed to take care of Renni and then everything would be like it was. But how?

He smacked his palm against the countertop, barely registering the sharp pain as he looked around.

A smile, one Doctor Seuss's Grinch would appreciate, split his face. *Of course. It's the perfect solution.* The barn was a replica of one that stood for decades before it blew up and killed Pop, an accident involving a careless two-pack-a-day smoker who drank too much and a leaky propane heater. If he worked it right, no one would think twice about a gas leak causing an explosion, let alone connect it to the earlier one. It would be sad and create a bit of excitement, but in the end, it would solve all the problems, just like when Pop died. Out of those ashes grew a perfect life for him and Karen. His Grinch smile broadened. It was poetic that their lives would again be renewed out of the ashes.

After he dealt with Renni, he and his twin would go on like normal. He'd take his annual vacation, but maybe he'd venture a bit further out. There wasn't really any reason to stick to the Interstate. Perhaps he'd choose locations more off the beaten path to leave the bodies, too. That would throw off the investigation and keep the cops from getting close. He laughed. They had no idea how close, literally, they were.

As he drove to work, his thoughts centered on how he'd been doing it. Successfully. Repeatedly. Yeah, maybe he shouldn't have pissed in his own backyard that night, so to speak, but when he saw the Cooper woman at the bar the very first day of last year's hunt, she was just so perfect he couldn't help himself. He got rid of the truck the next day. It wasn't like he used it all the time, anyway. He'd never been near it without gloves, and even if he'd somehow left a fingerprint on it, his weren't on file anywhere. There'd be no way to link anything to him. He was invisible.

Once Renni was out of the way, there was no reason to change things. He was smart enough to keep the cops from catching him—he'd already proven that. No need to change his methods. Maybe later he'd want to, but not until *he* was good and ready.

# Chapter Fourteen

Brody paused at the door to Delacroix Restorations. A handwritten sign taped to the inside of the glass said they were closed, but he pushed on the door and it opened into the lobby. A chime went off. He heard boots ring on the metal staircase, and a few moments later Renni appeared on the landing, the dog on her heels.

"Oh, it's you. Guess they don't teach cops to read," she said.

Her expression of disgust said a lot more. She stomped across the room and through the doorway to her office, giving the door a shove behind her. He followed and caught the door before it slammed.

"I assume you've seen the papers?" he said to her stiff back as she stared down into the shop.

"Wow. You really are an *amazing* detective." She spun around, eyes flashing, jaw rock hard. "So maybe you can find all the work I'm going to lose over that stupid article. Oh, and maybe my reputation too."

He opened his mouth, but she didn't even pause.

"Do you have any idea how long it's taken me to get where I

am in this industry? How hard I worked to be taken seriously? After this article circulates, I'll be a laughing stock. A broke, unemployed, whack job." Her eyes glittered, but he wasn't sure if it was tears or anger. "I can kiss my shop goodbye."

"I'm sorry. We didn't intend for the story to get out. It was a mistake. Best we can tell, the reporter was in a room near where an officer was discussing the case and overheard enough to get him started. I'm sorry about that, but the officer didn't know the reporter was there. He'll be disciplined."

Renni dropped heavily into her office chair. "Oh, well, in that case. Gosh. It's just peachy, then. No harm meant, is that what you're saying?"

"No, of course not. We'll do everything we can to clear this up." He frowned. "But in the meantime, I need to talk to you about some things."

She stiffened.

Brody had planned on asking her about the photos, but seeing her dog wander over and plop onto an oversized dog bed in the corner triggered a memory that had been bugging him. "You said you never got in the truck."

"No, I never got in the truck. Ever. Not once. Geez, are you deaf? You've asked me, like, five times."

"Then how do you explain the hairs your dog left in there?" Saying he knew the brown and white hairs belonged to a specific dog was pure bluff, but he didn't believe in coincidence.

She squinted at Buster, shaking her head slowly. "Buster didn't get in the truck. He was with me when Luke brought it in, but I'm the only one that got on the trailer."

"Well then, I think you have a problem." Brody smiled grimly. "Because when the DNA on the fur comes back to your dog, you're not going to be able to say it magically appeared there."

Renni frowned. Swiveling back and forth in her chair, she stared over his shoulder and chewed the inside of her cheek.

Now that he had her rattled, he pressed on. "And those

photos? You only identified five of the women as being in your *vision,* but you said you saw a total of seven. All the RMHK victims were in those photos. Who are the other two you claim to have seen?"

Bristling, Renni's eyes narrowed to slits at the word "claim." She stopped with a lurch and jumped out of her chair, striding toward him until she was only inches away, face turned up, green eyes dark and stormy.

"So, Mr. Detective," she snarled, "I don't suppose you bothered to find out if Lauren owned a dog? Maybe a brown and white dog? Maybe, just maybe, named Buster?"

Brody jerked back like he'd been slapped. "What?"

Renni turned and strode over to the windows, staring out but not appearing to see anything, hands on the windowsill white from her grip. "Buster was Lauren's dog. I found him when I went to her house to pack things up for her parents and took him home with me." Brody watched her reflection in the window as she swiped at her eyes. She sniffed hard and turned back to him. "You could have just asked me."

"I'll check into it," he said, impressed with how quickly she recovered from her shock. "But what about the pictures?"

She paced across the room, balled-up fists stuck deep in her pockets, then suddenly halted and turned to him. "What if there are two more? Maybe I saw two you haven't discovered yet?"

"Then why didn't you see the other victims, the two we've ID'd but you didn't pick up on?" he asked. She was quick to come up with solutions, or maybe she'd been waiting to put it out there and throw him off.

"You're just bound and determined I'm lying, aren't you?" Her pacing took her back to the window, and she stared into the shop with a far-off gaze before whirling around. "Wait, maybe those two were never in the truck. If they weren't around the truck, I wouldn't know about them, right?"

Again, she had an answer, almost like she'd read his file notes. "I have no idea if you would or not. You're the one who claims to be psychic, remember?"

"Oh, don't beat around the bush, Detective." Renni put her hands on her hips, her chin jutting toward him. "Go ahead and say it. You think I murdered not only my best friend but a bunch of other women I don't even know. I mean, hell, makes complete sense, right?"

Brody silently observed her. Waited to see how she'd react.

In three long strides, she was at the door and yanked it open. "Get out of my shop. Now! I have a lot of work to do, and I'm not wasting any more time talking to someone who doesn't want to hear anything I say. Go back to your office and get my lovely cell all set up so you can put me in it when you arrest me. But you're wrong." Tears, he was sure now, glittered in her eyes. "So totally wrong it's not even funny." She turned her back on him and walked out, clomping away down the stairs. Buster levered himself up from the bed, gave Brody what could only be described as a doggie glare, and trotted after her.

Brody sighed as he went out to his department-issued Explorer. If the dog belonged to Cooper, a DNA match wouldn't matter. Any decent defense attorney would claim it was transfer off Cooper's body. He was sure Delacroix knew more than she was saying, although her act was pretty damn convincing. Heaven help her if—no, when—he proved she was playing him for a fool.

On the drive back to the station, he mulled over what she'd said. There *had* been a couple of other badly decomposed bodies found early on, when the Fibbies were considering whether or not they had a serial killer. He couldn't remember the details, but it seemed like they hadn't matched up with any missing person reports, and the bodies weren't found in areas similar to the confirmed cases. In the end, they hadn't been included with the serial cases.

Back at the office, Brody went to his desk and booted up the computer. Using typing skills that were legendary in the detective division, his fingers flew over the keyboard as he pulled up and reviewed files on Jane Doe bodies logged over the last ten years. Eventually, he found what he was looking for. An unidentified female's body had been discovered near Helper, Utah, dumped off Highway 6 in a small rest stop. Unlike the RMHK's MO, the body had been buried about three feet deep and fairly well hidden in oak brush. If a tourist's husky hadn't dug up a leg bone, it's unlikely the body would ever have been found. With no fingerprints available and the skull never located, all they could tell was that the dead person was a female, aged late teens to thirty, who had never borne a child. The Feds had decided it didn't fit the MO. But when Brody compared the estimated time of death to the other RMHK victims since then, it was a close match.

Another body was found outside Moab. It was about fifty miles from Interstate 70, off a well-traveled dirt road in the sagebrush and grass-covered hills frequented by off-roaders. It, again, was badly decomposed, with less than half the bones ever found, many of which had been chewed by scavengers. The skull was crushed and the teeth, which could usually be tested for DNA, were missing, likely scattered and eaten by rodents. Again, the timeline fit, even if the MO didn't.

Was it possible there were actually more victims than they knew? That the RMHK had a larger hunting ground than the FBI profilers had identified? While some of the deaths seemed to come at a similar time of year, there were significant gaps and lags. But with decomposition, it wasn't always easy to get time of death with pinpoint accuracy. If the other two bodies were really related to the case, odds were good there could have been other murders too. Maybe the RMHK had more notches in his belt than anyone suspected. A lot more.

*Shit.*

# Chapter Fifteen

Renni was still fuming when she walked to her car with Buster after she and Luke put the shop back together. *Talk about arrogant!* That guy took the cake. She peeled out of the parking lot and Buster skidded against the passenger-side door. A moment later she slammed on the brakes when a car pulled out in front of her. Buster slid onto the floor. He looked up at her, his head tilted like he was confused. She patted the seat and scrubbed his neck when he crawled back up and laid down.

"Sorry, Butter Butts. It's not your fault and I shouldn't be making you suffer. You're such a good boy, I'm going to stop and get you some treats."

Familiar with that word, Buster sat and watched the passing scenery, wagging his short, stubby tail when Furr Balls Pet Store came into view only a few minutes later. He was prancing in the seat by the time Renni parked and came around to put his leash on.

They'd only taken a few steps inside, Renni looking at the overhead signs to orient herself to the layout of the newly remodeled store when the hair on the back of her neck stood on end and she realized someone had come up behind her. Close behind her. She turned and found herself staring at the middle button of a man's white shirt only inches from her nose. Renni tipped her head back as far as it could go and saw the chin and tip of a nose of an extremely tall, thin young man. From her vantage point, she could see downy hair on his jawline and a seriously bad case of acne. His long, wavy hair was pulled back in a greasy ponytail.

"Can I help you, miss?" He gazed down at her, his breath stirring the hairs on the top of her head.

She sidestepped a couple paces and waved her hand toward the store. "I'm just here to get some dog treats. I wanted to see what the store looked like after the remodel." She headed toward the dog aisle, and the young man stayed with her.

"What kind of treats are you looking for? Something for an older dog?"

Renni glanced at Buster, imagining how indignant the spaniel would be if he knew he was being considered an "older" dog. "You know, I'm not sure. I think I'll just look around and see what's new. But thanks for the offer to help."

"Okay. Just holler if you need anything. I'm Kendrick, by the way." He started to turn away, then stopped and stared at her for several uncomfortable seconds. Finally, he sidled off down the aisle but continued to throw glances over his shoulder.

Frowning, she wondered if the word "weirdo" had suddenly appeared on her forehead, to make him behave so oddly. She put these thoughts aside as Buster pulled at the leash like a plow horse and followed his nose unerringly to the dog food aisle, at the same time putting distance between herself and the clerk. There were at least ten feet of treats between the dry and canned foods, and she spent several minutes making Buster-approved selections. Wishing she had grabbed a cart or basket, she gathered up all the packets and cans and headed for the checkout.

Just as she rounded the corner, a woman with a large black

Labrador retriever came around from the next aisle. The Lab lunged toward Buster, barking loudly, and Renni struggled to hold on to the leash and her packages as Buster danced away from the threat.

Kendrick bounded out of a checkstand and put himself between the two dogs. The Lab growled and snapped its teeth, its owner tugging ineffectually on the leash and using baby talk to try and calm the big dog. Kendrick stood his ground and in a firm voice said, "Stop that. Sit!"

The Lab immediately sat, and its owner's mouth gaped open with apparent surprise. Kendrick turned to Renni, grabbing a can of dog food topper just before it hit Buster on its way to the floor.

"Are you two all right?" he asked as he snagged a basket from the end of the next aisle.

"Yeah. Wow. Thanks." She knelt, dropped her packages into the basket, and gave Buster a hard cuddle, her face sunk into his neck fur.

Kendrick turned back to the woman with the Lab. "Ma'am, if you want to bring your dog into the store, you must ensure that he is under your control at all times and does not behave aggressively. If I may suggest, there are cards on our bulletin board over there"—he motioned toward a wall at the front of the store—"where you can find some really great trainers."

"Baron certainly doesn't need training. It's this other ill-mannered dog that caused all the fuss." She pointed to Buster, stuck her nose in the air, and tugged on the leash. "Come, Baron, we're going to the *other* store. It's much nicer, anyway." Ignoring her attempt to head for the store exit, the Lab turned and trotted off, making a beeline for the Cat Adoption section. Kendrick called to another clerk, who raced after the duo.

Renni followed Kendrick to the checkout. "That dog could have done some damage. Thank you so much for what you did."

He smiled and shrugged. "Happens all the time. We get used to it." He rang up her purchases, dropping them into a bag as he scanned them. When he got to the last item, he hesitated before looking up at her, his face flaming red. "You're Renni Delacroix, right? The one in the paper?"

She was tempted to deny it, but since her photo was plastered all over the front page, she knew it would be a waste of time. "Yes, but . . ."

"Listen, I don't want to bother you or anything, but see, I think I can do that too. I mean, not with cars, but with animals. I get a sense of what it's been like for them, and what they're thinking." He blushed a deeper crimson. "Do you think, um, maybe we could have a drink or something and talk about it? I just turned twenty-one, so I can drink now. The real stuff, I mean." He stammered to a stop.

*And here we go again. Now everyone who has a moment of déjà vu will come crawling out of the woodwork wanting someone to understand. To tell them they're normal. Not a freak.* Then she realized she was seeing the kid through the haze of her own past. She knew how he felt but just couldn't deal with it right now.

"That's really interesting, Kendrick, and I'd say you work at a good place to use that kind of skill. But I'm really busy right now, and with the article, well, I just don't feel much like talking about all that. I hope you understand." She smiled to help ease her answer.

"Yeah. Sure. Maybe some other time." He took her credit card and looked at the back, where she'd written "see ID" next to her signature. He asked for her driver's license.

"Thanks for asking," she said, and dug it out of her wallet.

He stared at her license for longer than it should have taken, then handed it back and ran the credit card. After tucking her receipt in the bag, he set it on the conveyor and put the card into her hand. "You two have a nice day now."

Renni hustled out of the building and into her car. *What a day! I need a drink.* Buster let out a sigh and laid his head on her lap, like he fully agreed.

# Chapter Sixteen

He waited until she was a block from the store before slipping into his car and pulling out, careful to keep a few cars between her bright red Triumph and his borrowed, plain-Jane Hyundai sedan. He was hard-pressed to keep up with her, especially when she hit the switchbacks.

Twelve minutes later, she turned down a dirt drive. He continued past her driveway and went a half-mile up the road before taking the first paved right turn. The roads in this heavily agricultural area were set out on a grid, with letters for street names running south to north, and numbers running west to east, with quarter, half, and three-quarter mile increments. He kept turning right at each intersection until he came back to the road she'd turned off from.

He drove the square of roads again, paying closer attention to the street signs and stopping when he judged he was directly behind her house. He noted landmarks so he could find the spot again, in the dark if necessary. Then he went back to town, stopping at the grocery store to buy a family-sized Stouffer's mac and cheese, Karen's favorite, as well as some vanilla ice cream, hot fudge sauce, and cherry preserves. She'd be so happy.

# Chapter Seventeen

Renni was exhausted by the time she stumbled in her front door. A short time later, comfortable in a pair of lime green yoga capris and an "I'm lost, but I'm making good time" T-shirt, she fixed a drink and collapsed on the couch with a bag of microwave popcorn and apple slices for dinner. Her head was too full of crap to deal with anything serious at this point, including real food. She found a Harry Potter movie marathon and settled in, Buster content to sleep with his head in her lap. After nodding off herself a second time, she gave up before Dumbledore died and padded off to get ready for bed.

Her sleep was disturbed several times by nightmares, but instead of long, horrifying scenes, they were a strobe of images.

A familiar blonde head of hair hitting curved metal, hard.

The spans of a bridge flashing overhead.

An old man. A hand-rolled cigarette between fingers on an oversized steering wheel. The sound of a raspy voice cackling at something he found funny. A smile, revealing several missing teeth.

Renni woke with a jerk just as the sun breached the horizon.

A faint memory of spiders crawling over her sent a shiver coursing up her back and into her hairline. The dreams left her grumpy and out of sorts, and what was worse, they added nothing to the investigation. The only thing she'd bet on was the old man wasn't the killer. She wasn't sure *why* she was sure—maybe because he was so old and *small* somehow. Not right for the strong emotions Renni had felt. The rage just didn't fit him. But he *was* connected to the Marmon.

Even after her meager dinner the night before, Renni found herself without an appetite, so she dressed quickly in shorts, T-shirt, and a pair of heavy boots. She didn't want to stay at home, not after her unsettling dreams, and heaven knew there was plenty of work to be done at the shop. Buster allowed her to wave him through the front door, and she laughed for the first time in days as he bounded toward the garage with contagious enthusiasm.

# Chapter Eighteen

He parked the car on a canal bank out of sight from the road and prowled through weeds and over ditches to the old orchard behind Renni's house, tripping over the uneven ground in the opalescent dawn. A few hundred yards behind the house, he settled as comfortably as possible against the trunk of a thick, gnarled fruit tree, likely planted a hundred years earlier. The sun was spilling over Rampart Peak when a light came on in the house.

An hour later he heard the front door slam and an engine start. The red car rumbled down the driveway, leaving a thin trail of dust in its wake. Once it was out of sight, he hurried back to his car and drove sedately into town, stopping on the bridge. From there he could see the back of Delacroix Restorations with his binoculars. Her little car was sitting in the lot.

It only took ten minutes to drive back to her house. He checked to make sure there weren't any other cars in sight, then turned in her driveway. Parked, he grabbed his box of materials and went around back.

The back door was unlocked, as expected. People in this

small farm town rarely locked their doors, except the out-of-staters who moved there from the cities, yanked out all the fruit trees, and plunked huge, overdone McMansions in their place. There weren't any of those in sight, but he'd passed a group of them at the top of the hill.

He slipped into the house and headed for the kitchen. "Damn, it's electric," he said when he saw the stove. He went down the hall, checking doors until he found the water heater in a narrow closet. Setting his tools down near the enameled cylinder, he quickly closed all the windows in the house and turned off the swamp cooler.

Satisfied the house would keep the gas contained, he shifted his attention to the water heater. He turned off the pilot light, then connected the igniter and timer, setting it for fifteen seconds. In the living room, he twisted a small screw eye into the bottom interior of the front door and attached four-pound-test woven fishing line. The line unspooled as he walked backward to the water heater, where he cut the line off the reel and attached it, under tension, to the timer. His last task was to disconnect the gas line. The sickening smell of rotten eggs immediately wafted down the hall and curled into other rooms.

When too-snoopy-for-her-own-good Miss Renni Delacroix opened the door and let the tension off, BOOM! Arson evidence vaporized and problem solved. He nodded with satisfaction.

His watch confirmed he'd only been in the house for fifteen minutes. After gathering his tools into the box, he left by the back door, plucking a fragrant bloom off a shrub and waving it under his nose as he sauntered down the driveway. Head cocked, he listened intently for the sound of approaching vehicles. No one passed by before he reached the car. This time he stopped at KFC and picked up a bucket of extra-crispy.

# Chapter Nineteen

Renni went through paperwork for a while because if she didn't make herself do it, she'd never get it done. But the shop was where she really wanted—needed—to be.

As soon as she could, she went downstairs and surveyed the room, put back in order the day before, most of it before Brody interrupted. Luke had helped her move the cars around on their dollies, pulling them into position and driving the recalcitrant wheeled toolboxes, whose hard wheels tended to head off in the wrong direction, back to their assigned spots.

Now, the shop—*her shop*—beckoned. She went straight for the resto-mod, intent on installing the new Halibrand wheels and Diamond Back tires. Normally the effort of lifting the heavy tires and installing lug nuts and wheel spinners put her in the zone. But after realizing she couldn't remember which lug nuts she'd torqued, it was clear she was too distracted for even that basic task. Better to call it quits than have to redo work. Especially when the resto-mod was so close to completion. After writing herself a note to make a focused check later and sticking it to one of the wheels, she slogged back upstairs and checked her email.

The only message that needed a response was from Ed Benson, her best customer, asking if his 1930 Cadillac V16 Coupe would be ready in time for the haulers to pick up and take to the Amelia Island show. She crossed her fingers and sent a positive response. The painter was the only remaining major issue, and he'd never let her down yet.

The way things were going, this might be her last sizable job. Her chest tightened with the thought. Ed was her first customer, her *only* customer for nearly a year. He was Great-Uncle Oscar's best friend, and he'd sent her an old Edsel to see what she could do with it. Pleased with the result, he'd been sending her a steady stream of classic cars for the last four years. A self-made billionaire, inventor, and patent holder for several revolutionary solar energy products, he had money to burn. Luckily, what he spent it on was his addiction to buying, restoring, driving, showing, and selling classic autos.

Benson was a strong promoter for Delacroix Restorations as well, marketing her ability to cronies and strangers he met at shows. The work generated by his referrals had allowed her to hire Luke and buy equipment that made her place one of the best restoration shops in the Four Corners states. Her reputation, at least until the article came out, was on the fast track. She could only hope none of the national news services would pick up the Daily Watch's story and broadcast it across the very small classic car world.

Besides the Caddy, which Luke had dropped at the paint shop on his way home yesterday, the resto-mod was her only active project. For all practical purposes, it was complete. Up until a few weeks ago, Renni planned to take it to Santa Fe for a car show. The show, a fundraiser for St. Jude's, was a quality event with impressive sales numbers, and last year she and Ed had taken his Edsel.

She stared at the resto-mod, by far the best build she'd ever done. And it was all hers. The Chevy was rougher than a cob when she purchased it from a widow at a local yard sale, but there was never any doubt about what she would do with it. Like most builds, she saw it finished in her head the instant she laid eyes on it. Some owners didn't agree with her snap decisions, at least in the beginning, but so far, once she showed them a rendering of what it could become, they were all in. The resto-mod took more than a year to finish because work on it had to fit between other, paying, work.

Everything about the resto-mod was as near to perfect as possible, and it was worth a hefty price, at least a hundred and fifty grand—more if it had come out of one of the bigger, long-established, male-owned shops. She and Luke were hoping for at least high nineties to a hundred and ten or twenty since her shop wasn't as well known. They had talked over how to get the best price. A lot of auctions and shows were scheduled in late summer and early fall, which would dilute the pool of high bidders. The Santa Fe show's registration fee was high, and with added travel, hotel, and food costs, it would be a significant hit to the company's bottom line if no one made a reasonable offer. In the end, they'd agreed it was too risky.

Now, considering the situation with the Marmon, and the odds her shop was in for a long dry spell—if she was lucky enough not to lose the business entirely—she was glad of the decision. She was going to have to hoard her cash and assets. At the rate Brody's investigation was going, the car could end up as collateral for her bail.

Renni suddenly felt drained, like someone had pulled her energy plug and let it all leak out. She scrutinized the shop. Everything was where it belonged. Nothing out of place, no trash, no yellow crime scene tape. No reason to stay. She glanced at her fitness band. It wasn't even noon yet. She needed something to do, something to occupy her besides sitting at home watching TV, waiting for the other shoe to drop. Something that would take her mind off the strong possibility she'd be out of work very soon.

Deciding she should probably have some actual food in the house, she drove to a small, ramshackle fruit stand to stock up her fridge. It was a little out of her way, more so than Seth and Amy Hollister's neat, red, barn-shaped fruit stand down the road from her shop, but she hadn't been able to bring herself to go to Hollisters since Lauren's murder. Too many shared memories. Lauren did Seth and Amy's wedding photos, as well as photos for the stand's brochures and website, using Renni as a model customer.

Now every time they met, it ended up in a rehash of Lauren's life and times. It was too painful. Instead of Hollisters, Renni had started going to a fruit stand that didn't even have a name, located in an old cinder block and corrugated metal building between the Interstate and the railroad tracks. What it lacked in ambiance, it made up for with a pretty good selection.

Renni strolled up and down the aisles, tucking fruits and vegetables into the plastic basket over her arm. When she glanced up, she noticed the guy behind the counter was staring at her. She knew the owner, but she didn't recognize this clerk. He was attired in a T-shirt with a monkey dressed to look like Bob Marley and a Jimmy Buffet baseball cap. His skin was deeply tanned, his eyes a washed-out blue with crinkles at the corners from too much sun, or a lot of laughter. The way he was watching her seemed kind of creepy, but maybe he was worried about shoplifting. She hurriedly picked up the last few items and placed her basket on the counter.

He rang up her purchase and stuffed everything into two full bags. Renni winced. She'd have bruised plums and smashed tomatoes by the time she got back to the shop.

"You got an account, babe?" he asked in a California drawl, as he pulled out a small wooden box full of alphabetized index cards. Before she could answer his question, the woman who usually waited on Renni stepped out of a backroom. She recognized Renni and waved.

"Hey, Miss Delacroix, how are you? Lovely weather, isn't it?"

Without waiting for a reply, she hurried out through another door.

Renni turned back to the clerk, struggled for a moment to remember his question, then said, "Yes, I do, but I'll pay cash." She handed over a twenty and he returned a card to the box.

When she held out her hand for the change, he grabbed her wrist with one hand and dropped each coin and bill slowly into her palm, staring into her eyes as he counted, "Twenty-three, twenty-four, twenty-five cents and four ones make twenty dollars. Nice doin' business with you, Miss Renni Delacroix. You be sure to come on back now. It's cool we're only a few miles from your place. Nice and convenient." He smiled, showing a mouth full of perfect teeth. They were slightly pointed.

The image of a surfing shark planted itself in Renni's brain. *I need chocolate. I'm beginning to lose it.* She jerked her hand away. "Thanks."

She hurried back out to her car, vowing she would brave Hollisters from now on, and that she'd have Maisie call and ask these guys to tear up her account card.

Renni munched on a plum as she turned toward home, but before she headed across the river, she decided to pull off at Riverside Park and treat Buster to a swim. She parked the car under a tall, widespread cottonwood to keep the sun off it and followed as Buster made a beeline for the shallow, slow-moving Colorado River. She waded out with him, the lukewarm water washing over her bare feet and calves. Fine silt sifted between her toes, and the current sucked at her. She smiled at Buster's antics as he bounced out to chest-deep water, stuck his head under for a moment, then raced back to shore and shook like he'd swam the entire width of the river.

When it felt like her nose and shoulders were starting to burn, she looked up at the sun, surprised to see it was straight overhead. She sighed. *Time to go.*

She called to Buster. As he reluctantly turned and came toward her, the hair on the back of her neck prickled and a sudden chill ran down her spine. She looked up again, but there weren't any clouds blocking the sun's rays. Turning in a circle, Renni spotted a man staring at her from the edge of the trees. He wore a ball cap, T-shirt, and shorts, and while the shadows made it difficult to see any details, she was pretty sure it was the guy from the fruit stand. He put his hands up, held something to his face, then dropped it back down. Like he was using a camera. Uncomfortable, she quickly clipped on Buster's leash and headed back to the car.

Nearing the parking lot, Renni caught a flicker in her peripheral vision. She ducked as a carelessly thrown Frisbee missed its disc golf target and skimmed close enough to ruffle her hair. Her effort to keep from being clocked by the disc resulted in tripping over Buster's leash and stumbling several steps before regaining her balance.

When she stood to continue to her car, she found herself face to face with the man who had been staring at her. Up close, it was obviously the guy from the fruit stand. He wore an old-style SLR camera on a lanyard around his neck.

He put his hand on her bicep to steady her. "You okay?" he asked.

"Yeah, um, fine, thanks. Excuse me," she stuttered, skirting around him and hurrying toward the Spitz, tugging a reluctant Buster behind. As she neared the car, she glanced over her shoulder. He was still standing in the same place but had his camera up and appeared to be shooting photos of the kids playing Frisbee golf. *Thanks to that damn cop, I'm seeing trouble everywhere. The guy likes to get out in the fresh air, just like me. So what? Nothing mysterious about that, right? Still . . .*

"I don't know why, but that guy gives me the creeps, Busty. You better keep an eye on him, okay?" She ruffled his fur and wheeled the Spitz out of the crowded parking lot, headed for home.

—

He watched her load the dog into her itty-bitty sports car, feeling kind of sad. It was a shame Renni needed to die. But she threatened his plans. Threatened Karen. She would ruin everything, and he couldn't let that happen. It was hot in the car, so he strolled over to a picnic area under a shade tree, hiked himself up onto a concrete table, and watched the Frisbee game.

# Chapter Twenty

Renni pulled up in front of her garage and debated leaving the car out. The hour by the river hadn't done much to relieve her exhaustion, and it seemed too much effort to try and squeeze the car into the old shed. The structure wasn't built to accommodate three vehicles, even small ones. When all of them were inside the garage, she was forced to climb over the car door to get out. Besides, the space in front of the garage was nicely shaded by cottonwoods.

She was pretty much convinced of her decision when a wet, white blob splattered on the hood of the car. "Oh, yeah." She nodded, lips pursed. "*That's* why I never park outside."

Moving quickly before the crow could drop another bomb, which might land closer to home, she slipped the car into its usual narrow slot. After she climbed over the car door, she lifted Buster out. He ran around sniffing everything in sight as if a whole parade of critters had trooped through the yard. Renni flipped the garage door down and fastened the latch.

"Come on, you goof. It's the same bunnies and toads from yesterday." Buster trotted over to her side and they went up the steps to the porch. The instant the door swung in, she got a strong whiff of a noxious odor. "Whew, Busty, what did you eat today?"

Buster barked and scrabbled backward. It took a few seconds for the smell to register, but when it did, Renni started backing away too. She pulled out her cell phone and hit 911. "Buster, come on!"

As she put her foot over the first step, the spaniel darted between her feet. The next thing she knew, she flew ass over teakettle down the flight of concrete steps. Her shoulder, hip, and forearm connected with one or another of the five steps, and from the yips Buster let out, he hadn't escaped a bounce or two. They came to rest in a pile at the corner of the steps and stone foundation, Renni's legs tangled in a thorny barberry bush, Buster draped over her chest.

"Holy shi—"

And then the world ended.

# Chapter Twenty-One

He slowed the car to a crawl once he was on top of the plateau. The explosion would be massive, so there was no reason to get any closer. Even expecting it, the actual event made him flinch.

The flash of flame was much smaller and more fleeting than expected, but the enormous plume of debris that flew up and out, raining down—now *that* was amazing. A thunderous boom followed the flash and probably rattled windows for miles.

He pulled onto the shoulder and stopped, watching as flat pieces of walls and roof fell in slow motion, fluttering back and forth on their descent like ginormous butterfly wings. Smaller pieces tumbled down like huge raindrops, thudding and crashing into the ground.

He hadn't been able to enjoy the explosion that killed dear old Pop since he was still living in Utah at the time but based on the photos he'd seen of the aftermath, this one was almost as good. When he first came up with the idea, he wasn't sure how he'd pull it off. But thanks to the Internet, he'd been able to find all kinds of interesting information, not to mention great prices and free one-day shipping. The trigger. The ignition source. Instructions. All of it. Gotta love Google and Amazon—*life made simple,* just like the commercials said.

Sirens jarred him out of his reverie. He shook himself, focused, and started the car. He steered toward town, using the busiest roads available. There were several sports bars on the I-70 Business Loop, and he pulled into one in hopes the local news would have a special report. He was rewarded with an excited reporter nearly hopping up and down as she recounted every movement of the firefighters behind her as if the viewers couldn't already see it for themselves.

# Chapter Twenty-Two

Brody leaned back in his chair, tuning out the noise around him in the task force center as he flipped through DNA reports. They'd shown up a day later than promised, at least to his desk. The reports were dated yesterday, meaning the CBI took a whole day to send them over.

He took a deep breath and pursed his lips, nodding along as he read that several tests had come back positive for known RMHK victims. But there were some unknowns. That played right to Delacroix's claim to have seen other women. He was so engrossed he almost missed what the dispatcher said when the hand-held radio on his desk crackled.

"10-80 at 10632 Thirty-Seven Road, 11-41 requested. Code 10."

As a detective, he rarely went out on emergency calls, but he'd paid more attention to them since putting in for SWAT earlier in the month. There was something about the address that seemed familiar. He keyed it into the computer, and ten seconds later bulled his way down the hall and out to his black and white.

Fast-paced radio calls crackled back and forth over police channels, and he hoped the call about an explosion with critical trauma and rolling a "bus," short for ambulance, was the result of an overzealous dispatcher, or the address was wrong. As he got closer to Renni Delacroix's address of record, the road became narrowed by looky-loos parked along the nonexistent dirt shoulders, half in and half out of the barrow ditches. He was forced to slow. A perimeter had been set up a quarter mile from the house, but the patrolman guarding this end of the road opened the barriers as Brody approached, his identity advertised by the bright band of flashing emergency lights set in his grille. A section of fence inside the perimeter was down, and deep tracks led through the old orchard toward the house. He turned in and followed them.

Brody parked a hundred yards from the smoldering ruin and hiked the rest of the way. There were several fire department vehicles parked at odd angles, hoses, and other equipment strung out. There weren't any flames and not much smoke. Not that there was anything left to burn; it appeared the majority of the structure lay in an irregular circular pattern around the foundation. Most of the debris showed scorch marks.

Red and white strobes flashed near the front of the house and Brody hurried toward them, slipping and sliding through the mud and tripping over deflated fire hoses.

He arrived just as the doors of the ambulance slammed shut. Its siren began to wail as it pulled out. He took a few jogging steps after it before acknowledging the futility, then turned to search for the fire chief.

Chief Ray stood at the back of his command vehicle, the rear hatch open, keying data into his laptop.

"Chief? Detective Brody."

The chief didn't turn as he said, "Yeah, Detective, I'm kinda busy here. What do you need?"

"This residence belonged to a person of interest in a serial murder case. I need to know ASAP if it was an accident or arson."

"When I have information, I'll pass it along."

Brody squeezed his eyes shut, biting back a sharp retort. "Do you have ID and condition of the critical trauma case?"

"Young woman and a dog. The dog was taken to a local vet. He didn't appear hurt much, considering he was ready and willing to bite the hand trying to rescue him." The chief finally turned and interpreted Brody's impatient glare. "The woman . . . Well, we'll have to wait until we hear from the trauma center." The chief tilted his head, and Brody saw a smear of ash across his cheek. "Woman of interest in a serial case? Would that be Renni Delacroix?" he asked.

Brody nodded.

"Saw the article. I've met Renni, but I didn't see the victim. The EMTs were already at work by the time the crew was lined out. Good kid. I can't believe she had anything to do with any murders."

"She's not a suspect." Heat rose on his neck at the lie. "But she may have information to advance the case."

"That why you want to know if this could be arson?"

Brody nodded again. "If there's a chance this was deliberate, it could mean the murderer wants to prevent her from talking to anyone." He clenched his jaw. "If it turns out the killer got the information from that reporter, and I get my hands on him, you might need more than an arson team to sort it out." Given her involvement with an ongoing murder investigation, Brody doubted her house exploding was mere coincidence. Especially since he didn't believe in them. It might not be a bad idea if the killer thought she was dead. "Can you keep the fact she survived quiet?"

The chief grunted. "Too late, I'm afraid. The reporter, Lassiter, was here almost before us. Probably has a scanner in his car." He jerked his head toward what was left of Renni's house. "If it's arson, I'll get you a report as soon as I can." A slow, evil grin skittered across his face. "And if I get a call related to a guy named Lassiter, I'll make sure the units roll real slow."

Brody waved his thanks and turned away as the chief went back to his computer. He radioed dispatch to get the phone number for Lassiter, then keyed it in.

"Lassiter here. Speak. I got deadlines."

"Mr. Lassiter, this is Detective Brody. I'm working on the RMHK case. I need to ask you to keep a lid on the Delacroix property explosion. You could be putting Miss Delacroix in danger." It was all Brody could do not to accuse him of causing the explosion in the first place.

"Sorry, man, I already turned my story in."

"Get it back."

"No can do. Once it's in, it stays."

Brody stabbed the End Call button with his index finger, wishing the reporter's flesh was taking the beating instead of the inanimate phone. There wasn't anything he could do about Lassiter and his story, so he headed for the hospital. His badge got him past the volunteer and emergency room gatekeepers, but no further than the trauma center waiting room. With cell phone use banned, he called Luke using the handset on the waiting room table.

"What do you mean Renni's in the hospital? What happened?"

"Did you hear about the explosion—"

"It was Renni? Where is she?" Luke hung up before Brody could tell him, but since there was only one hospital in the area with a trauma center, it wouldn't be too hard for him to find her.

Sure enough, less than twenty minutes later, Luke and Vicki burst through the door into the waiting room. Maisie arrived shortly after, clutching a soggy tissue, her wrinkled face blotchy and red. The expression on Luke's face when Maisie made a beeline for him would have made Brody laugh under other circumstances. Abject fear was replaced by relief when Vicki intercepted the older woman, steering her to a row of garish, upholstered side chairs.

They waited. Fetched lousy coffee from the machine. Sat.

Stood. Paced. Hour after hour.

Early in the evening, a figure stepped into the waiting room doorway and they all turned, expectant. Instead of a doctor, they saw a tall, thin white-haired man in an untucked shirt covered with brightly colored cartoon cars. He moved farther into the room and eyed each of them. His gaze rested on Maisie. "Mrs. Fletcher?"

"Oh my God! Thank goodness you're here!" She ran over to the newcomer, threw her arms around his waist, and burst out bawling.

He stood, arms akimbo, shock on his face. When she showed no sign of stopping or letting go, he reached down and gently disengaged her arms. Vicki came to the rescue again. Another man, only an inch or two shorter and at least forty pounds heavier, stepped out from behind him.

"I'm Oscar Wallace," the first man said, "Renni's great-uncle, and this here's my boy, Bubber, er, Elmo, officially." He nodded at the redhead. "Mrs. Fletcher called and told us about Renni. We got here as fast as we could."

Brody stepped up and offered his hand. "Mr. Wallace, I'm Detective Brody."

The amiable expression on the old man's face changed to one of wariness. "What's a detective doing here?" he demanded.

"Renni is . . . well . . . involved in an investigation, sir."

"What kind of investigation?"

Brody could see the old man wouldn't accept a standard *I can't discuss an ongoing investigation* type of answer. "We have a potential serial killer."

Wariness became downright anger. "Is that the reason she's here?" Oscar asked. "How she got hurt? Is it something to do with this *investigation?*" Father and son stepped up close, making Brody, who was above average height, feel short.

"We don't know what happened, Mr. Wallace. I spoke to the fire chief, but they don't have enough information yet to determine if it was an accident or something else."

"If it wasn't an accident, then I think we all got an idea about what that there something else would be, right?" Bubber snapped.

Luke came forward. "Renni was the one who went to the police." He paused, and Brody could swear he blushed. "Well, anyway, she considered it important the police be told."

Bubber opened his mouth, but just then another door into the room opened, one marked "No Admittance." A man in a clean white coat over red scrubs with darker red smears stepped into the waiting room. Deep lines covered his face, but his eyes were bright blue and earnest.

"I'm Doctor Moore. You're all with Miss Delacroix?" At their nods, he continued. "She's a very fortunate woman from the sound of it. The EMTs told me the condition of her house. She has a moderate concussion, hairline fracture of the left radius, er, forearm, dislocated right shoulder, and a bruise the size of a dinner plate on her right hip. In addition, she suffered a few small first- and second-degree burns to one side of her body, though not extensive, along with a variety of contusions and abrasions. There's also a potential for temporary hearing problems."

He looked around at them, then fixed his gaze on Oscar. Brody wasn't sure if it was because Oscar was the oldest or tallest person present, or due to the intentness of his gaze.

"She'll need to be here for a day or so to let us monitor her concussion and run a few tests. Her arm is being cast right now, but it should heal quickly. We've performed a reduction on her shoulder, which will require a sling for one or two weeks at most. The burns can be treated topically. Scarring and pigment change should be minimal. We don't believe she has tympanic membrane rupture . . ." At the frowns this term brought, he clarified, "Burst eardrums. But I wouldn't be surprised if she has some ringing in her ears or difficulty hearing for a week or so, as well as headaches, and possibly dizziness or vertigo. She'll need a few stitches for the penetrating wounds and will be a veritable patchwork of bruises, but nothing life-threatening. We'll set her up with pain meds for a while and get her on an antibiotics series to be safe."

"I saw the house, Doc," Brody said. "There's basically nothing left. I'm surprised she doesn't have more serious injuries." As soon as he said it, he wanted to bite back the words. *Wow, Brody, you're so very sensitive.*

Doctor Moore nodded. "As I said, she's incredibly lucky. Normally someone close to a major explosion would have very traumatic damage and burns. From what the EMT told me, the house sat on a stone foundation with a steep set of steps. Miss Delacroix was discovered at the bottom of the steps, off to the side. With the wrist, hip, and shoulder injuries indicating impact with something hard and relatively sharp, my guess is she fell down the steps and ended up below the major blast wave. Otherwise . . ." He shrugged and turned to go.

"Can we see her?" Oscar asked.

The doctor stopped halfway out the door. "It'll be a while yet." He checked his watch. "Why don't you all go somewhere for a bit? Have some dinner. I'll leave orders that if she's up to it, any family members can get a few minutes with her later tonight even if it's after visiting hours." He ducked out of sight.

The six of them trooped out together, stopping under the portico where they were shaded from the slanted, still-bright sun and ninety-five-degree heat.

"We ain't real familiar with this place," Oscar said. "Anyone got an idea where we can get something to eat? I'd like to hear more about this investigation stuff and why the hell my girl is mixed up in it." He fixed Brody with a hard stare.

"If you like Mexican food, there's a great place about five minutes away," Luke said. "Or there are several chain restaurants by the mall and the airport. They're fifteen to thirty minutes away."

Bubber stuck up his hand. "I vote Mexican. They got margaritas?"

Luke laughed. "Yeah. Good ones. Handmade."

Everyone agreed to follow Luke to the restaurant. Brody considered heading back to the station but decided it would be an excellent opportunity to pump Renni's friends and family for more background on her. Maybe get a feel for if she had a propensity to be an attention seeker.

He didn't much like the twinge of conscience chewing his ass as he headed after them.

# Chapter Twenty-Three

The décor was typical for a family-owned Mexican restaurant. Pottery, carved and painted benches, statues of mariachi bands, woven blankets, and vibrant paintings adorned the walls and decorated colorful niches. The menus were large and so were the margaritas. The waitress advised them it was happy hour with two-for-one pricing, and Bubber's face broke out in a grin from ear to ear.

They ordered, arguing about split bills until Oscar slammed a fist on the table and gave everyone the stink eye, eliciting a giggle from the waitress and a promise he'd be the one she gave the ticket. After baskets of tortilla chips and saucers of *pico de gallo* and cabbage salsa arrived, Brody settled in to begin his interrogation.

Before he could open his mouth, Oscar beat him to it. "So, what does our Renni know about a serial killer?"

Being questioned by someone else was a novel, and not particularly pleasant, experience. Brody tried the standard line. "It's an active investigation and I can't—"

"Hell you can't. My girl is in the hospital. Seems to me like maybe someone tried to blow her up. You better damn well tell me what's goin' on, boy." Oscar's voice was gruff and gravelly, his eyes hard.

Brody considered the dining area. They were in a small alcove at the back of the restaurant, with the nearest diners on the other side of a five-foot wall, two tables down. He surveyed the group around their table. Everyone was either related to or close friends with Renni. They all had her best interests at heart.

Except him.

"Apparently she has this idea she can touch a car and 'feel' stuff. She thinks a serial killer owned a truck she bought," he began.

"Ain't no 'apparently' about it," Oscar snapped. "Renni has had the gift since she was a kid. Started when she put her hand on the car that hit her parents and killed 'em. What'd she see this time?"

Luke chimed in. "Renni finally found a Marmon—"

Bubber chuffed a laugh. "She's been searchin' for one of them since high school."

"It was in an online auction," Luke continued, ignoring Brody's frown, "but the company has a solid reputation. Anyway, she was too busy to pick it up, so I fetched it. When I pulled in, she could hardly wait to get her hands on it. But as soon as she did, it knocked her clean off the trailer."

Brody raised his eyebrows. He hadn't heard that part. He waved Luke silent and took over the story. "Luke called me and said his boss might have some information on the death of a local woman, Lauren Cooper."

Bubber nodded. "I remember her. That photographer Renni met right after she came here. They was good friends. Renni was real tore up after she was found, wasn't she, Pa?"

Oscar nodded impatiently and motioned Brody to continue.

"Anyway, the Cooper death is linked with several others, and we suspect a serial killer is operating along Interstate 70, mostly on the Western Slope, but possibly over to the Front Range, or into Utah. The internal name we've given the file is RMHK."

"Yeah, it stands for Rocky Mountain High Killer, you know, from the song?" Maisie added.

Brody tamped down hard on his impatience at the interruption. "After I interviewed Renni, one of the detectives on the case was trying to impress an admin at the station and told her a local psychic had information on the RMHK. There happened to be a reporter in the station on another matter who overheard the conversation. He ran a wildly sensational story, mostly garbage, but it's possible—unlikely, but possible—the killer saw it and came after her. Until the arson investigator gives me his report, I can't say for sure."

"So she could still be in danger? Whyn't you lock the sumbitch reporter up or tell everybody she died, you know, like they do on TV?" Bubber demanded.

"We can't lock him up for running news stories, and he'd already turned in a second story about Renni surviving the explosion before we could stop him. He probably has a scanner and was on-site before the ambulance arrived. At this point, there's no way to keep it quiet."

"Well, God damn it, we sure as hell can't let him get another crack at her. We'll load up all her stuff and take her back to Missouri with us, right, Pa?" Bubber said, leaning back in his chair and crossing his arms.

Luke shook his head. "You're closer to Renni than me, but I can't imagine there's any way in hell to get her to pack up and leave the shop, not after working her ass off to get it up and running. She's got some tough deadlines right now."

Oscar nodded, a wry smile on his face. "She always was a stubborn little thing." He rubbed his chin. "You're right. She won't go. Me 'n Bubber'll stay awhile, keep an eye on her. One of us will be with her all the time." He slapped the table and sat back, settling the issue.

"You think Renni is going to stay in your hotel room?" Vicki asked. "I don't think she'll go for that. Besides, with all the other people staying there, maids and whatnot, you'd go crazy trying to make sure no one gets near her." She shook her head. "No, the best thing is for her to come home with us." She turned to Luke, who nodded his agreement.

Maisie, who'd been conspicuously quiet, piped up. "She can stay with me. I got the best security system ever made."

"I have a feelin' there's one thing we ain't considered." Oscar sighed. "Our girl won't put anyone at risk, and she ain't much for hidin'. Or being told what to do. She's got a stubborn streak a mile wide."

Luke rolled his eyes at Vicki, who giggled.

Brody held up his index finger to get their attention. "For now, Renni's safe in the hospital. We don't have to come up with a half-assed plan yet. I'll make sure we have an officer outside her room for the time being. From what the fire chief said, I think he'll have something pretty quick one way or the other. If he determines arson, Renni will need professional protection. The RMHK is smart. Smart enough to have operated for over a decade, and likely to know his way around explosives. If it comes to that, I'll contact the FBI and arrange for protective custody."

By the time dessert arrived, the conversation had deteriorated into arguments over who was best qualified to keep Renni safe, and the restaurant manager all but chased the boisterous group out. Brody excused himself and started for the station. The others headed to the hospital, but Brody didn't want a crew of overly protective family and friends around when he talked with Renni. Besides, there was always the chance new information had come in about the explosion or one of the queries he'd sent out to the FBI.

The office was quiet. The heavily staffed day shift was long gone, and most of the night shift was out on patrol. Other than the RMHK task force office, all the lights were off in his wing of the building. It only took a minute to boot up his computer. He scanned through messages, dragging most of them into other folders or deleting them. Only a scant few related to the RMHK were left, and none of them held anything of interest.

Brody sent an email to Hatten updating him on the explosion and Renni's condition. He requested twenty-four-hour protection for her upon release from the hospital. But even if Chief Wilcox agreed to it—which was slightly less likely than seeing a pig fly—the department's budget wouldn't stretch to any place decent. He also mentioned Renni's great-uncle and cousin were in town, then logged out and shut down. On his way out, he arranged for one of the night shift patrolmen to be stationed outside Renni's room for the night and turned toward home.

# Chapter Twenty-Four

He sat down in his recliner and opened the Sunday paper, anticipation raising his heart rate several ticks. The explosion would be all over the front page. Nothing exciting ever happened in this little farm town. Well, not in about fifteen years, anyway. He smiled. When he flicked the page flat, the smile slid off his face.

The jumbo black headline read, "Explosive Escape." Large photos of Renni's house—or what had been her house—filled the front page, showing the explosion had utterly obliterated the structure. There wasn't anything left above the old stone foundation. How in the hell did she not get vaporized? He read the story twice, but there were very few real details. The only one that mattered was Renni Delacroix was alive.

Then four other words caught his eye: *Arson possible . . . Investigation ongoing . . .* He grunted. They'd be picking through bits and pieces of the house scattered over at least a half-mile radius for days. Good luck finding proof.

He stood and paced the room, chewing his lip. But what if they did find something? What if he hadn't been careful enough? He rubbed his hand over his chin, the tented newspaper forgotten on the floor. His fist slammed into his thigh over and over as he became more agitated. *Damn it!* The problem with Renni should have been over by now. It was a good plan. Well thought out. Perfectly executed.

She'd made him fail. Pretended to be all nice to him. Tricked him into trying to make it quick and painless. *I'll have to do better next time. And it won't be quick or painless.*

—

From her usual place in the corner, Karen watched him surreptitiously. His stunned expression, violent movements, and angry snarls surprised her. He was usually happy and upbeat. Except the week before he went on his annual vacation; he could get pretty worked up then. But it was months before he was scheduled to go. Something was different. Something had upset him.

Or someone.

# Chapter Twenty-Five

Brody was back in the office early the next morning, checking his email and hoping to talk with the FBI task force members, but it appeared they kept banker's hours. They still hadn't shown up when Hatten stopped in.

"Hell of a day yesterday, eh?" Hatten said.

"Not one of my favorites."

"How's the girl? You hear anything?"

"Not yet, I'm going there shortly. I'm waiting on a response from Chief Ray. He knows Miss Delacroix, and I think he'll get back to me as soon as he has anything, but the place was a mess. I can't imagine how long it will take to get through it all and make a determination."

Hatten eyed the room. "Kind of the Lone Stranger around here, aren't you? Where is everyone?"

Brody shook his head. "Hell if I know. I haven't heard from the Fibbies since they came in and set up. Maybe they're not even still in town."

"I'll see if I can light a fire under them to get on the explosion." Hatten grinned. "Pun intended."

As he turned to leave, Brody said, "Sir, what about the protection I requested?"

Hatten paused in the doorway. "We don't have anything resembling a safe house around here. And no budget for twenty-four-hour surveillance. If we ask the FBI for coverage, they'll ship her over to the Front Range and the RMHK will be well and truly theirs. Besides, I'm still not convinced she isn't involved. This whole 'car whisperer' thing is too far out there for me. I think she knows a whole lot more about the killer and we need to get it out of her." He slanted his head, a speculative expression on his face.

Brody didn't like the look. He'd worked with Hatten long enough to know the sergeant could be very Machiavellian when he wanted to be.

"Renni Delacroix is attractive, isn't she?"

"*Yeeeaaaah . . .*" Brody said, even more convinced he wasn't going to like whatever came next.

"You're a good lookin' guy, at least that's what some of the admins say."

Brody snorted. "So?"

The smile splitting Hatten's face would have done the Cheshire Cat proud. "I think I have the perfect solution." He headed out into the hall. "I'll give you the details once I have them all worked out," his voice echoed from the hallway.

"Wait—" Brody started to follow, but a ping from the computer notified him of an incoming email. He opened it. Fire Chief Ray. The email was short and to the point.

*Suspicious evidence on-site. Front door located fifty feet behind garage; eye screw on interior leading edge, nylon line attached. Similar material melted on floor. Trace leads to water heater/main ignition point. Gas connecter undamaged indicates disconnect before explosion. More tests needed but high probability of criminal arson. Best guess is trip-wire-triggered ignition. Thought you might be interested.*

Brody sent thanks and leaned back in his chair. Attempted

murder by explosion. A serial killer who suffocated his victims. It was an unusual combination of modus operandi. Would Delacroix blow up her own place? Would the RMHK change his method that dramatically? He scowled, muttering, "Goddamn FBI." Where were they when he needed to talk to them about profiling or checking their database for anything similar?

He stood and kicked the wheeled chair, sending it careening across the room. Maybe an interview with Miss Delacroix would turn up something interesting.

# Chapter Twenty-Six

After stomping around the house most of the morning, growling and snapping at her when she tried to ask what was wrong, her brother balled up the newspaper and took it outside with him. She watched out the window as he stuffed it down in the big trashcan set out front for pickup and then disappeared into the barn.

Knowing the trash truck could be by any minute, she got up the nerve to sneak out and retrieve the newspaper. It was her only chance to see what he was so upset about. A series of hard sneezes hit her as she walked back into the house, the blooms on the Rose of Sharon reminding her it was time for an allergy pill.

After reading every article, she buried the paper in the bottom of the kitchen trash, rather than risk going out to the big bin again. The only article that wasn't the usual recap of city council meetings, business openings and closures, politics, or sports, was the front-page story about the explosion. It must be what upset him so much. She paced through the house, arms hugged tightly to her chest, as she mentally compared the recent explosion to one from years ago.

The explosion was big news back then. Not so much because Daddy died, though. Most people in town considered him a pain in the ass. But the blast rattled windows for more than a mile, and several head of livestock were injured running through fences. Finding Daddy's remains in the debris seemed almost incidental in the newspaper reports. As for her and Mom, their lives changed for the better with his death. He'd been a distant, unapproachable man who spent most of his time in the barn like her brother did now.

It wasn't too long after the explosion that Mom died in the nursing home. There was a lot of life insurance money, and when her brother showed up out of the blue, he appropriated a chunk of it to rebuild the barn. Since then, it was just the two of them.

If he hadn't come back when he did, she wasn't sure how she would have gotten along. Her transcription business paid well, and she could order most of what she wanted or needed on her computer. But some things needed doing in person, like meeting with repairmen, or going to doctor appointments, and she'd never learned to drive. Her brother handled the in-person meetings, picked up takeout, and did other shopping she couldn't do online.

He was good company most of the time too. He made sure she had library books to read and movies to watch, and they spent most evenings watching TV together just like they had when they were growing up. Before the spider.

But lately, something had changed. He was moody and snapped at her all the time. Karen wrung her hands as she fretted about the changes. She didn't want to be alone again. It would be so much more difficult.

She found herself in her room, peering out the window toward the backyard and the two-story barn, identical to the one destroyed more than fifteen years ago. She'd never set foot in it. After rebuilding the barn, her brother, like her father before him, told her it was *his* space and she wasn't allowed. Like some kind of "boy's club." Like she cared.

Now she wondered what she would find out there if she looked. Not that she'd ever get up the nerve to try. At least not while her brother was around.

# Chapter Twenty-Seven

When Brody entered the antiseptic-tinged room, Vicki was sitting next to Renni's bed. The second bed was empty. She stood and stepped over to him, leaning in for a hug.

"Ren's sleeping, but I think she's beginning to wake up. The nurse stopped in a few minutes ago and said the pain meds would be wearing off and to let her know if Renni needs more." She peered at her watch. "I have to get going. I'm supposed to pick Buster up from the vet as soon as they open and take him to our house. Will you stay with her until she wakes up? Make sure she's doing okay?"

"Sure. I wanted to talk to her anyway, if she's up to it." He bussed Vicki on the cheek and listened as her sandals flip-flopped down the hallway. When he turned back to the bed, Renni was awake and watching him.

He stepped over and sat in the chair. "How're you feeling?"

Frowning, she touched her ears while shaking her head. Remembering what the doctor said about her hearing, he raised his voice and repeated the question.

Renni closed her eyes a moment, and a deep dent of pain

bisected her forehead. "I don't have a mirror, but I think possibly worse than I look," she said, overly loud.

"Too bad, because you look like hell."

She gave him a wan smile. "Gee, thanks."

"The nurse told Vicki you could have some pain meds. Want me to call her?"

Renni nodded, then winced. He went to the door and made eye contact with the nurse at a nearby station, angling his head toward the room behind him. The nurse finished making some notes and then came over.

"She's in a lot of pain," he said. "Vicki said you could give her something for it . . ."

The nurse nodded. "You bet. I'll be right in."

He went back and sat, assuring Renni the nurse would return soon. "You probably don't feel like it, but if there's anything you can tell me about yesterday, it might really help."

Her brows drew together and she stared out the window, unseeing. "I remember going to Riverside Park with Buster. We came home. I parked the car. Buster was being a doofus, and then . . . that's it."

"You don't remember going into the house?"

"No." She squinted harder. "Wait. I remember the smell. A bad smell. Buster acting crazy." Renni frowned. "It was rotten eggs, so it was a gas leak, right?" She shrank back on the bed like a balloon with its air let out. "My house blew up. I remember Oscar telling me last night, but I was kinda out of it. But you already knew, I guess."

"Yeah. I got there after the firemen. The ambulance was leaving to take you to the hospital." He leaned in close. "Renni." His tone made her sit up a bit straighter. "It wasn't a gas leak. The arson inspector thinks it was deliberate."

Her bloodshot eyes, surrounded by black, green, and yellow bruising, flashed. "I didn't blow my house up, Detective Brody. I didn't, I swear. I loved it."

Tears filled her eyes and overflowed. He frowned and shook

his head, touching the shoulder not in a sling.

"That's not what I'm saying. We think the explosion was meant to blow you up, along with the house."

"Me?" The word came out in a squeak. "Why would anyone want to blow me up?"

Brody was impressed with the innocent expression, the hurt surprise in her voice. She should be on stage. He played along. "There's a good chance the guy who killed Lauren did it. There was an article in the paper . . ."

Her eyes squeezed shut. "That article! I remember now. It's gonna kill my business."

He frowned. Under the circumstances, most people would be more worried about the article getting *themselves* killed.

The nurse bustled in with a tray containing a pink plastic jug, matching sippy cup with bent straw, and small paper pill cup. She tipped two pills into Renni's palm and offered the sippy cup. Renni popped the medication into her mouth awkwardly with her left hand and sipped on the straw to wash them down, drawing Brody's attention to a futuristic plastic cast on her forearm.

He'd seen an article about the technology on the Discovery Channel but was surprised their small-town hospital was so advanced. He pointed at her arm and said, "Pretty cool."

Renni nodded as she sucked another long slurp of iced water. "They 3D-printed it right in the exam room this morning after they did a computer scan. It's waterproof, and I can scratch an itch through it." She followed up the statement by sticking a finger into one of the holes and scratching her arm.

"It's called Active Armor. We're a test market," the nurse said as she wheeled a one-legged table over, positioning it so it extended over the bed and placing the jug on it. Renni took one more drink and set the cup down.

"Hungry?" the nurse asked.

"A little."

"I'll bring a tray in shortly. You'll want to eat soon because you'll probably get sleepy once the meds kick in. You need all the rest you can get."

"Can I get up? I need to . . ." Renni flicked an uncomfortable glance at him.

Brody wasn't sure, but he thought there might be a blush somewhere under the bruises. He quickly stood. "I've got some calls to make. I'll be back in a few minutes to ask more questions."

Even though it was an excuse to give Renni and the nurse privacy, Brody used the time to call the fire chief, thanking him again for the early report and checking if there was anything more he could pass along. There wasn't.

Next, he called the direct line to the task force office and was surprised when it was picked up by AIC Tanner. Yes, the FBI knew about the explosion. No, they hadn't talked to the fire chief yet today. Yes, they'd offered their forensics people to assist with the arson investigation. No, it wasn't yet confirmed as arson. Yes, they planned to question Miss Delacroix as soon as her doctor okayed it.

It was like pulling teeth. Tanner didn't seem inclined to tell him anything of interest, so Brody wasn't inclined to advise him Renni was awake and cognizant or that the fire chief had a determination. At the end of the call, Brody had no more information than before.

Deeming enough time had passed, he returned to her room and found Renni picking through a bowl of what might be overcooked oatmeal with some mystery dried fruit in it. Her lackluster attempt to eat told him it wasn't any tastier than it appeared.

He leaned against the doorjamb. "How you feeling now?"

"Better after those pills." She gave him a lopsided grin. "As long as I don't actually do anything."

"You up to a few more questions?"

She nodded, then grimaced. Apparently, the pills weren't wholly blocking the pain.

"Do you remember seeing anyone following you, or hanging around your house or the shop?"

She pondered his question, nose wrinkling as she forced another bite of the mush. "No, but then I wasn't looking for anyone." Renni paused, brows furrowed. She set the spoon in the bowl, her hand shaking a bit. "You don't think the person who killed Lauren is here? In Rampart?"

Brody waggled his head back and forth. "Might be, might not be. It's pretty odd, don't you think? The day after a newspaper article comes out pegging you as knowing something about a serial killer, your house, along with you, gets blown up?" He watched her face closely.

"I can't believe it was intentional." She frowned. "You said they haven't finished the investigation. Maybe it was an accident. A defect in the hot water heater."

Brody tensed. "You think the water heater was the cause?"

"Well, the water heater is the only thing I have that runs off natural gas. Everything else is electric, except the old boiler, which uses coal. I assumed . . ."

*Good explanation or fast thinking.* "The investigator found a tripwire, and the water heater's gas line was disconnected. It didn't malfunction or break off."

She sighed and let her head sink back against the pillow, eyes closed tight. "I loved my house. I bought it from Maisie when I bought the packing plant. They both belonged to her husband's parents. She showed it to me after I said I needed to find a place to live, and I fell in love with it."

"Insurance?"

She waved her hand weakly. "That's not the problem. How am I ever going to rebuild a hundred-year-old house with hand-scraped wood floors and handmade molding? It had real calcimine walls and everything." Her voice took on a dreamy quality.

"What?" he asked. Interrogating her about the fire was a waste of time now the pills were kicking in.

"It's like plaster. They put it on thick and made patterns in it. Maisie said mine was broomed." At his frown, she gave a sloppy smile. "They used a real broom to make swirly patterns. Pretty cool, huh? Nobody does that anymore."

"Have you given any thought to where you're going to stay once they release you?"

Renni's eyelids flickered, then closed. "I'll get a hotel room. No, wait, I'll put a bed in the shop. Or sleep on the couch in my office. There's a shower downstairs, and I can cook in the breakroom . . ." Her voice faded.

"You won't be safe if . . ." Brody stopped. She was out, or at least past the point of comprehending what he was saying. He'd have to try again later.

# Chapter Twenty-Eight

Back at the station, Brody found a note on his desk that Hatten wanted to see him. With a sinking feeling, he headed down the hall.

Hatten's head jerked up when Brody knocked on the doorframe. "Come on in. Shut the door," he said. Once Brody was seated across the desk from him, the captain leaned back and put his feet on an open drawer. "Anything new on the car whisperer?"

Shrugging, Brody said, "She's too drugged-up to get much out of her. Says she doesn't remember seeing anything or anyone hinky before the explosion. Hell, she can barely remember conversations from last night after the accident. Maybe in a day or two. I'll keep trying."

"Yeah, I'm sure you will. And to make damn sure, I'm going to help you out."

Brody raised an eyebrow.

"You got that nice two-story house on a quiet street. A fancy security system you bragged about all spring. You're the best interrogator we have. And Miss Delacroix needs someone to keep an eye on her, and at the same time, find out what she's not telling us. You've got everything we need."

"Wait a minute," Brody said, leaning forward in his chair, "you want me to have the Delacroix chick live at my house? That's your brilliant idea?"

"Yep. Solves several problems. We'll reimburse you for extra food, but since you have a spare room you're not using, we won't need to pay rent or any other expenses. A cop's house with a security system is as secure as anything we could come up with, probably more so. You can transport her back and forth to her shop. I'll have patrol increase their drive-bys. That friend of yours who works with her can keep watch while she's there. I don't see any problems. Do you?"

"Hell yes, I do. My job description doesn't include babysitting."

"So you'd rather we send her to Denver and the FBI takes over?"

Brody ground his teeth. "Shit."

Hatten did the Cheshire Cat thing again and waved Brody out of his office.

—

Two days later, Renni found herself in a rental car with Oscar and Bubber, staring at a two-story Victorian house in an old residential area populated with large, well-maintained homes. Trimmed shrubs edged the neatly mowed lawn. Two large pots filled with bright annuals sat on either side of the front stoop. From somewhere close by, she could hear neighborhood children playing and dogs barking.

"This is stupid—" she began, but Oscar held up his hand.

"We've been over this. You agreed it was the best choice." She opened her mouth again, but he shushed her. "Get over being stubborn and so damn independent, Ren. We ain't gonna let anything else happen to you. *End of story.*"

She'd heard those three words many times over the years.

They signaled Oscar was finished discussing a topic and there was no changing his mind. Considering the old man—a sixty-something widower at the time, living with his confirmed-bachelor son—had one day found a young girl dropped on his doorstep, literally, he was an exceptionally understanding guardian. Oscar would listen to her arguments and, if they were compelling enough, was always willing to change his mind or a decision. But when he'd heard enough and not been swayed, those three words put paid to any further discussion.

"But . . ." She snapped her mouth shut when he glared and waggled his index finger at her. She groaned. "Come on, Buster. Let's go find some shoes or furniture for you to chew up." The spaniel jumped down and bounded along as she went slowly up the walk, Oscar beside her, while Bubber pulled large shopping bags with brand name logos from the trunk.

The door of the house opened before she got to it, and Brody stepped out onto the stoop. Buster charged up and stood on his hind legs, doing his pogo stick thing. Renni couldn't help a smile but quickly wiped it off her face as Brody unbent from petting the dog. He stepped to the side and waved her in, waiting as Oscar and Bubber entered behind her. Buster trotted in ahead of everyone like he owned the place.

"If the stairs are too much for you, Miss Delacroix, I have a rollaway bed I can set up for you down here. It's pretty comfortable," Brody said as he shut the door and engaged a security system.

It was on the tip of her tongue to ask why he would sleep on a rollaway bed in his own house, but she bit back the question. "No, I can walk fine." That wasn't exactly the truth. Her hip still hurt like a son of a bitch, but the physical therapist said she needed to get plenty of movement every day to loosen up the muscles. "And you might as well call me Renni since we're going to be roomies for a while."

The grin he gave her as he waved her up the stairs made it clear he'd noted how hard those words had been to say. "It's the door on the right."

She went up, Buster preceding, sliding her fingers along the smooth banister held up by elaborate, carved balusters. The steps squeaked gently underfoot. She inspected the high-ceilinged space, admiring the plaster rosette from which an antique, wrought-iron chandelier hung on a chain. The room she'd been assigned was large and airy, with floor-to-ceiling windows on two walls. They were old-style sash windows with wooden blocks set on the sills to prop the heavy windows open. A soft breeze stirred the cotton curtains.

A gaudy floral bedspread covered the queen-sized mattress, along with at least a dozen decorative pillows. A frilly bed skirt peeked out from under the edges. Renni peered over her shoulder at Brody.

"You decorate the room yourself?" She grinned at his blush and eye roll.

"The bedding came with the house. I've never used it before." He motioned to the door on the left of the headboard. "Closet in there." To the right, "Bathroom there. If you need anything, holler."

He backed out of the room. Bubber muscled the bulging bags through the doorway and hefted them onto the bed.

"You want us to unpack things for you?" Oscar asked.

She shook her head. "Nah, I need to practice doing stuff for myself."

"Okay, then. We'll be downstairs. Come down when you're done, and we'll get our schedules figured out." He gave her a raised-eyebrow frown that made her hold her tongue about what they could do with their schedules.

It took an annoyingly long time to empty the bags and get her new clothes hung in the walk-in closet or stowed on the numerous shelves. The frustration of not having full use of her dominant right hand, which was strapped to her stomach to keep her shoulder in place, was driving her crazy. She would be able to take the shoulder harness off for short stints in a few days, but she was still a week from being free of all entanglements. Buster spent the time snuffling every square inch of floor space, including wriggling under the bed.

By the time all her clothes were unpacked, she'd taken up about two total feet of closet space. Compared to her phone-booth-sized closet at home, it was like having a whole house for her clothes. Thinking about her nonexistent house nearly brought her to tears again, but she forced them back. What was done was done, and no use crying about it. She laid out her toiletries and what little makeup she used in the bright white bathroom. The shower curtain and rugs were a neutral shade of brown, a relief after the bedding.

Finally satisfied with her arrangements, she called Buster and went downstairs, following the sound of masculine voices through the kitchen and out a screen door to an expansive redwood deck.

# Chapter Twenty-Nine

Brody waved the two men out to the patio, nodding toward the cooler of ice and beers. Once they were all comfortably seated with drinks in hand, Oscar cleared his throat.

"We gotta sort this feller out, Brody. I ain't gonna let him have another go at Renni."

Bubber nodded emphatically.

"Maybe you could take her—" Brody started.

"Hell, if you knew her, you'd know better than that. She don't back down or run away. Never has. She stayed at that university until she graduated, puttin' up with all kinds of shit from them boys and teachers instead of takin' off." Oscar leaned back and gazed up at the sky. "All she's wanted since she got out of school was to find a place she could call home and set up shop."

An airplane dragged a fuchsia contrail, and the setting sun painted the clear blue sky faintly pink. Brody felt a pang, wishing he *did* know Renni better.

The old man continued. "This town. Her house. They're what she's wanted all her life—a home. Me 'n Bubber couldn't give her one, not with the racing. When she came to live with us, it was because we were her only family left. An old widower and his grown son weren't the right people to raise a little girl, but we was family. And family does for each other. We dragged the poor kid all over creation for almost ten years. She never had a proper house to live in. Mostly it was campers or motels. Folks, people from my hometown back in Missouri, sent us school stuff for her. She was smart enough to figure most of it out on her own, and it was a good thing 'cause we sure as hell couldn't deal with things like algebra and all that." He took a long sip of his beer.

"When she bought the shop and her house here, she musta sent me more'n a hundred pictures, and more every time she refinished a floor or painted a room or planted something. She was so damn proud of the home she finally had. She ain't gonna give it up."

"She doesn't have a home anymore," Brody argued.

Oscar smirked. "You'd be surprised what can happen in a few months."

Before he could belabor the point, Brody heard footsteps, and Renni came into view.

"All settled?" he asked.

She nodded and eased herself onto a thickly padded chaise lounge. Buster headed off to explore the large yard, yipping excitedly.

Brody motioned to the cooler. When she didn't pick up a cold beer, he asked, "Can I get you something to drink?"

"Do you have any iced tea?"

"Sure do. It's unsweetened, that okay?"

She nodded.

He went into the kitchen, puttered around a few minutes, and came out with a tall glass of tea with a lemon wedge on the lip and a long straw. She smiled her thanks.

"So, we was talkin'," Oscar started.

Renni rolled her eyes conspicuously.

Her uncle frowned at her and continued. "We"—he jerked

his chin toward Bubber—"decided Brody here can bring you to the shop in the morning. Me or Bubber or Luke will bring you home, take you to lunch, run errands. Whatever. At least one of us will be at the shop all the time you're there."

"And how long is this going to go on? Don't you and Bubber have a business to run? You can't hang around here forever being my bodyguards, and I'm sure Detective Brody has better things to do than be a taxi driver."

Oscar grinned. "We been talkin' about that as well."

Bubber nodded. "This is a nice place. Not too crowded. People are real friendly."

"What have you two been up to?" she asked, eyes narrowed.

"Now that we have some good fellers to manage the race teams, we can do what we want. I'll call me a real estate person and have them find a house for me and Bubber. We ain't gonna stay here all the time, mind you, but I'd like to do more than come visit you for a few days now and then. Eddy Benson's always trying to get me to go to shows with him, and this is a central location, so to speak."

Renni was the one grinning now. "Really? That'd be great. I know a good realtor. What kind of house do you want?"

"Now settle down there, Ren. We ain't in no hurry. We're staying at that Old Winery Inn. It's a nice place. Convenient to the Interstate, and close to here and the shop. The food's good. And they have some pretty damn good wine there."

"It's expensive, isn't it?" Renni asked.

Oscar shrugged. "I think I've earned the right to spend my money keepin' myself in comfort. At least for a week or two."

"I could stay there w—"

"Nope," the old man said without hesitation. "Me 'n Bubber don't need no female tellin' us to pick up our clothes or when it's time to eat or when it's time to quit drinkin'. You'll stay here, and we'll stay there, at least until we get a place. Besides, strangers will stick out a whole lot more in this neighborhood than they would at a hotel. We'll help you get your place put together in the meantime."

"I don't think there's any way to put Renni's house back together," Brody reiterated, shaking his head.

"Maybe not. But she can rebuild it."

A short time later, the two older men said their goodbyes and headed out, leaving Brody alone on the deck with Renni. They eyed each other, then studied Buster's antics in the yard. Listened to the noises of neighbors and birds. Brody suggested dinner. Renni declined. After several more awkward minutes, Renni made her excuses, noting it was time for a pain pill.

"I'll let Buster play if you'll let him in when you go to bed," she said. "Is that all right?"

"Sure." He watched as she slowly made her way into the house, wishing they could have had a real conversation for once.

# Chapter Thirty

There was a strange greenish tint to the air. Half of her was freezing, the other burning. She wanted to lick her lips but found her tongue so dry it stuck to the roof of her mouth.

There was the sudden sensation of arrested movement, and her temple slammed into something hard. Pain jarring her from a stupor, she began to comprehend what she saw. The green color came from faint dash lights. She was sitting on the floorboard of a vehicle, her back against the passenger-side door. A flow of hot air blew against her side, the fan on high causing her long blonde hair to swirl and tangle. Her head had bounced off the curved metal dash, and she could just make out the shape of an old-style glove box.

Her legs were tied at the ankles and knees, and her feet, one missing a shoe, rested against the transmission hump in the middle of the floor. A crooked floor-mount stick shifter protruded from the hump and ended beside the driver's knee. A man was driving the truck. She was pretty sure it was a truck. Pretty sure it was a man. The green dash lights were too dim to make out features in the dark. The hair was long and matted, or maybe curly. The nose in profile was straight and pointed, the jaw heavy, not feminine. The hands on the steering wheel had thick fingers.

He, she was sure now, suddenly turned his head. His eyes glittered, but the rest of his face was in deep greenish shadow. He turned away without a sound.

She couldn't talk, couldn't move her mouth, and she realized there was a tight band across her face. Tape. Some kind of tape. Her shoulders ached from arms drawn back behind her, also secured at the wrists and elbows with rope or tape. She tilted her head down, wincing as something pulled at her hair. Her blouse was a familiar pattern she recognized. Was it even still the same day? It took a moment to retrace her memories. She remembered leaving work and stopping at the bar by the bus stop for a drink and a sandwich. Casual conversation with Carson, the bartender. Some guys hit on her, but she was tired and not up for the standard bar dance that led to screwing a virtual stranger. Leaving around 8 p.m. with a little buzz on. Walking toward the bus stop. Then . . . nothing.

The truck slowed, and her head whacked the same place as before. She moaned against the tape. The driver spared her a glance and then concentrated on steering the truck over rough ground. They stopped. He turned off the engine, and the dash lights went out. The door handle wrenched up as the man climbed out, his movements sensed more than seen in the blackness.

A moment later, the door behind her opened. She gasped as she fell backward, tensing for the pain of crashing onto the ground, but he caught her. Threw her over his shoulder, which dug painfully into her stomach. Carried her what seemed a long way. Gently lowered her to the ground. There was no moon, but bright stars twinkled. She couldn't see what he was doing behind her, but she could hear the sound of a shovel slicing into dirt, then the thud of clods of earth falling.

Her heart thundered, her chest vibrating with the effort.

Sweat oozed out of her pores, and her mouth lost whatever bit of moisture it previously contained. Her mind fought to find a solution. A reason. An explanation for what was happening besides the thing her brain refused to accept.

The sounds stopped. The sudden silence was worse than the noise. It meant he was done. Was ready for what came next. She wriggled like a worm, even as her brain told her there was nowhere to go. Tears streamed from the corners of her eyes and dribbled into her ears, and she sniffed at the overflow. Tried to cry out. To beg. Nothing but muffled groans made it through the tape.

He grabbed her under her armpits and she flinched, jerking and twitching away from him. Her bare foot scrabbled in the dirt, beating against rocks and sticks.

He dragged her toward where she'd heard him digging. Her butt scraped over pebbles and sharp sticks, then abruptly slid down an embankment into a shallow depression. Her legs and feet followed. He let go of her shoulders, and her head fell back into soil. It was soft but cold. So cold. It seeped through her hair and raised goosebumps on her skin. The pain of her arms pinned behind her was overshadowed by abject fear as he knelt beside her, using one hand spread over her chest to hold her down. With the other hand, he reached inside his clothing and pulled something small out. He fumbled one-handed with a vial that glinted in the scant starlight. With a grunt, he shifted until his knee rested on her chest, enough pressure to keep her pinned but not enough to restrict her breathing. He then used both hands to fiddle with the lid of the small container and placed it against her cheek.

She heard a clicking sound and realized he was flicking his fingernail against the glass. There was a prick against her skin. Like a bee sting. The man reached inside his clothes again and brought out another object. There was a muted snap, and the beam of a flashlight blazed into her eyes. She blinked and squinted, trying to turn her head away, but he still had the bottle pressed against her cheek. The light flickered, and she realized he held it in his mouth because she could see both his hands again. He made a motion of tossing away the little bottle, but a reflection showed it still in his hand. He capped the vial and put it back in his pocket.

A new sensation intruded into her fear and shock. Even though he'd taken his knee off, the pressure on her chest increased. A band tightened around her until she couldn't draw breath. Bile swirled in her throat. She feared if she vomited, she'd drown with the tape over her mouth. She tried to swallow it down, but her throat wouldn't respond. Her tongue swelled to the point there wasn't any room left in her mouth. Her face was hot and sweaty, and itches prickled all over. The racing of her heart pounded in her ears.

She struggled to draw wheezing breaths through her nose, but it was too little. And too late. Her frantic thrashing slowed. She tried to focus on his face, but her vision blurred, then froze. Just before the darkness settled over her like a blanket of thick, heavy silence, she heard him utter, "That was . . . unexpected."

—

Renni gasped like a fish out of water. Her lungs were heaving, but it was as if something was lodged in her throat. She was being buried alive by a malevolent shadow.

Inexorably. Unfeelingly. Permanently.

With the last of her strength, Renni threw back her head and screamed.

# Chapter Thirty-One

Brody's eyes snapped open. He snatched up his forty-five auto and mini Maglite from the bedside table as he rolled out of bed and hit the floor running. His door crashed against the wall seconds before he slammed Renni's open. Pistol up, Maglite cupped beside it in his left hand, he scanned for the intruder. Faint dawn light seeped through thin curtains. Renni was sitting up, eyes wide, Buster crouched defensively beside her. Brody ran to the closet and ripped the door open, searching the nearly bare interior. Nothing. Not bothering to run the extra steps, he leaped over the bed in two bounces and landed on one knee at the open bathroom door. Empty.

He let out an explosive breath and flicked on the light switch next to the bathroom. The overhead light illuminated Renni, shaking, in the middle of the bed. Buster leaned against her good shoulder, not helping the situation as she struggled to untangle her feet from the twisted blankets one-handed. The sling had fallen off her elbow, but her injured shoulder was still caught in it. She stared up at him, her eyes reflecting residual fear and a touch of embarrassment. She also had the green-around-the-gills color of someone about to be sick.

"You okay?" he asked. She didn't seem remotely okay, but he wasn't sure what else to say under the circumstances. Reaching over, he gently untwisted the sling so she could ease her elbow back into the pocket.

Renni flinched away until she realized what he was doing. Letting him help, she took a deep, shaky breath. "Hell no, I'm not okay! *Soooo* not okay. It was one of them."

"One of who?" he asked, confused.

"One of the women. He was killing me. Her. It was like I *was* her." She scrubbed her face with her left hand, then ran her fingers through her hair. "Sorry." She blew out a breath. "Give me a minute."

She finally managed to kick free of the blankets twisted around her legs and pulled them up with her good arm, covering bare skin. Her hand shook, and she slipped it under the fabric. "Buster, lie down," she told the fretting spaniel. He instantly complied, snuggling against her legs.

Brody watched her closely. Her behavior was consistent with the nightmares Oscar described at dinner the night of the explosion. He tried to imagine what it would be like to go through life aware that, at any moment, you might be forced to witness something horrible that had already happened. Something you had no control over. Something you experienced alone. In the dark.

He shook his head. When he'd been in the military, and now on this job, things could morph into a real mess in seconds. And sometimes after a particularly tough day, he experienced nightmares. But even then he maintained some semblance of control. Some power. What Renni claimed—no control over when or what—it must be worse. If it was real.

Her color was coming back now, and her breathing had become more regular. Sitting on the bed next to her, he said, "Did you . . ." His conscience twinged over what he was doing, but he shoved it down deep. No matter how uncomfortable it was, he had to get her story, then try to trip her up on it. "Did you recognize which one it was?"

She swallowed hard and gave a little shake of her head. "It wasn't Lauren. It was one of the women in the photos you showed me. I just can't remember which." She shivered again and pulled the blankets up tighter.

"I'll give you a few minutes to get yourself together. Take your time. I'll have breakfast ready."

"I'm not hungry."

He nodded. "I understand. But I'm still going to need you to recheck the photos and point her out if you can. Maybe tell me about what you saw in your, um, dream. Sounded like it was pretty ugly. Are they always like that?"

Renni slanted a glare at him. "You don't have to pretend you believe me. I get you're just stuck with me until you guys find out if there's really a killer around here."

As Brody tried to think of how he should respond, Renni scrubbed her hand through her short hair again, leaving it sticking out in all directions, and he had the random thought that she resembled a garden fairy sitting in the middle of a hideous field of flowers.

When he didn't reply, she quirked a brow. "Can I have a little privacy? Watching me get dressed seems to stretch the definition of keeping an eye on me a tad too far."

He complied, feeling a burn on his ears when he admitted to himself he would like to have stayed.

# Chapter Thirty-Two

Renni stared at the faint glow of sunrise through the curtains. It was just like before. Once people knew about her, she became the neighborhood freak. Only this time she was the freak the cops suspected of being in on serial killings.

Brody had asked if it was always like this. She assumed he meant always scary. It wasn't. But what was the point of telling him about the purple 1969 340 Wedge 'Cuda, and the guy who owned it proposing to his girlfriend in the backseat? How happy they were and all the plans they made for after graduation? Then Renni remembered she'd also had flashes of the same couple, the girl massively pregnant and crying over his draft notice for Vietnam. And later, the woman, a baby in a stroller beside her, taping a "for sale" sign on the 'Cuda after learning he'd never be back to drive it. No. It wasn't always scary. Sometimes it was horribly sad.

She checked her watch. 5:30. *Crap.* There was no chance she could go back to sleep. As she swung her feet over the side of the bed, it dawned on her she was wearing only a thin, hip-length T-shirt with "Well, aren't you just a ray of pitch black?"

printed in bold letters—Oscar found it for her when they went shopping to replace her burned-up wardrobe—and skimpy bikini underwear. *Damn. Those pills must be pretty potent because I don't remember getting undressed or into bed.* Renni thought back, trying to remember how much Dudley Do-Right saw when he came flying into her room. Nothing he hadn't before, she was sure. Just like she was sure he wasn't the hottest guy ever in tighty-whities, with long, muscular legs, tight buns, and the broadest shoulders she'd ever seen.

Except he was.

Renni soaked in a bath for a bit to loosen her muscles, letting hot water melt away her stiffness. The full-length mirror on the back of the bathroom door showed her, in living color and painful detail, how much damage she'd received from the explosion. There were very few places showing normal skin tone. She was a lousy camouflage job of bruises ranging in color from deep purple-black to yellow, green, blue, and rose. Small, bright red burns and swatches of white bandages covering the more substantial injuries completed the picture.

The hospital had sent her home with a packet of fresh gauze, antibiotic ointment, and instructions on how to care for the cuts and burns requiring more than just being kept clean. She doctored herself up and decided there wasn't much she could do with her hair, not having thought to buy shampoo and conditioner. As she ran her fingers through the short strands, she realized there were not only small bumps and scabbed-over nicks on her head but several singed patches. She would need a trip to the salon to get the fried strands cut off. "Guess we're going even shorter than normal for a while," she said, thankful her head didn't require shaving for stitches.

A sudden loud rumble in her stomach reminded her it had been more than twenty-four hours since she'd eaten any real food. It took a while to get dressed and put the harness on after her bath. Then she made her way downstairs, following the siren scent of cooking bacon to the kitchen. Buster bounded past her and pranced impatiently at the screen door until she let him out.

Brody appeared surprisingly at home amidst pots and pans. Coffee clunked away in the Keurig, and there were jugs of milk and OJ on the table. What looked like a full pound of bacon sizzled in a large skillet, an open carton of eggs next to it.

"You planning on feeding an army?"

He chuckled and spoke over his shoulder. "Luke's dropping by. Between me and him, you'll be lucky to get anything. You want coffee?"

"Any chance you have tea? Or cocoa?"

Brody rubbed his wrist under his nose and pointed with the spatula. "Second cupboard, second shelf, I think. Been a while since I checked."

Finding a slightly dusty box of Constant Comment with only one packet missing, Renni heated water in the coffee maker after removing the used coffee pod. She sat on a tall stool at the bar counter and watched as he fussed with the bacon and then forked it onto a paper-towel-covered plate, poured most of the bacon grease into a ceramic cup, and started cooking eggs. A pair of low-slung jeans rested on his hips and he wore a thin, snug-fitting white T-shirt. His back and arm muscles rippled as he moved.

"How do you like yours?"

His question caught her off guard, and she felt a blush as she bit down a saucy retort. A quick flick of her eyes to the back of his head confirmed he hadn't caught her stare or the blush. "Um, scrambled, thanks."

The front door rattled. Brody stiffened, putting down the spatula and taking a step toward a towel-covered lump on the counter.

"I'm hungry," Luke's voice hollered down the hallway. "Anything left?"

They glanced at each other, and Brody gave her the first genuine smile she'd seen. It was a nice smile, reaching clear to the crinkled corners of his eyes and exposing a single right-hand dimple. As Luke strolled nonchalantly into the kitchen, Renni asked why he was up and about so early.

"Hell, I been patrolling the neighborhood all night. Didn't see anything suspicious." His self-satisfied smirk made it obvious he figured he'd saved the day, or night.

"You do know the night patrol has instructions to come by here frequently, right? They're watching for strange activity. You're lucky they didn't arrest you, or at least pull you over," Brody chastised him.

Luke ducked his head. "They did. Pull me over, I mean. It was Fred, though, so it was okay. He told me I was scaring the neighbors. After that, I drove around normal with my lights on and all."

A burble of laughter escaped her, and Renni wondered how much trouble Luke would be in when the night shift turned in their reports.

They consumed the entire pound of bacon and almost a dozen eggs, along with several cups of coffee and three cups of tea for Renni. Afterward, she tried to insist on washing up, but Brody wanted to talk to her.

"Luke can do it. Payment for his gourmet breakfast."

Luke frowned and grumbled, but gave up quickly and set about the chore. She saw by the practiced way he rinsed the plates before loading the dishwasher he was an old hand at helping in the kitchen. Vicki was no dummy.

Out on the patio, Brody booted up his computer and opened the photo file of RMHK victims. Renni blanched and bit her lip, but pointed to one of the blondes onscreen. "That's her."

"You're sure?"

Renni bristled at the question until she realized he wasn't doubting her ability so much as wanting clarification on how it worked.

"The best way I can explain it is that I *was* her, so I know who I was. Does that make sense? It's not always that clear.

Sometimes I just get little bits and pieces. But this . . ." Renni shivered at the memory. "This was really clear."

He nodded. "That's Celia VanGundy. She was found six years ago at Island Acres in De Beque Canyon. Disappeared on her way to a bus stop in Carbondale." Brody rattled off the details without pause.

"So the killer hauled her all the way from Carbondale?" Renni took a deep breath. "She was alive right up until he was burying her. Oh God, Brody, she was so scared. So confused. She knew . . . She was sure he was going to kill her, but she just kept hoping. He put something on her face. Then something happened, I think. Something he didn't expect—he seemed surprised. She couldn't breathe, and just . . . died." Her voice dropped to a whisper. "How did he kill them? I mean, he didn't choke her, or shoot her, or anything like that."

Brody's eyes fixed on her, intense. "Did you see his face?"

She rubbed her eyes, letting her hands slide down her cheeks, and then crossed her arms, hugging herself tightly. "No. I was seeing through her eyes, and she never got a good look at him. He's pretty good-sized, though, with long hair. Big hands. That's all I saw." Again she asked, "She wasn't suffocated, was she?"

He paused like he was trying to decide if he should say anything more. He sucked in a deep breath and blew it out. "She died of anaphylactic shock."

"From, like, allergies?"

"The coroner said it was likely a bug bite."

Renni thought a moment. "But it was cold out. Freezing. She was so cold. There wouldn't have been any bugs. He put something on her face, something that fit in a little bottle. I couldn't tell what he was doing, but he acted weird. And something stung her cheek."

Brody made some notes on his computer. "I'll check into it."

Yawning, Luke wandered out onto the patio. "You ready to go to work?"

She eyed him and said, "I am, but you aren't. Go home and get some sleep. I don't need you falling asleep while you're tuning the carbs on the resto-mod. And no more nocturnal wandering. Leave it to the cops, Luke."

"Hey, I was just helping out." His jaws cracked with a huge yawn. "But maybe I'll run home for a little nap."

# Chapter Thirty-Three

After Luke left, Renni gathered up her backpack, called Buster, and climbed into Brody's police Explorer. When they arrived at the shop, Maisie's hot pink VW sat in the lot next to Oscar's rental, a non-descript gray Chevy sedan. Inside they found Bubber and Oscar playing cards in the lobby while Maisie made coffee in the breakroom. Buster made a beeline straight for his bowl of kibble in Renni's office.

Brody eyed the two men. "Don't leave her alone, right?"

"Got any fours?" Bubber asked.

Oscar waved to Brody carelessly in acknowledgment, then told his son, "Go fish."

Brody shook his head and left.

As soon as Brody pulled out of the lot, Oscar set his cards down, frowning at Bubber. "Don't you be peekin'!" he said, and put his arm around Renni, steering her toward her office. He gently shoved her down on the sofa.

He flipped one of the client chairs around and sat on it backward, laying his forearms across the back. "How'd it go last night?"

She shrugged.

"Had a nightmare, didn't you?"

Renni gave him a questioning look.

"It's in that there line in the middle of your forehead. It's always there when you have a dream. How bad was it?"

"Pretty bad," she admitted. "It was one of the women he killed." Renni slammed her palm on the seat cushion, glad it wasn't a hard surface when pain reminded her of her injuries. "If I could only see his face! See something that would help the cops find him. But, damn it, all I see is what he does to them."

Oscar reached out and laid his hand on her shoulder. "Hell, if it weren't for you, the police'd be in the dark about all this. You'll find him. They'll stop him. There's a reason you have this gift, child."

"Curse, you mean."

"No, sir-e-bob, I do not. I know it's hard on you, but being able to do what you do might save lives. Help people. I ain't sayin' it's fair to you, but you gotta make the best of it."

She leaned her head back against the seat, eyes closed. "You're right, I guess. I'm grumpy, that's all." Then she bent forward, eyes open. "It's getting worse. It seems like the longer this goes on, the more I feel what's happening. It's not just a movie where I watch the events scroll by. I *feel* what they feel. Their horror. Pain. Even, I think, some of the killer's excitement. It's always been that the things I see are mostly inside a car, maybe once in a while outside but close by, and pretty much always linked to one person. This isn't like that. It's almost as if anyone who's been affected by that damn truck is linked, and they're all starting to, I don't know, talk to me." Her head drooped.

Oscar leaned in, putting his forehead against hers for a moment, then dropped a kiss in its place. "You gonna be okay?"

She sucked in a deep breath. "Yeah. Gotta be, right? And I got work to do. Best be at it."

"What can me and the nitwit do to help?"

"Hey, I heard that," Bubber hollered from the lobby.

Grinning, Renni headed to the lobby, the old man following. Bubber and Buster trailed along behind as they went down to the shop. In no time at all, the two men were settled next to the WWII motorcycle, stripping parts and putting them into the washer. Renni picked up the checklist for the Caddy and started making notes on what was complete and what still needed doing.

It annoyed her to be sidelined with the shoulder harness. It kept her from doing the things she enjoyed and left her stuck with office work, which she hated. She checked off the slanted two-piece windshield she'd installed earlier. The newly re-chromed Goddess radiator mascot, wheel center caps, fold-down rear luggage rack, and dual horns were all sitting in boxes ready to go on as soon as the Caddy came back from the paint shop. She made a note to call about the replacement Waltham dash clock and the custom leather golf bag and trunk to verify they were still on schedule and would arrive before the end of the week.

Luke showed up after lunch, looking considerably friskier than at breakfast. Renni left the three of them, with Luke in charge, and went up to talk with Maisie.

"So how much business have we lost over the damn newspaper article?"

Maisie shrugged, grimacing. "Well, I got an email sayin' the '63 'Vette won't be comin' in from Moab. Owners said they changed their mind about having it done right now."

Renni slumped and let her head fall back on her neck.

"Now, don't get all dramatic on me. No one else has canceled, and you didn't want that job anyway—they're the ones always tryin' to get bullshit discounts and claim warranty work. Otherwise, there were two idiots asking if you'd help them find the fortune their grandpa buried somewhere on his forty acres. I can handle that crap, don't you worry, and it'll blow over when the next issue comes out with a new front-page story."

"You say that like it's no big deal, but since this is the most exciting news the Daily Watch has seen in a long time, we could be dead in the water by the time some other excitement takes the pressure off."

Maisie *tsk*'d and stood, giving Renni a close inspection. "How you feelin'? You look like shit."

Renni laughed. "Thanks. You're not the first to say so. I'm doing okay. A little stiff and sore in the mornings, but it's better every day." She ran fingers through her hair, grimacing at the crispy sections. "Can you call Sam and ask if she can get me in for an appointment as soon as possible? I need to get all the burned stuff cut off."

"I'll do it right away."

Renni went into her office and booted up her computer, determined to find out more about the Marmon and its owner.

# Chapter Thirty-Four

Karen watched him pace but kept her mouth shut. He'd been in a bad mood for days now, and she'd learned asking him what was wrong upset him more. After a while, he stomped out of the house. She watched through the window as he headed to the barn. Lately, he'd been spending hours every day behind the broad sliding door.

She shivered. Whatever was wrong was getting worse. *He* was getting worse. She went up to her room and carefully pulled the dresser out a few inches to retrieve her journal. She opened it to the first empty page and began to write, keeping an ear out for his return.

—

He prowled down the center aisle of the barn, past empty stalls to the tack room. Inside, batts of insulation and a heater kept the temperature warm and the room dark, no matter the time of year. Large, lidded glass terrariums sat on shelves in the dim red light. They contained dirt, pieces of wood, rocks, small plastic plants, and spider houses of his own design. He stopped at one and smiled at the sight of a gray web comb with an egg sac tucked in a shadowed corner. Soon he'd have more pets. He wondered if he should order something a bit more lethal but then shook his head. "No. I'm not going to change all this because of her. I'll deal with little Miss Renni some other way," he said as he fished cockroaches out of a large metal box and dropped them, squirming, into each of the terrariums.

He stayed to see if any of them would let him watch them eat and was gratified to have one taker. Back at the house, he found Karen sitting in her recliner in the living room, the TV on. He grinned at her. "How about some popcorn and a movie tonight, sis?"

She gave him a small smile and nodded. "Sure."

—

He went into the kitchen, not noticing her eyes follow him. Unconsciously she chewed her fingernails, most of which were already gnawed to the quick.

# Chapter Thirty-Five

Renni checked her email and found one from Maisie regarding the Marmon's VINs. They were all registered to Jon Davis in Layton, Utah. Maisie's notes said Jon Davis purchased six different Marmon-Herringtons and Marmon-outfitted-Fords, vintage 1939 through the early '50s, over a period of nearly three decades. The registrations all listed the same address.

She wrote down the address and then started googling the US Census Bureau files as well as genealogy sites. She opened *familysearch.org* because she'd heard it was run by Mormons. Odds were, they would have information on a man who lived in Layton, Utah, whether or not he was Mormon himself. She filled in the data fields, and little by little began to build a file.

Google Earth showed the address to be in the middle of a large subdivision of brick mini-estates. Going back through assessor records, she found that the Davis property had been agricultural before it was developed, Jon Davis running an equipment repair shop out of his barn as well as managing a large farm.

She located an obituary for Davis dated sixteen years earlier.

The accompanying photo showed an elderly man with a snow-white crew cut, weak chin, and small dark eyes. It was the old man who'd been smoking a hand-rolled cigarette in one of her dreams. Clearly, he wasn't the killer.

She dialed the phone number for the Layton Standard-Examiner newspaper, which had printed the obit. After a lengthy wait suffering through really bad on-hold music, she was connected to the newspaper's morgue. An unusually helpful man kept her on the line while he puttered around and unearthed the paperwork for the obituary.

"It was placed by Deacon Thaddeus Johnson of the Layton LDS Stake House," he said, then gave her a quick rundown of the Church of Latter-day Saints' organization and how various parts of it functioned. Armed with more information on the Mormons than she'd ever wanted to know, she called the number listed for the deacon and got a secretary who told her the man was semi-retired. She had no idea when he was due to come in.

"Give me your number, and I'll have him call you when I see him."

Renni complied, hopeful a church secretary wouldn't break a promise and forged ahead. Document after document flashed over the screen as she went from one ancestry site to another. Then, out of the blue, a new name grabbed her attention. Bill Davis. The document was a generic school immunization record listing Jon Davis as guardian/next of kin, but no school was listed. She couldn't find any indication of how they were related or even proof it was the same Jon Davis. Nothing in Jon Davis's file indicated he'd ever been married or had children, and the name "Bill" hadn't appeared anywhere else in Davis's information.

Two hours later, she stood and stretched, gingerly touching her toes and bending backward to loosen tight muscles. She gazed down into the shop and smiled. Her uncle, cousin, and Luke were sitting on stacks of tires jawing with each other. Luke should have been working, but Renni left him be. They were on schedule with Ed's Caddy and the resto-mod was as good as done. Besides, with Oscar and Bubber staying in town, she would have some extra hands—experienced ones—if they needed more help. It wouldn't hurt for the "boys" to take a break.

Renni sat back down and started a specific search on Bill Davis, but quickly realized he was more a ghost than a person, except for that one document. She was about to give up for the day when she found a temporary learner's permit in the name of Bill Davis, with the same address as Jon Davis. It was a poor copy of a small piece of paper with only basic information and not even a photograph, but it was enough to prove she was on the right track.

She checked the clock. 3:55. She'd been at it most of the day, with next to nothing to show for it. She sat back in her chair, tapping a pen against her lower lip. How could she get a photo of a kid who barely existed? Then it dawned on her—he was high school age. And if he was in high school, he probably had his photo taken for the yearbook.

Renni went to the window and looked at the men down below. They were still engrossed in their stories and likely paying no attention to the time.

Confident of remaining undisturbed, she started researching high schools in the Layton area ten to fifteen years ago. There was plenty of information about where the schools were located, including maps of the districts and records of when those maps had been changed due to population growth. Eventually, she decided Layton High School, home of the Javelins, was the only one close enough to Davis's place. She went to their site and signed up so she could access their data. Not sure how far back to go, she started with 1990 and scrolled through the digital yearbooks, finding the pages of last names that started with "D."

The school was large and apparently names starting with "D" were popular in Utah. She scanned more than a dozen pimply-faced teens in each class. Each time she finished one class level, she had to repeat the effort twice to get through all three grades.

She went year by year. Faces became a blur. It surprised her that nearly all the boys wore short hair and the girls didn't appear to have on much if any, makeup.

When she finally did stumble upon his photo, she almost missed it, thinking he was a girl due to the hair.

She found him in the 1998 book, as a junior. The black and white picture was small, only about one square inch, so the features were slightly blurry. Bill Davis had long, light-colored hair, parted in the middle. It hung limply, creating a narrow frame along his face and partially hiding his eyes. He might have been good-looking if he hadn't been glowering so hard at the camera. A group photo on the facing page included Bill Davis in football uniform, positioned a little off to the side from his teammates. He was tall and slender, with wide shoulders made even wider by the pads, and he held his helmet under his arm.

Renni picked up the phone and started to dial Layton High School's number, then realized it was way past school hours. She'd have to wait until tomorrow.

She smiled at the thought of telling Brody what she'd found out. Maybe it would convince him she was on his side.

# Chapter Thirty-Six

Bubber waited in the car while Oscar went inside with her, checking the hall closet and under the beds. He made a production of opening a few drawers and cabinets in the kitchen, chuckling when she finally shooed him out the door.

The refrigerator yielded pork chops, fresh tomatoes, and mozzarella. After rooting around in the pantry, she came up with potatoes, balsamic vinegar, and olive oil too. A basil plant grew in a pot on Brody's deck. It only took a few minutes to make a Caprese salad, and she put the potatoes in the oven to bake. Brody could grill the chops when he got in. Renni fixed herself a gin and tonic, let Buster out into the backyard to play, and went upstairs to change into more comfortable clothes.

At the sound of the front door closing and footsteps in the hall, she shimmied into her shorts and hurried to pull on an "If you met my family, you'd understand" T-shirt. She smiled, both because of the very appropriate text and because she'd finally be able to tell Brody something about the killer to convince him she was innocent. Barefoot, she started down the stairs, instinctively skipping the first step to prevent the usual loud squeak. She hugged the edge of the staircase so she could run her hands down the smooth, warm banister.

She was almost to the bottom when she heard Brody's voice from the dining room around the corner.

"Yeah," he said. "I just got home. She must be running late." There was a pause. "I know. I'll push harder tonight. Trip her up on her story. She has some pretty specific info about one of the dead women related to an allergic reaction." A pause. "You know I can. I have to get her to trust me enough she's not guarding everything she says." Then, "Give me another day, and I'll have it."

Renni turned and tiptoed silently back up the stairs. She sat on the bed, hands fisted in her lap. *The son of a bitch!* How convenient it must be to have their suspect sitting there, answering whatever questions he asked. Babbling about what she'd seen in her dreams. All it did was convince them she *was* involved. *Well, I'm done.* She grabbed her cell phone and scrolled through her contacts until she found the right one. She hit the call button.

Ten minutes later, she sent a long text to Luke and received an even longer one back. She thought hard before composing a reply.

*Luke, you're going to have to choose sides here. Either I can trust you, or I can't. You work for me, or you work for Brody. He's your friend, but I need you to have my back on this. I guess I'll know what you decide in the morning.*

—

Brody put his phone in his pocket and went to the fridge for a beer. The first things he saw were a colorful tomato salad and a Ziploc bag with marinating pork chops. He headed for the patio and pushed the screen door open. "Renni?" he called, but there was no response. Buster romped by in exuberant pursuit of a butterfly, and Brody realized she must be in her room. Wondering if she was feeling all right, he went upstairs and knocked on her door. "Renni? I'm about ready to put the chops on."

"I'm not hungry. Headache." Her voice shook.

"I'll bring a plate up in a bit. You okay? It's not anything from the explosion?"

"It's only a stupid headache. I'm going to bed. I'll probably go in a little late tomorrow. Luke'll pick me up and take me in. Don't worry about breakfast, either."

"Need some Tylenol or anything?"

"No."

Brody was surprised at her tone. She sounded angry, but then, she *had* mentioned having a headache even before the explosion. Maybe she was one of the unlucky ones who got migraines. He didn't know enough about her. Not yet.

"If you change your mind . . ."

"I won't."

—

Renni listened to the steps creak as he descended. A while later, Buster whined at the door and she let him into the bedroom. She took one of her prescribed sleeping pills, hoping this time it put her out so deep she couldn't dream.

# Chapter Thirty-Seven

Renni was awake when Brody went downstairs the next morning. Buster danced at the bedroom door as she listened to faint sounds from the kitchen, then the front door shutting. As soon as Brody's car drove off down the street, she let Buster out.

She packed clothes for the next few days in the paper bags Bubber had left and put them by the door. As she waited for her ride, she made a jumbo-sized cup of chai from two of the drink pods in the rack by the Keurig and toasted a pair of cherry Pop-Tarts, a breakfast treat she'd loved since Bubber introduced them to her when she was ten.

When Luke texted her that he was pulling into the driveway, she called Buster in from the backyard and grabbed her bags. After opening her door, he motioned Buster into the back seat. As he backed out, Luke looked over at her, frowning.

"You sure you want to do this? He's going to be mucho pissed."

"I'm tired of Brody's games. He can arrest me and prove I've done something wrong, which I haven't, or leave me alone and actually find who's doing this. No matter what, I'm done being played." She bit her lip and stared out the side window. "If you call him and tell where I'm going . . ."

Luke shook his head emphatically. "I'm not going to call him, Ren. I'm not a cop. It's not my job." He elbowed her and grinned. "What I want to know is how the hell you got space at the Santa Fe show the day before it starts."

She shrugged and laughed. "Pays to have friends in high places. Last year when I went down with Ed, he paid a record price for a car, then donated it back to St. Jude's so they could auction it again. Mr. Wilson, the promoter, told me if I ever needed a favor, to just ask. So I did. There was a last-minute cancellation, and he gave it to me. Not exactly 'gave,' but he didn't charge me more than I would have paid if I'd reserved on time."

"You sure Oscar and Bubber will go? You can't go by yourself. I won't let you do that."

"Are you kidding? Those two live for road trips, and they'll have a blast at the show." She patted his leg. "I'll be fine. And maybe I'll get enough for the resto-mod to keep us going, or at least for you to keep the shop afloat while I'm in the hoosegow, or whatever it is Oscar calls it."

As they turned into the shop drive, she said, "Can you take the truck and rent me a trailer? The cops don't seem to care they still have ours. Oh, and will you and Vicki take Buster for me?"

"Yeah, and yeah. I'll go get the trailer right now." He squirmed and grimaced. "Listen, Ren. I said I won't call Brody, and I won't. But I won't lie to him, either."

"I'm okay with that," she said, joshing his shoulder. "If I'm lucky, I'll be long gone before he checks."

Both Oscar's sedan and Maisie's VW were in the upper lot when Luke dropped her off. As she headed toward the door, the bags of clothes knocking against her thigh, she heard the Dodge start up in the lower lot. The chime went off as she burst through the door, and she discovered Bubber sitting on the corner of

Maisie's desk, both of them laughing to beat the band.

"So glad my business is in good hands when I'm not here," she said.

Maisie startled so hard she nearly fell out of her chair, and Bubber jumped up, sloshing coffee from the cup in his hand. He did a little jig, swearing profusely and swiping at his crotch as he scrambled toward the restroom. Renni laughed until tears ran. It took several minutes to get herself under control as she let off pent-up emotion. It felt good. Really good. She'd needed that laugh.

Finally, she managed to ask, "Where's Oscar?"

"Don't ask me," Maisie said primly as she started opening and closing desk drawers at random. "Elmo was alone when he showed up."

Renni shook her head as the use of her cousin's real name sunk in. *No one ever calls him Elmo.* She went to her office, wondering if there was something going on between the two sixty-somethings. The concept was too much to dwell on, and she distracted herself by gathering the resto-mod file, including title and provenance, build sheet, and before and after photos. She started to set an out-of-office message on her email and work phone, then shook her head. *I'm not giving Brody a chance to find out what I'm up to. I can check for messages on the road.*

Then she remembered her lead on Bill Davis. Shocked that it hadn't been the first thing she thought of that morning, she quickly tapped in the school's number from her notes. All she got was a recording saying Layton High School was closed for a teacher workday and to call on Monday. *Damn it!*

Sighing, she stuck her laptop and chargers into one of the clothing bags, added ice packs from the breakroom freezer, and headed down to the shop. A wheeled file box on a shelf was kept stocked with marketing materials for Delacroix Restorations, and she put the resto-mod's paperwork, laptop, and charger inside, and parked it by the door. Her show kit, consisting of a small set of folding chairs and matching table, a Delacroix-logo'd golf umbrella, and a cooler, which she filled with ice packs and bottles of water, went into the pile as well.

There wasn't anything else to do until Luke brought the trailer. Renni surveyed the gleaming resto-mod waiting to be loaded. She ambled around the once-upon-a-time 1940 Chevy Coupe. After chopping the top to lower the upper profile and channeling the body to make it sit even lower to the ground, she'd added custom bumpers and fenders to give it a sleek, rakish profile. She'd modified the interior too, incorporating the nostalgic details of the original dash design with the convenience of contemporary features such as electric windows, leather split bucket electric seats, padded center console, Bose system with Sound Touch, and a nav system.

It was striking. Luke, a master carpenter, had handcrafted the new dash and interior door panels from glossy exotic Bubinga wood. The base color was a high-shine metallic deep green. The swooping fenders were highlighted with a unique, stretched, and twisted checkerboard in several shades from lime to evergreen. The design, one she'd come up with after Luke wore a pair of Vans shoes with a checkerboard pattern one day, was perfectly executed by the amazing local painter she'd stumbled on not long after setting up her shop.

Both she and Luke had put a lot of time and effort into the resto-mod, and she knew it was the best work either of them had ever done. Having the car at a high-quality show was as much to market Delacroix Restorations as it was to find a buyer. She hoped a high score at the show would drive traffic to her shop. It might keep them afloat until the serial killer was found and she was vindicated.

The rumble of a car engine approached. Hoping it was Luke and not Brody, she pushed the button on the overhead. What waited for her on the other side was something she hadn't expected.

# Chapter Thirty-Eight

Sitting on the concrete apron was a futuristic silver sports car, its idle echoing in the cavernous shop. As she watched, the scissor doors flipped forward. Oscar climbed out, along with an equally white-haired but dark-skinned man.

Renni snapped her hanging jaw shut and ran over to the car. "Ed! What are you doing here?" Before he could answer, she said, "A Koenigsegg One:1? Seriously? How in the hell did you get your hands on one of these?" She ran reverent fingers across the hood, nearly salivating. "Holy shit. These cost, like, three million bucks."

"And change," Ed Benson said, a self-satisfied smirk on his face. "And I have my sources, dear heart."

She shook her head, eyeing one old codger and then the other. "You two are certifiable, you know that? You don't drive one of these around like it was a Honda."

"Why not? It's a car, ain't it?" Ed countered.

"Hey, Renni, guess what?" Oscar said, pointing to the car. "It comes with custom leather suitcases and diamonds on the key fob. Far out, huh?"

She rolled her eyes.

As if on cue, Luke wheeled the diesel with an attendant enclosed trailer down the drive and circled it around, backing it up to the other overhead door. With a last longing look over her shoulder at the gorgeous car, Renni ran the door up and guided Luke in. He climbed down and sauntered over to her, a sly grin on his face.

"Where'd you get a box trailer and how much is it going to cost me?" she asked.

He shook his head and chuckled. "Don't sweat it, boss lady. I was almost to the rental place when I remembered this kid I went to school with, Freddie More. He used to build and race dragsters, and his dad owned a body shop. I swung over where the shop used to be, and sure enough, they were still there. Freddie runs the place now. The car hauler was sitting in the back lot. After I explained to Freddie where I worked and that I needed a trailer to haul a really special car, he said I could borrow it as long as your insurance will cover any damages. It will, right?"

"I'll have Maze call Betty and make sure we're good." She squeezed his arm. "That was smart thinking. I hated the thought of taking the resto-mod all the way to the show on a flatbed trailer."

Luke helped her open the trailer's doors and attach the ramps. She carefully drove the gleaming car into the trailer, taking it slow because of the resto-mod's limited clearance. While Luke secured the car with wheel straps, Renni checked the lighting harness and taillights.

After verifying the lights and trailer brakes worked—and double-checking the tie-downs, to Luke's amused annoyance—Renni headed for the stairs. She chuckled as Luke went the opposite direction, making a beeline for the One:1.

Upstairs, she asked Maisie to call their insurance agent, then went into her office and booted up her computer to check possible routes to the show. After reviewing the distances, weather, and drive times, she decided to take Highway 50 through Gunnison, then 285. It had fewer steep passes. That settled, she logged into a cheap travel site to find a hotel room. With the show in town, nothing but a no-tell motel on the outskirts of Santa Fe was still available. Wrinkling her nose in distaste, she went ahead and booked it.

A car door slammed outside, and Renni nervously looked out her front window into the customer parking lot. It wasn't Brody, as she'd feared, but Kevin Green, climbing out of a beat-up Gremlin, an enormous bunch of flowers in his arms.

She hurried out through the lobby on her way down the stairs, hollering over her shoulder, "I'm running late for my appointment with Sam and need to check in with the guys before I go. Can you take care of this?"

"Take care of what?" Maisie yelled back, but Renni had already hustled out of sight. She heard the front door chime just as she hit the bottom step.

Outside, she found Oscar grinning as Luke struck a series of silly poses next to the One:1 while Ed egged him on.

"So, Unc, you and Bubber up for a road trip?"

Ed sauntered around the silver car, stopping right in front of her. "I roll into town, and already you're running out on me. That the deal?"

"I'm headed to the Santa Fe show in about an hour, but you're welcome to tag along if you like."

"Well, hell, I'm already packed, 'cause I ain't unpacked, and you know I like that show," he said with an impish grin.

"Bubber can stay and hold down the fort. Me 'n Ed can handle guard duty," Oscar said, nodding to his partner in crime.

"Guard duty?" Ed tipped his head back and narrowed his eyes.

"I'll explain on the way," Oscar said hastily, then turned to Renni. "Let me fetch my stuff, and we'll meet you here in forty-five." They climbed back in the car, and Ed spun it around in a haze of smoking rubber.

Knowing Renni was without her own wheels, Maisie had offered her VW for any trips. Since she always left the keys in it, Renni snuck up the drive and climbed into the hot pink VW, making sure Kevin's car was still parked outside. She drove toward the salon, hoping Brody didn't decide to drop by in the meantime—and that Kevin would be gone when she returned.

—

An hour later, she pulled back into the shop's empty upper lot. No sign yet of her two geriatric bodyguards. She ran inside to print out the hotel directions and confirmation information, as the Dodge didn't have GPS and she never liked to depend on her phone when driving.

In her office, she was greeted by an overwhelming blast of floral scent. There were three humongous bouquets scattered around the room, each with more than two dozen roses in a riot of colors. Sighing, she picked up the one on her desk and moved it into the breakroom, bringing back paper towels to mop up water that had sloshed onto the wood top and some paperwork.

Maisie appeared in the doorway. "Sorry about that. I was on the phone and couldn't get off fast enough to stop him from making a mess. That boy, he never has had a lick of sense. His mama always told him he was every girl's dream and he could have whoever he wanted. His father was another story. I guess old Kevin decided you were the one. What you want me to do with all those flowers since you're leavin'?"

"Take what you want home and drop off the rest at a nursing home or three. You might have to hand out hay fever pills while you're at it." She barely got the sentence out before a series of three hard sneezes hit. Renni shook her head at the sensory overload.

"You bet," Maisie said with a laugh and gathered up the other bouquets.

Throwing the wet paper towels into a trashcan, Renni went to her computer, poised to enter her password, but saw she'd forgotten to log out in her hurry to escape a meeting with Kevin. She opened her itinerary and printed what she needed, locking the computer screen when she was finished. After double-checking she had everything, she went down and joined Luke in the shop in time to see the One:1 come screaming down the drive. It screeched to a halt inches from the Dodge's bumper.

She rolled her eyes at Luke as she climbed inside the Dodge. "Keep a sharp eye on the shop. Without Oscar around, Bubber's likely to get into all kinds of trouble. I'll be back Sunday if I survive these two."

"Okay, but keep me posted as to how the show's going."

The One:1's horn honked.

"I gotta get out of here before these two lunatics do something crazy," she said.

Luke hopped onto the running board and leaned through her window to give her a peck on the cheek. "What could be crazier, or cooler, than showing up with that car?" he asked.

Laughing, she started the truck. He gave the door a slap and jumped down. The sports car reversed in a "U," burning rubber again, and pulled up beside her, Oscar grinning up at her from the passenger side.

"Men," Renni groused. "Bunch of little boys playing with toys." All the while thinking, *Damn, that old son of a bitch has the best toys.*

The drive south toward Santa Fe was uneventful if Renni ignored the honks and ogling that accompanied the One:1 wherever they went. Nothing made Ed happier than to have a gaggle of looky-loos surrounding the car when they stopped for gas or food. He puffed up like a banty rooster and strutted around, Oscar egging him on, whether there was an audience of one or twenty-one.

A few hours into the trip, they stopped at McDonald's in the small college town of Gunnison for a quick bite, then hit the road again.

"Ah, crap," Renni grumbled when she spotted a billboard

advertising an annual road bike race set to take place over the weekend. It would mean a choice between returning on the same route or taking a high, narrow pass that would be populated with a bunch of slow-moving RVs this time of year. However, the thought of dealing with a mob of hard-pedaling road bike racers, support cars, and a few thousand spectators lubricated with beer and pot who would run into the road to get pictures, not to mention one-way road closures, convinced her the RVs would be less of a headache.

*Guess it'll be Red Mountain on the way home.*

By the time they hit the state line, she figured Ed had averaged at least one speeding ticket per hour, repeatedly flying by her only to be pulled off several miles down the road, accompanied by the flashing blue and red lights of the Highway Patrol. She wondered if they were radioing ahead to each other to be on the lookout since she'd never noticed so many patrolmen in a whole month, let alone a single day. They'd probably made their entire month's quota off the compulsive speeder.

He zipped past again just as a green roadway sign telling her she was only a hundred and twenty miles out of Santa Fe flashed by, but by then she'd lost track of the number of times he'd done it. She called him on her cell and suggested he add another million to the car's cost to pay for the tickets. He laughed and reminded her there was a raft of lawyers on retainer to deal with such minor inconveniences.

Even when they pulled into the Santa Fe golf course, the show's venue, where there were already dozens of rare, high-end cars, heads still turned to stare at the One:1 with its venturi tunnel side panels and distinctive rear wings. While Ed basked in the attention, Renni took care of the paperwork for the resto-mod and drove to her assigned spot. It only took a few minutes to unload, and after being assured there was twenty-four-hour security, she followed the sports car to a fancy hotel near the golf course. Ed and Oscar insisted she have dinner with them even though it was nearly 10 p.m. She was tired, but with little to eat since the fast food place, she didn't have much inclination to argue.

Climbing down from the cab of the truck, she eyed the sports car parked next to her, then Ed, and said, "Just going to park in the lot, are you?"

The old man looked uncomfortable. Clearly, he hadn't considered how he would store the multi-million-dollar car when he wasn't driving it.

She took pity on him. "We can put it in the trailer overnight, but I'm staying at the Drove 'Er Inn out on the I-25."

Ed choked on a laugh. "Hell you are. We got two rooms here, and one has two queens. Me 'n Oscar can bunk together, and you can have the other one. You ain't gonna stay at some by-the-hour dive."

Renni opened her mouth to refuse, but he held up his hand.

"I don't want my little baby that far away, and just so you know, I ain't talkin' about the car. I wouldn't be able to sleep a wink for worrying. And I'm old. I need my beauty sleep." He pouted, trying to appear pathetic.

She shook her head, but Oscar joined in. "How we gonna be your bodyguards if you're way off somewhere in some rickety dump? Brody'll have our asses we let anything happen to you. It's settled. End of story."

Renni stood by, hands on hips, her arguments falling on deaf ears as the two men opened the trailer and set up the ramps. Ed gingerly drove the One:1 in. They didn't bother with the wheel straps since it would be parked, but they made sure the door and hitch lock were secure.

"Who's ready for a drink?" Ed asked, pulling a still-protesting Renni along toward the glittering hotel entrance.

# Chapter Thirty-Nine

Brody spent the morning bringing the RMHK file up to date, including the information regarding Celia's bug bite and the small details Renni provided about the suspect. *If only she could see the guy.* Then he realized somewhere along the line he'd started to consider Renni might be the real deal.

An email came in from one of the coroners. He'd gone back over earlier autopsy videos at magnification per Brody's request and found a small contusion in the victim's skin below her eye, high on her cheek. The tone of the email was slightly defensive, and Brody read between the lines that the man was upset at having missed a clue, whether or not it was significant. Brody replied, reassuring him that with no discoloration and the cause of death being obvious, it wasn't surprising the tiny mark was missed.

Unfortunately, the victim's body had been cremated, so the remains couldn't be exhumed and examined. Still, the "small contusion" was pretty close to a smoking gun in Brody's mind. He was angry, however, that a specific signature of the RMHK had been missed. What would have happened if all the coroners caught it early on?

By early afternoon, two more coroners replied. *Amazing what results you get from the FBI making calls. A lowly, small-town police detective never gets results like this.* In each case, closer inspection of their photos showed a small bite on the victim's cheek, more or less in the same location. The good news was both victims had been buried and could be exhumed, assuming a judge would issue the paper. Brody would leave that task up to the FBI since they had the juice to make things happen, no matter which state's jurisdiction it fell under.

He was adding notes about the bites to his murder book when AIC Tanner stepped into the office, a broad smile on his face. It was a day of surprises. Brody had to force himself not to glance at his watch or the clock on the wall.

"Wanted to tell you congrats for finding the bug bite thing," Tanner said as he sat down at his own workstation.

More surprises.

Brody was feeling pretty good about the kudo until the AIC took credit for the find on a call with his superiors only a few minutes later. After he hung up, Tanner clapped Brody on the back. "By the way, we'll be having a conference call here at four. The profiler and a couple of our serial specialists are going to give us their insight. If you're handy, you might want to sit in."

Brody bit his tongue and nodded as Tanner left. He wasn't going to give the FBI agent the satisfaction of knowing how pissed he was about having the credit for a major break in the case pulled right out from under him. Then he calmed down. He might not like it, but if finding the bug bite meant they nabbed the bastard, he'd let Tanner, or even Renni's dog, take the credit and be happy about it. Besides, getting invited to the conference call meant he'd still be able to keep a hand in the investigation.

He rocked back and forth at his desk, thinking about the case. It all seemed to hinge on what Renni could tell them. The RMHK was too careful for any amateur mistakes to break the case open, and the clock was ticking. They needed to catch the killer before he left more bodies, more grieving families. Now that Renni was on the killer's radar, she was at considerable risk, not to mention going through a lot of mental anguish reliving the women's last moments.

An idea occurred to him and he scooted up to the desk. He pulled up his contact list on the computer and searched for a name, then punched the numbers into his phone.

"Phil Logan."

"Help, I've fallen and I can't get up," Brody said in a poor falsetto.

There was a moment of silence. "Brody, you shit, is that you?"

Laughing, Brody said, "Yeah, it's me. How could you tell?" But he knew Logan, an agent with the Colorado Bureau of Investigation, would remember when they'd gone to FBI-sponsored training together in Vegas. Logan knocked Brody on his butt during a hand-to-hand combat class and Brody made the quip, getting Logan to laugh so hard the instructor made Logan the "crash dummy" on the next set of maneuvers. It wasn't something the Cibbie was likely to forget.

"How the hell you been, man? What's it been, a year?" The CBI agent was a big Hispanic man, tough, with a mean right cross but a happy disposition, and more than twenty years on the force.

"Closer to eighteen months, I think. We gotta do it again sometime."

"Yeah, but minus the bruised kidney, please. So what's up? Somehow I don't expect you're calling me up to ask for a date."

*Right to the point. There's a reason I like this guy.* "I need to find a hypnotist. Somebody who's worked with law enforcement."

"You know it's harder 'n hell to get evidence obtained through a hypnotist admitted in court, right?"

"I don't need it for evidence. We have a pretty strange—"

"RMHK?"

Brody sat up straight. "How the hell—"

"Don't you know I work in the strange case department? I'm like the CBI's Fox Mulder of strange cases." Logan laughed. "Problem is, the Dana Scully of strange cases is about four-ten, *weighs* about four-ten, and has a mustache and beard. Seriously, though, a serial falls into my bailiwick. I saw your name in the file and was thinking of calling you."

"Did you happen to read anything about Renni Delacroix in that file?"

"I saw her name mentioned. She was the one who bought the truck, right? The truck with DNA from some of the victims?"

"Yeah. But she didn't *just* find the truck." Brody explained how Renni came to his attention and what she'd learned. The violent nightmares she experienced and the pieces of information that came from the dreams. How he hoped a hypnotist could help her fill in the blanks without having to go through the nightmares.

"I got a name for you. She's good. Everybody she's worked with liked her. She's retired from practice but still works with law enforcement. You want me to give her a call and tell her you'll be getting in touch?"

"That would be great. I'd appreciate it if you didn't give her any details—"

"I know the drill. I'll make sure not to influence her. What's your email?" After Brody gave him the information, Logan said, "I'll send you her contact info. Keep me posted. It might be we'll be working together on it eventually, anyway."

"Sure," Brody said, but he knew while the CBI might share with the Feds, the only thing they'd give local yokels like him was legwork and heartburn.

They talked a bit more, made promises to get together that would probably never pan out, and hung up. Five minutes later, an email from Logan came through with the hypnotist's name, phone number, and email address. Brody dialed the number.

A woman answered with a brisk, business-like, "Doctor

Richard, how may I help you?"

Brody explained he had a potential witness, but there were unusual circumstances, and then elaborated.

"Well, Detective, that's quite a story. I have to admit it would be interesting to work with the young woman, as much to find out how deeply she believes in her ability as to find out what kind of evidence she would provide. I've never worked with anyone who believes they can 'channel' the observations of actual witnesses or victims. It would be quite a coup to research." She sighed. "However, I'm afraid I've just returned home from hip surgery and my old bones just don't heal like they used to. I won't be going anywhere for at least several weeks. I'm sorry."

"No problem, Doc. I appreciate your talking to me and hope you heal quickly."

Disappointed, he hung up and checked his watch. Two hours to kill before the conference call and a couple more before he'd have a chance to talk with Renni. It would have been nice to tell her he'd found a way to help her avoid the bad dreams.

# Chapter Forty

The show wasn't as large as some, but the quality was undoubtedly high-end, and the competition would be stiff. After setting up her table and gear Saturday morning before the judging started, Renni wandered the rows, admiring the other cars. Her cell rang several times with calls from Brody, but she quickly declined them. She'd deal with him later. Besides, she reasoned, he probably couldn't get any madder than he already was, right?

The aging dynamic duo rode to the venue with her and then disappeared within minutes. Renni wasn't worried. They all had cell phones, and she was pretty sure she'd find them in the VIP bar after the judging.

The trio of judges made their rounds throughout the day, along with thousands of showgoers. Renni stood by the resto-mod to make sure no one got overly close and to answer questions. She was there when the judges came by to give her the second place trophy.

Immediately dialing Luke, she told him, "We got second in the open class!" Luke let out a whoop that had her holding the phone away from her ear. She placed the trophy on the table and sat, giving him details of the winning car and other placers.

Once the announcement of the winners went out over the PA system, a crowd began to gather around her car. She told Luke she'd call him later and spent the next few hours in the broiling sun talking to showgoers. A few made offers on the car, but none were for what it was worth. She began to sweat from more than the temperature.

Late in the afternoon, a scruffy-looking man approached, asking detailed questions not related to the car but about her and the shop. Even when she broke off to talk to other attendees, he stuck around and resumed the conversation as soon as he had her attention. Finally, she said, "I'm sorry, but I need to talk to the people over there," nodding to a wizened little man and his wife. The old man was leaned over the resto-mod's engine, muttering to himself.

The man handed her a business card. "I'll call you in a couple weeks."

Tucking the card in her hip pocket, Renni went over to introduce herself to the woman, who shook her head at her husband's puttering.

He turned to Renni. "Can I sit in it?"

She was on the brink of refusing, but his eyes lit up like a little kid who found the hoped-for bike under the Christmas tree. She didn't have the heart to say no. "Sure, but please be careful."

He wasted no time clambering inside, and quickly adjusted the seat closer. When he found the steering wheel was modified to allow telescoping and tilting, he adjusted it to fit as well. "Hey, Lenore, get on in here. See what you think."

Lenore smiled at Renni and held her hands out, palms up, and with a little shrug did as he asked. Renni hovered nearby, trying to make sure he didn't get carried away.

Eventually, they climbed back out. The bliss on his face gave her a twinge of guilt that she'd considered denying him the pleasure. He strode up to her and stood, hands on hips, head thrust forward.

"So. You take one-eighty for it?" he demanded.

"One hundred eighty thousand?" Renni frowned, not sure she'd heard him right.

"All right. A hundred eighty-three. But that's my final offer." He crossed his arms and scowled at her, as if daring her to turn him down.

"You want to buy the car? For one hundred eighty-three thousand dollars?"

"It isn't worth a penny more."

Renni almost blurted *You're right about that*, but managed to keep her mouth shut long enough to get her excitement under control. "Let me call my partner and ask what he thinks." She stepped a few yards away and speed-dialed Luke's number, fighting to keep from looking back to make sure the old guy was still there.

"Hey, there's a guy here who offered me a hundred eighty-three grand for the car. I told him I needed to talk to my partner." She peered over her shoulder at the old man, who was keeping an eye on her and smiled, nodding.

"You . . . you . . . you're kidding," Luke stuttered out. "I didn't think you'd even get the one-ten we were hoping for."

"Oh ye of little faith." She laughed. "Hell, I didn't either. I'm afraid I'll start hyperventilating. I'll call you back and let you know if I close it or not. Wish me luck."

"You got it."

As she started to put her phone away, she noticed there were a bunch of messages, all from Brody. *I don't have time to listen to him bitch about anything right now.* Renni stuck the phone in her back pocket and went over to the couple, smiling at the anxious look on the man's face.

"It took some convincing, but he agreed." She waited for the old guy to break out laughing and say it was all a joke. Instead, he introduced himself as Lee Pacheco and his wife as Lenore and suggested they head to the tent housing the business end of the show, with the insurance agents, car transporters, and finance companies needed to transact buying, selling, and shipping cars.

"Let me pack up." She put her table and other stuff in the resto-mod's expansive trunk and drove the three of them over to the enormous white tent. Inside, Lee produced a letter of credit. The financing clerk made some phone calls, helped them complete the paperwork, and witnessed signatures. Lee went back out to admire the soon-to-be-his car while they waited for the bank transfers to go through.

Lenore's faded eyes gazed lovingly at her husband as he ran his hands over the car, opened and closed doors, and inspected the engine. She leaned close to Renni and whispered, "Lee owned a car like that when we first met. Not all fancy, of course. He bought another one about twenty years ago and was going to fix it up—he says just like you did . . ." She grinned and shook her head. Then the smile faded. "He had to sell it to pay for medical care for our grandson. He has cerebral palsy, you see." Tears glistened on her cheeks. Renni put her arm around Lenore's shoulders, and they watched Lee until the clerk called them back to her table.

Less than an hour later, Delacroix Restoration's bank account was close to a hundred and sixty thousand dollars heavier than before, which was going to make a huge difference in whether or not the shop shut down in the very near future. Renni got a hug and a kiss from Lenore, and a tearful "Thank you" from Lee, before they climbed into the resto-mod. She barely got her things unloaded before the car rumbled away down the road, a grinning Lee peering over the steering wheel. Glad the file box had wheels, Renni stacked everything as best she could and rolled it to the truck, locking it all in the backseat.

Everything set to go, she wandered the VIP area until she spied a pair of familiar white heads of hair. Oscar and Ed were talking with several other men, all on the high side of sixty.

When Ed saw her coming, he beamed her a smile and stepped over to take her arm, leading her to their table.

"Here she is," he said.

Renni's head swam as Ed made rapid-fire introductions. She knew she'd never be able to remember a single name.

One man, the youngest of the group, said, "Yours was the resto-mod Chevy Coupe? The one that took second?"

She nodded.

"You was robbed. It should have taken first, hands down," the man said.

"Hell, the paint job alone shoulda clinched it," another added. The others nodded in agreement.

All she could do was thank him as she tried to field all the questions they threw at her about why she'd done this or that to the original coupe, asking what kind of wood was used in the interior, and trying to trick her into revealing her painter's name. She finally excused herself, saying, "I need to get cleaned up before dinner. It's been a long, hot day. And I need to call Luke and give him the good news. You coming?"

She started to ease out of the circle.

"We're all headed to the hotel bar shortly," Oscar said. "We don't need a ride."

"What a surprise," she said to herself and waved over her shoulder.

She drove back to the hotel, updating Luke on the way. "After using your friend's trailer, I think we'll get one. It will be a lot safer for the cars, and less work too. Unless . . . you know . . ."

"Cool," he said, ignoring her pessimism. Renni asked the status on the Caddy, and he told her everything else on her list had arrived. "Oh, the painter said they discontinued the Vermillion paint you picked, but he showed me a substitute and I couldn't tell the difference. He's used the brand before and says it's just as good, maybe better, so I told him to go ahead. Hope that was okay. I know you want it to be perfect."

"If he thinks it's as good, I trust him. He's never screwed us yet," Renni said, hoping it was true but knowing there wasn't enough time to do anything else.

"Um. Also, Brody's been calling," Luke said. "He's left me a bunch of messages, but I haven't called him back. I think I better, though, because he said if I don't, he's gonna put an APB out on you."

*Well, shit. So much for having a fantastic day.* "Go ahead and call him. Sorry to put that on you, but if I call him, he'll probably make me mad enough to say something I might regret later."

Luke laughed. "No problem. I can deal with him. Have a safe trip back." He disconnected.

Back at the hotel, Renni took a long, cool shower before changing into a light sundress with matching sweater. She started to stuff her jeans into the laundry bag before remembering the scruffy man's business card. She pulled it out. Her eyes widened as she read the guy's name, "Feature Writer" title, and credits listing *Classic Motorsports* and *Auto Restorer* underneath. She did a little shimmy of excitement. Having an article on her shop in those magazines would be a real coup. Then she frowned. Unless he found out about the newspaper article. Maybe he already knew? But he hadn't acted like he thought she was loony or a serial killer. She shook her head and grabbed her bag. He'd probably never even call.

She went down to the hotel bar, giving it even odds the incorrigible old men had already managed to get thrown out as she went inside.

# Chapter Forty-One

After Ed and Oscar's marathon night, first in the VIP tent and then the hotel bar, Renni was surprised the pair were capable of getting on the road by ten the next morning. Especially after drinking several decades-younger men under the table into the wee hours of the morning. Renni explained why she was taking a different route back, and after perusing a map on her laptop, as well as some dramatic pictures of the narrow, twisting turns of the Coal Bank, Molas, and Red Mountain Passes, Ed asked Oscar to drive, grudgingly admitting the former stock car driver had better reflexes.

It didn't take long for it to become clear her uncle's lead foot was as bad or worse than Ed's.

As she began the switchback climb outside of Durango, Ed called and said they decided to stop for some pie and they'd catch up. She laughed and asked him to bring her a piece. Even with the delay, she figured they'd get to Silverton before her. An empty trailer was still a hard pull for her old workhorse of a truck at this altitude. She patted the steering wheel of the '89 Dodge and smiled at the memories it conjured. She'd chosen to rebuild it because 1989 was the first year Dodge utilized the massive straight six Cummins turbo diesel. The truck made a ton of power but not a whole lotta speed, and it was showing its age.

Renni quickly realized tourists in their RVs tended to swing wide on the snaking corners, unsure of where the ass-end of their long vehicles were in relation to the towering rock face beside them. She was careful to pull as far to the right as she could on the turns as a preventative measure. Each time, she was acutely aware of the narrow dirt shoulder, cut with washouts, no guardrails, edging a thousand-foot drop on her passenger side. A couple near misses left her hands white with tension as she gripped the wheel, praying she'd still have a side mirror after the behemoths passed.

The One:1 still hadn't made a reappearance, and Renni began to wonder if they'd gotten into more trouble than a traffic ticket. She was checking her side mirror again when movement caught her eye in the reflection. She frowned as a light-colored van pulled up fast until it tailgated her.

"What the hell is he trying to do?" she muttered. The box trailer prevented her from getting a good look at the driver. "Idiot. He's going to get someone killed."

Ahead of her was a long straightaway. The van pulled out to pass, even though the centerline was a double yellow. *Better to have him ahead of me now, before there's an RV full of kids in the other lane.*

As the van's front bumper came even with the diesel's front end, it suddenly swerved left, then back right, careening solidly into the Dodge's front quarter panel. The van kept pushing until the truck was forced toward the cliff's edge. Taken by surprise, Renni battled the steering wheel as the right front tire dropped onto the soft shoulder. She strained to keep the truck from veering further, aware the soil would quickly fade to nothing but air.

A car appeared in the distance, and the van pulled ahead of

her and accelerated away. Working the wheel hard, she forced herself to lay off the accelerator and not send the truck into a skid by mashing her foot on the brake pedal. Gradually, the Dodge's power and bulk allowed her to ease the steering wheel left. Her shoulder sling impeded her ability to maneuver, forcing her to keep her right hand on the bottom of the steering wheel. With a welcome chirp, the truck's right-side tires regained the asphalt, but there was no time to relax as she fought to keep the empty trailer from whipping over the edge and pulling her off with it.

After another hundred yards, both truck and trailer were lined up safely between the solid yellow-and-white painted lines. She let out a long, wavery breath and rolled her good shoulder, relieved to note the van had disappeared from sight. Sweat trickled from her hairline, between her breasts, and along her spine.

"Holy shit," she said, after smacking herself in the forehead with her cast as she wiped sweat from her brow. The oncoming car, which had very likely saved her life, went by, and she had the road to herself the rest of the straight stretch. She took the next turn carefully, scanning ahead to a long, shallow curve.

Her feeling of relief was cut short. The van was tucked against the wall on the inside lane, lying in wait.

He ambushed her as she drove past. Renni floored the accelerator, and the diesel answered with a billow of gray smoke and a grossly inadequate surge of speed. The van came up hard on her left. Her eyes flicked between the rearview mirror and the next curve, which approached too fast for comfort. She prayed the road stayed clear as she settled herself into the broad bucket seat, gripped the wheel, and prepared to swerve to keep him from coming up beside her again.

A silver blur slipped in the narrow gap between the back end of the trailer and the front of the van, then screeched to an abrupt halt.

It was a perfect Bump and Grind, in reverse, one of Oscar's signature moves from back in his circle track days.

The van smacked into the right rear corner of the One:1, sending the little car into a 360-degree spin. Renni's gaze was glued to the mirror as she slowed the truck to a crawl. The sports car spun closer to the sheer drop. She watched, heart in throat, as the left rear wheel slipped off the edge, the left front hanging on by half a tread. With a masterful show of skill, Oscar pulled it out of the spin. He accelerated into the empty left lane beside her.

"Thank God the tires on the little sucker are so wide." Renni uncurled her white fingers from the wheel as she waited for her heart to slow down.

Through the sports car's windshield, Oscar grinned and waved cavalierly. Ed did not appear quite as calm. His eyes were wild, whites showing all the way around the pupil. His teeth were bared in a grimace, and he had a tight grip on the dash and grab strap beside his head.

Tan movement captured her attention, and she braced for another strike, but the van made a quick three-point turn and disappeared back down the road toward Durango. Oscar stuck his hand out the window and waved her on, then dropped back and tucked in behind the trailer. She picked up speed, the One:1 staying close, but a safe distance off her tail.

It was only a few more miles to Silverton. Renni pulled over at a gas station parking lot at the bottom of the hill, jerked to a stop, and put the truck in park. She laid her forehead on the wheel. Choking sobs built up in her chest and she fought them down, with only a hiccup or two escaping. A glance in the rearview mirror showed white, tight skin around her mouth, and glassy, staring eyes. She took several deep breaths to calm herself, then chugged the last of a bottle of water sitting in the cup holder, the uncontrollable quiver of her hands causing her to spill a couple drops.

Gravel crunched as the One:1 pulled in behind her. She climbed out of the cab on shaky legs and stumbled toward the back as Ed flipped up the passenger door and levered himself out. His dark face was sheened with sweat and had a gray tint that made the dermatosis spotting his cheeks stand out. Deep lines bracketed his mouth, which was turned down at the corners.

"You okay, Ed?" she asked. She took his arm as he tottered over to the trailer.

He shook his head. "Hell no, I'm not okay. I only brought one pair of clean skivvies and they ain't much good to me right now." He sagged onto the trailer's bumper, looking all of his eighty-eight years. Renni's eyes teared at his attempt at humor. Hopefully humor.

The driver's door pivoted up and Oscar clambered out. Unlike Ed, he was smiling ear to ear. "*Whooeeee!* What a ride. Reminded me of turn two at the Big Piney track when Billy Bob Shuman tried to knock me outta the race by givin' me a kiss on the ass and I beat him to it just to make sure he didn't win."

She shook her head, laughing as tears rolled down her face, and stepped in for a hug. He gladly obliged. It wasn't until she was tight against him that she felt his heart thudding at an accelerated pace and the tremor in his hands.

He finally let her go and turned back to the car. "Guess I better see what I did to Ed's toy, huh?"

They walked around and inspected the rear end. The gleaming carbon fiber material was cracked, chunks missing from several places. How much additional damage there was to the frame or drive train components was another story requiring specialists to determine.

Ed ambled back toward them, shoulders slumped. "Guess this pretty baby is gonna have to finish the trip in the trailer," he said. "I wonder if I have to send it back to Sweden to get it fixed?"

"Hell, that's the least of our worries. I'm more concerned about finding a store so you can get some more shorts. Otherwise, you'll be ridin' in the back of the truck," Oscar quipped.

"Please tell me you have insurance, Ed." Renni didn't want

to hear what her agent would say if she put in a claim on the One:1.

"Course I do. Besides, I have proof it wasn't our fault."

"What do you mean?"

Ed pointed to the car. "Dashcams. Got it all on video—front, back, and sides. Uploads to my phone."

"Oh, Ed, I could kiss you."

He held out his arms, bushy white eyebrows waggling to match the leer on his face.

She shook her head with a slightly hysterical giggle, glad to see he was feeling better. "Later. I need to make a call first."

# Chapter Forty-Two

"So fucking close!" He pounded his fist on the steering wheel. If that damn car hadn't gotten in the middle of things, Renni would be splattered along the bottom of the gorge, and he'd be home free.

He took several deep breaths, willing his heart to slow so he could think. Plan. Decide what to do.

It wouldn't take long for the Highway Patrol to start searching for a van with a wrecked front end, and that was if the crappy hunk of junk's wheels didn't fall off first. He turned on a narrow dirt road marked with a county sign and drove until he found a place where the track hugged the mountain on one side and dropped off sharply down a brushy hillside on the other. He pointed the nose of the van down the steep embankment, stepped hard on the emergency brake pedal, and put the van in neutral. He climbed out and released the brake lever. It only took a shove with his shoulder to start it rolling. The van built up enough momentum to carry it deep into the brush before it ground to a halt. He checked the road a few yards each direction, verifying someone would have to really be looking to find it.

He set off downhill, heading cross-country when he reached the bottom of the gorge. It was hard going, but he didn't care. A challenge, something that confirmed how much better he was than the others—tougher, smarter—was what he liked best.

It was late afternoon when he arrived at the outskirts of Durango. At a gas station, he found a rare public phone and ripped a map from the dog-eared book hanging by a cable. He followed the map to a bus station and approached slowly, mixing with the masses of tourists who swarmed the open area. There were two men in suits standing together sipping coffee from paper cups and scrutinizing the crowd, eyes covered with aviator sunglasses. He sneered. *Stupid cops. Might as well wear a sign.* He withdrew and headed to the ticket counter for the Durango-Silverton narrow gauge railroad several blocks away.

When he finally arrived at the head of the long queue and asked for a ticket on the next train, the clerk asked if he had a reservation. He shook his head.

The clerk frowned. "We're sold out. This is the last train until tomorrow morning. I can set you up for that, though."

Cursing, he turned, shoved through the next few people in line, and stalked across the crowded staging area. Taking deep breaths to calm himself, he moved into a shadowed corner and watched families with their loud, obnoxious kids, and the equally offensive, overly demonstrative young couples milling about. It took a while to find the right mark. An older man, alone, at the end of the line, ticket in hand. Foreign-looking, with too-short shorts for a guy and white socks under his sandals. He walked up to the man.

"Excuse me, sir, I need a huge favor."

The man glanced up from his train brochure. "*Ya?*" he said in a guttural European accent.

He gave the stranger a self-deprecating shrug. "My son lost his ticket. They're sold out, and now none of us can go if he can't. We have to leave early tomorrow to catch our flight. He's only eight. Would you consider selling me your ticket? I'd pay extra, including putting you in a nice hotel for the night. Please." He smiled. It was a disarming expression he'd practiced often over the years.

The man stared at him, frowning.

"Dinner at whatever restaurant you want."

That seemed to do it. The man nodded and handed over his ticket. *People are so gullible.*

"Come meet my son. I'd like him to thank you personally." He took the man's arm and steered him toward an alley. As soon as they were shielded from the tourists, concealed by a low wall that enclosed a dumpster, he pulled out his stun gun and touched the man's neck. The German's knees buckled and he lowered him to the ground.

Within minutes, the man was propped up in the corner between the wall and the dumpster. For effect, he pulled one side of the man's shirttail loose, ripped open the front, and propped a beer bottle he found on the wall in the man's hand. Anyone who saw him would think he was sleeping off a night of drinking. Assuming someone was crazy enough to wander down an alley reeking of garbage too long in the sun.

The PA system announced the final train of the day was loading, and he hurried to get in line. He climbed aboard the last car on the train. It was nearly full. The ticket-taker tried to direct him to another car, but he said he wanted to be at the end so he could get better photos. The porter shook his head but waved him onboard.

# Chapter Forty-Three

Brody answered on the first ring. Before Renni could say anything, he snapped, "Where the hell are you?"

She flinched.

"I've left you a dozen messages. I can't believe you just took off without telling me. You have any idea the extra man-hours we put in trying to find you after you didn't show up back at my place? You're damn lucky Luke finally called me back and told me where you were. I was all set to put out an APB on you." His voice vibrated with anger.

"I'm sorry I didn't let you know sooner, but I was busy. I figured you'd bully my whereabouts out of Luke, anyway." She could hear the murmur of several other voices on Brody's end. Cops, no doubt. Remembering *why* she'd felt the need to leave in the first place, her temper flared. "I have a business, Detective, in case you forgot. This show was very important to me, and no one said I couldn't leave town. I'm in Silverton, on my way back. The only reason I'm calling now is something came up and I thought you might want to know about it."

"What? Another *vision?*"

Renni ground her teeth at his smarmy tone. "I'm sure it's a disappointment to you, but no, it wasn't a vision. It was a van. A tan one to be exact. It tried to run me off Molas Pass."

The background voices went silent, and Renni assumed he'd signaled them somehow.

"I'm putting you on speaker." There was a short pause. "Go ahead."

"A tan van tried to bump me off, literally. It almost succeeded. I kept the truck on the road, but he came back for seconds. I'm not sure what would have happened if Oscar hadn't got in the middle of it in Ed's new sports car." Her voice started to shake as she remembered the horror of watching the little car, and her beloved uncle and his best friend, head for the edge. "By the time we all got straightened out, the van had turned around and took off. I couldn't call then because there wasn't any cell service."

"Give me the best description you can."

"I can do better than that. Ed's car has cameras. I'll have him send the video as soon as I get off the phone."

"No license plate?" an unknown female voice asked.

"I don't remember a plate, but I was a little busy at the time. It was a Ford Econoline. Late '70s or early '80s. Cargo van with no rear or side windows. The passenger seat window was heavily tinted."

"Any decals, markings?" Another stranger.

Renni closed her eyes and tried to envision the van. "Maybe something on the rear bumper, left side. The van will have pretty significant right front damage. My Dodge sits high and is built like a tank. I'd be surprised if he has fully functioning steering. I saw a bad wobble as he drove off. At least one tire probably won't last long, and he might lose the radiator. For sure the headlight is gone."

"Send the video," Brody said. "I need to make some arrangements. Call if you spot the van again."

She opened her mouth, preparing to tell him she might be

smart enough to do that when something tripped in her head. "Wait a minute. No one but Luke knew I was coming here until right before I left." She paused. "Except maybe this one guy. And he has long hair."

"Who?" Brody's voice was taut with interest.

"He's related to Maisie somehow. Works at the post office."

"Okay . . ."

She could almost see Brody making circles with his finger to get her to the point. She hurried on. "He came into the office while I was getting ready to go to the show. I had my itinerary up on my computer while I was out of my office, and he was in there. He might have seen where I was going."

"Give me his name and anything else you got. We'll check it out."

She told him Kevin's name and occupation. "It's probably a waste of time. I mean, he's kinda creepy, but more like a nerdy geek who has a hard time talking to girls. I'm sure he couldn't do anything, you know, like . . . like the killer does."

"We'll check it out anyway, just to be safe. I'll make some calls. Send the video, then get yourselves home and try to stay out of trouble for a change." He hung up without a goodbye.

Renni went over to where the men were leaning against the trailer drinking beers that had mysteriously materialized. Ed sent the file to Brody, then the three of them got the car in the trailer and tied down. Ed rode next to her in the front seat, with Oscar in the back hugging the cooler he'd taken from the One:1's minuscule trunk. The old men lamented the destruction of several bottles during the altercation with the van, but otherwise were back to their normal obnoxious selves.

It turned out the underwear issue was an exaggeration, so they headed toward Montrose. Oscar and Ed gave Renni a ribbing for trying to play chicken with the van and kept up a running commentary of one-upmanship on cars, women, and bad jokes. The atmosphere lightened, but Renni still kept a sharp eye on the mirrors.

As they closed on Montrose, a pair of black SUVs pulled alongside. The passenger in the first vehicle put his window down and flashed a badge, waved her to continue on, and pulled ahead, the other tucked in behind. From that point on, the trio drove precisely the speed limit, much to the old men's annoyance, but they made it back home with no further incidences.

# Chapter Forty-Four

Three hours after he'd boarded the train, cabins began to appear, dotted here and there in the trees, and an announcement came over the speakers that they would be in Silverton within a half hour. He couldn't have timed it better when a kid on one side of the train yelled, "Look! A bear with babies!" The entire car full of tourists scurried to that side and crowded the windows, jostling to spot the animals. He slipped out the door to the narrow landing on the rear of the car, ducking down so no one inside would spot him. The train slowed for a turn, and he scanned both sides of the railbed. One side was a rock-strewn bank, but the other was a grassy drop-off to a swampy area bordering a sinuous stream. Without wasting time to think, he jumped into the grass, rolling and bouncing until he came to a stop with a wet splat in black, stinky mud. He lay still until the train was out of sight around the curve.

The sun was down, but there was still an hour or two before full dark, and he used the time to scout out an empty cabin. Through the trees, he spied a small one that had a run-down, unused look. Lights came on further up the valley. Glad now for the coating of odiferous mud on his neck and arms, he swatted at masses of hungry blood-sucking mosquitoes as he made his way to the cabin. There were no lights within a half-mile or more.

He kicked open the flimsy back door. The cabin appeared to have been vacant for weeks, if not months. It didn't have running water or power, but he found a battery-operated lamp. After covering the windows with towels from a cabinet, he rummaged around and found a case of bottled water and a cupboard of canned goods. A closet in the one tiny bedroom yielded a flannel shirt, threadbare jeans, and boots only one size too large.

He used several bottles of water to wash the mud off and changed into the clean clothes, except for his own underwear and socks. Dinner was cold Beanie Weenies, Townhouse crackers, and a jar of green olives. He'd eaten worse living on his own. He slept on the couch, secure in the knowledge no one would be looking for him anywhere near the cabin.

As the tips of the mountain peaks were tinted gold by the rising sun, he gathered up several bottles of water, more cans of food, and a crank can opener. Stuffing everything into a ratty backpack that looked like its usual duty was to carry firewood, he trekked away from Silverton back toward Durango, using the train track when the going got too rough. It took all day, but he managed to get back to Durango right at dusk. This time no suspicious suits loitered around the bus station. He got a ticket to Salt Lake City via Grand Junction, which would put him within hiking distance of Rampart well after dark. As he climbed the steps into the Greyhound, he chuckled under his breath. He'd be home in a few hours, and the Keystone Kops would still be stumbling around searching for the van.

The bus was full, and he didn't have a choice when an elderly woman took the seat next to him. When she started to drone on about cats and grandchildren, he turned his shoulder into the window and leaned his head against it, pretending to sleep to get her to shut up. In the relative quiet, he focused on what went wrong on the pass.

It was only a fluke that let him discover Renni was out of town and where she was going. Since he knew exactly where she'd be, he stayed at a cheap motel and watched for her outside the show, following her from the Santa Fe golf course to a fancy hotel. It was easy to then track the distinctive truck and trailer when she headed back to Rampart. There was plenty of traffic to hide in as he followed her north, but it also prevented him from realizing the silver sports car was with her. He'd noticed it, of course. Who wouldn't? It zipped past at high speed time and again, then he'd see it pulled over a little further down the road. He'd been happy it was there—it kept the cops occupied.

Traffic petered out once he left Durango, and since the little sports car had disappeared by then, he'd forgotten about it as he closed in on her. The plan had been a good one, considering he'd put it together in a hurry. It wasn't his fault it didn't succeed. The old bastards in the car, they were extenuating circumstances. Old men like Pop. He wasn't a failure. Not like Pop always said he was. And next time he'd *prove* it. No more hurried plans. This one would be perfect, and Renni would no longer be a problem. Everything would be like before. He could go on his annual pilgrimage to honor Karen. The *before* Karen. When she was the prettiest girl in school. When *they*—the two of them—were the ones everyone wanted to be around.

He drifted off. Dreamed of being holed up in a cave below the Bookcliffs after he ran from the spider incident. Of creeping home after he figured Pop had got over being pissed. His surprise at finding the house empty and wandering around in the silence. The unused feel of Karen's room. Not dusty, but lacking her presence. How, with no one to stop him, he raided the refrigerator, gorging on cold fried chicken and a cherry pie. The crunch of tires on the gravel drive as he swallowed the last bites.

It was Pop, Ma . . . and Karen. A bandage covered half her face, but she appeared fine otherwise. He panicked, grabbing the dirty plate from the table and throwing it in the trash bin under the sink. He ran upstairs to hide in Karen's closet behind her clothes, a place where the two of them hid as kids, reading Dr. Seuss with a flashlight while their father raged beneath them.

Karen arrived a few minutes later. He'd left the closet door open enough to see through the crack and watched as she shut her door, sat on the bed, and sighed, fiddling with the bandage on her face.

As soon as he was sure his parents weren't going to come in, he whispered, "Karen, it's me."

She jerked around, staring at the closet, then crept over and slowly opened the door. He crawled out on his hands and knees and stood up.

"Where did you come from?" she asked.

"I've been camping out in the hills. I thought maybe Pop might have gotten over . . . well, you know." He tilted her head up with a finger under her chin. "Did he do this? Did he hurt you?"

She jerked her head away and turned to the window. "No."

"What happened?"

"It was the spider. It bit me."

He went over and peered at the side of her face. "Why did they put such a big bandage on a little spider bite?"

Her hands were shaking as she reached up and grabbed a corner of the adhesive tape. She peeled it away.

In his sleep he shivered, fists clenched as he remembered the crushing shock. Recoiling. Trying to turn away but unable to force his eyes from the horror. The *thing* she'd become.

"What did they do to you?"

Tears ran down her ravaged, pitted cheek. "Nobody did anything. It's all the bite. Those spiders have a poison. It ate my face. They call it some fancy name. Necrotizing venom, I think. It's stopped eating now, but there's nothing they can do about the scars."

"You mean you're always gonna look like that?" he

demanded, the disgust in his voice clear even to him.

She stumbled back, like he'd slapped her. He'd hurt her feelings for sure, but he just couldn't bear to see her. Not the monstrosity she'd become.

Right then he decided to leave. He wasn't sure which was stronger—the fear of what his father would do to him if he found him, or the inability to bear the sight of Karen. His no-longer-perfect twin.

After hitching a ride with Old Man Davis and settling in Layton, he went to the local library and used a computer to hook up with Karen on AOL. She kept trying to get him to come home and offering to get on a bus and come see him, but he didn't want to look at her. He needed to remember what she used to be like, when she was perfect, like him. He convinced her they needed to keep his whereabouts secret to make sure Pop never figured out what they were doing or where he was living. Never knew the prodigal son kept an eye on the happenings back at the old homestead.

Karen worried about him. Worried Mr. Davis would turn him in as a runaway or might be a pedophile or something. She warned him to be careful. And she was right, in the end. Karen also kept him updated on what was going on at home. How Pop sent Ma to some nasty nursing home because she started to forget a few things.

It was only a few months later when Davis told him he'd sold out and was moving away, abandoning him like he was a disposable razor or something. That was the straw that broke the camel's back.

When he told Karen what happened, she suggested he try to get Davis to pay for the time spent working for him or do something to show he valued all his "son" had done.

But Davis laughed at the idea. "You're not family. I don't owe you nothin'. I taught you a trade. Gave you a place to stay. You can have one of the trucks. It's more than you have a right to expect."

It made everything after much simpler. He knew then that Old Man Davis was the same as all the rest. Not appreciating what they had in him. First his father, then the girls he'd gone out with in school who made up stupid reasons not to stay with him, and now the old man.

Everyone was like that, he realized. Even him. He hadn't appreciated Karen, *before* Karen, like he should have. He decided then and there he'd make sure people regretted not valuing those they had when they had them. When they were whole.

It took him a few tries to get it just right. That first one at the rest stop was totally unplanned, and he'd been lucky there wasn't anyone else around. She was beautiful even with her eyes red from crying. She told him all about her husband's plans to divorce her for no good reason. The jerk was going to throw her away just like Old Man Davis did to him. It made him want to help her.

When she offered to give him a blow job in exchange for a ride, it almost spoiled everything. But he'd made a promise to himself, and he was going to keep it. It made it easier, too, because she wasn't pure like Karen. What he had to do to her was her own fault. And the husband would still wonder what happened to her and realize what he'd had once but never would again. Maybe blame himself for her being gone.

When it was over, he knew it was something he needed to keep doing. To honor Karen, the old Karen, the one that was gone. The one he missed more than anything. The second time was easier, and by the third, he had a pretty slick system down.

By the time he got home, both Ma and Pop were dead. Pop from the explosion, Ma in her sleep. His and Karen's lives seemed to come together then. He even found the spider living in his old bedroom. Like it was preordained. Karma.

He smiled in his sleep. K-1. K-2. Karma. A trifecta.

# Chapter Forty-Five

Renni backed the trailer into the shop and locked it up, the damaged sports car still inside, while Ed called a car shipper and arranged transport to Sweden. He paced around the parking lot, phone to ear, arm waving dramatically.

Oscar leaned against the wall and stared out the open overhead toward the field out back and the river beyond. She reached out and put her hand on her uncle's arm. "How's Ed? I'd hate it if my favorite client had a heart attack."

Her uncle gazed down at her, his soft smile telling her he was aware of how truly worried she was about Ed. He snorted. "He's fine. Already huntin' another car."

She rolled her eyes. "He'll probably fire me for getting him mixed up in this mess."

"Not gonna happen. When I told him about your little housewarming last week, he was ready to call the Marines right there and then. I got him simmered down some, but it didn't stop him from rousting his pilot and getting the plane ready so he could fly me 'n Bubber here." Oscar laughed. "'Sides, me 'n him got important things to do around here."

Renni gave him a dubious stare. "What important things?"

"This 'n that. You don't need to fret none. When we got our shit together, we'll let you know."

Renni pursed her lips and shook her head, but before she could say anything, footsteps tapped on the staircase. Maisie sashayed down to the shop. Her oversized caboose stuffed into a pair of skin-tight hot pink capris made Renni wince, even though her office manager's wardrobe choice, including the sequined T-shirt that featured dancing, glitter-bedecked teddy bears stretched too tightly across her broad bosom, was pretty standard fare.

Surprised, Renni asked, "What are you doing here?"

Maisie's eyes darted around the room, anywhere but at Renni. "I . . . um . . . I left something here and wanted to pick it up. What are you doing here?" she demanded.

"We just got back from the show." Renni wondered why she thought she needed to justify coming into her own business. Before she could ponder further, Bubber thundered down the stairs behind Maisie. *What's the deal? I'm the only one who ever works weekends, and I like it that way.* "What are *you* doing here?" she asked.

He stumbled to a stop, flashing a look at Maisie before stuttering out, "I, um, wanted to work on the motorcycle. It wasn't any fun sitting around that hotel all by myself."

Right then, Luke wheeled into the parking lot with Vicki and Buster. It took several more minutes to get everyone settled down and organized, then they all trooped upstairs to the lobby.

Sitting at the table, surrounded by her friends and family, Renni forced herself to relive the last few hours and days. Oscar and Ed kept a close eye on her, and whenever she appeared to be struggling, stepped in and added humorous comments or elaborated on the story to give her a few minutes to pull herself together. When Oscar launched into a vivid description of the One:1's wild ride, Renni made a lame excuse and headed to the ladies room, locking the door securely behind her.

Putting the seat down, she sat on the toilet and let her pent-up emotions flow. She held her hands over her mouth to muffle her cries, knowing the whole group would be at the door in an instant if they heard her. After shedding a bucket of tears over what seemed like an hour or two, but which her watch confirmed was only a couple minutes, she stood up and splashed cold water on her face before blotting it with paper towels. A few neck rolls loosened her up, and a few deep breaths calmed her enough to return to the breakroom.

Oscar gave her a sharp look but kept quiet, and the rest were still engrossed in Ed's description of how heroic he was, giving Oscar instructions on how to drive the sports car during the excitement. Renni stood in the doorway looking at all of them with love and wonder. Here she'd dragged them smack into the middle of a serial murder case, and they were taking it like it was just another day at the office. They'd risked their lives for her. They believed in her.

And then there was Brody, who maybe didn't believe in her, but he *had* gone out on a limb to convince his bosses that there was something to what she'd told him. Not to mention he had to put up with babysitting a stranger who was living in his house.

She grabbed the bottle of Fireball from her office and a handful of cups from a breakroom cupboard. As she distributed drinks around the table, Luke, Vicki, Bubber, and Maisie continued to pepper the other three with questions, getting shushed so many times it sounded like a bunch of balloons being let loose. Two hours later, after the story had gotten more and more outrageous with every retelling, as well as louder, Oscar banged the table with the flat of his calloused hand.

"Okay, folks, that's enough for today. It's been a long one, and us old folks need our beauty sleep."

Ed frowned. "Speak for yourself, you old codger. I'm ready to start hittin' the bars for a couple hours. Maybe shoot some pool."

Given the lines of exhaustion bracketing his mouth and

bisecting his forehead, Renni knew this was all bluster.

Everyone packed up and headed out, Renni locking the shop behind them. Bubber, Ed, and Oscar headed to their hotel, and Luke and Vicki dropped Renni and Buster off at Brody's.

# Chapter Forty-Six

The video from Ed Benson was sent on to the conference call members in Denver and viewed several times, repeatedly run backward and forward to check for details. The FBI sent it over to their digital specialists to see if they could enhance it enough to get a face or license plate. Even from a distance of several hundred yards, the video was clear enough to eliminate any doubt it was a deliberate attempt to run Renni off the cliff, and it showed how close she came to going over before getting the truck back on the road.

The second attack was recorded from much closer, with the car right in the middle of the action. From the expressions on some of the other viewers' faces, Brody didn't think he was the only one feeling queasy after trying to concentrate during the spinning ride.

While they watched, the FBI techs got started researching Kevin Green, and they soon had his full name, address, social security number, printed copy of his driver's license, and fingerprint card from his application to work at the post office. The information was distributed to the team members, and

Brody knew not one detail of Kevin's data would be overlooked once they all started digging.

The FBI profiler spoke up. "On the surface, Mr. Green appears consistent with my profile. He's a white male, between the ages of thirty and sixty, with some education, who likely hasn't been very successful with women. He's located within the area of our 3D unsub map, and we're confident the RMHK is a Hunter, sticking to a confirmed comfort zone along I-70."

Chief Wilcox looked confused, and the profiler elaborated.

"I'm sure you're familiar with the Ted Bundy case. He was a Hunter. He looked for women in a fairly specific area. Disposed of them in specific areas. Most of them were within a day or two of his home, so he could go back and visit the bodies. We don't think the RMHK has any interest in going back to the dump sites because he's leaving the bodies in relatively high-traffic areas. It's likely he wants them to be found quickly. It's critical we ensure the media doesn't get ahold of too many details because just like Bundy, the RMHK might abandon that comfort zone if there's too much attention."

He waved a sheaf of papers related to Kevin Green. "Once I know more about this subject—his family history and hobbies, things like that—I can determine if he shows indications of the degree of sophistication and risk tolerance indicated by the previous kills."

The call closed with the Fibbies promising to forward their findings on the video after closer review, but it was likely an empty promise, as always.

Brody called the post office and asked for the supervisor. Rather than inquire about Kevin and possibly tip his hand, he asked to have the last thirty days' schedule for all staff emailed to him to investigate recent allegations of misuse of a mail truck. The supervisor could have required a subpoena, but he seemed so upset about one of his vehicles being misused he didn't hesitate to say yes. *Lucky break.* The schedule arrived a half-hour later. With a grim smile, Brody put in some additional data requests, as well as a request for a search warrant on Kevin's house. It was unlikely he'd get it before morning, even if the FBI threw their weight behind it, so

he left the office and went home.

He stopped in the mudroom, silently observing Renni on the back deck through the screen door. Her shoulders were slumped and she seemed to be studying her hands in her lap, but he couldn't tell if it was weariness or depression. After everything she'd been through, either was to be expected.

He pushed through the door, and she jerked around.

"Sorry. Didn't mean to startle you. I need a drink. How about you?"

"Yeah, that'd be great."

He returned a few moments later with two tall glasses and handed her one with clear liquid and a wedge of lime. "I made you a G&T. Hope it's okay."

She took a deep drink. "It's fine." She let her head fall back against the seat cushion. "I can't believe this is happening. It's bad enough to know there's a serial killer out there, but now I've put my family and friends in danger too."

Brody slid onto a seat next to her. "None of this is your fault. Honestly, if there was some way I could go back to the day you told me about the truck, I'd never tell anyone about you. I'd find a different way."

"Yeah, right. Without me as your only suspect, what would you tell your boss?" She smiled to take the sting out of her words and shrugged, sipping her drink. "Did you find the van?"

He hesitated.

Renni shifted away. "Oh, right. Sorry. You can't tell me. I get it," she said, her tone disgusted, clearly regretting letting him off the hook a few moments before.

"It's not that." He set his drink down a little harder than necessary. "Damn it, Renni. I have a job to do, and sometimes it's not very pleasant." He took a deep breath and unclenched his fists. "The van was found outside Silverton by a county worker. Driven off the side of a hill into the brush. It was clean. We figured he'd maybe jacked someone out four-wheeling, but there weren't any reports of missing persons. The local LEOs staked out the bus station but didn't see anything." He took another sip. "I got to thinking about the Durango-Silverton narrow gauge train. They sent some deputies over there and found an uproar about a kid whose parents found him peeing on a homeless man in an alley."

She gasped. "He didn't."

Brody nodded. "Yeah, he did. Lovely family from what I heard. Anyway, the guy turned out to be a German tourist who couldn't remember anything after agreeing to sell his ticket to a guy who said his kid lost his. There were stun gun burns on his neck. Surveillance cameras at the train station were old, but we got a hazy picture of a man in a Levi jacket and baseball cap with the tourist, no detail. The cameras in Durango don't show the man at all."

She opened her mouth, a question clear in her eyes, but he held up his hand.

"We studied the photos. Either he wasn't there or he'd completely changed his appearance. He could have gotten off the train before it actually left the station, or somewhere before it stopped at the other end. Who the hell knows? We've got more than a hundred people searching for him. Dogs. Park Rangers. The works. Maybe he's hitchhiking, caught a bus in another town, or stole a car that hasn't been reported yet." He shrugged. "I'm pretty sure we missed him."

"Did the tourist give a description?"

"We set him up with a sketch artist, and the guy swears the drawing is perfect." He sniggered. "Now all we need to do is find a guy who looks exactly like Pee-wee Herman, and we've got him."

"Pee-wee Herman?" Renni bit her lip, but the corners still curled up.

"Everyone who's seen it says it. Apparently, the tourist

watched a movie with Herman the night before, so, you know . . . Anyway, we'll circulate it to law enforcement all over the Four Corners region. Maybe there's a Pee-wee impersonator running around out there somewhere."

"A scary thought all by itself," she said, laughing, and relaxed back into the chair cushion, the smile still on her face. Brody laughed with her, and they sipped their drinks.

Setting her glass down, Renni asked, "What about Kevin?"

"We don't have a lot yet. Except he called his boss the day you left for Santa Fe and said he was sick. He's still gone. We have an APB out on him. We should have a search warrant for his house by tomorrow. Until then . . ."

"So what's next?"

Brody didn't answer for a long time. Finally, he said, "We'll see if we can connect Kevin to the van somehow. Keep following the crumbs." He yawned. "It's late. I think we need to get some sleep. I have to be in the office for a debriefing with the chief by eight."

He waved her in ahead of him and followed her up the stairs. He couldn't help but admire the view. Clad in a pair of cut-off jeans and a tank top, she was *way* better than the thought of a good night's sleep. But he imagined even wearing a pair of hip waders and a down parka, she could still pull off sexy.

# Chapter Forty-Seven

The next morning, Brody steeled himself to bring up the topic he'd avoided last night as he heard Renni padding down the stairs, Buster's nails scratching on the wood.

He handed her a cup, teabag floating in the hot water, as she came through the doorway. He still hadn't gotten used to having such a distraction each morning. Before Renni, he'd always been in a hurry to head into the office. Now time flew. When she gave him a searching look, he turned back to the oven so she wouldn't see his face flush at getting caught staring and bent to pull a pan of blueberry muffins out of the oven. After setting it on the stovetop, he removed the cammo-patterned silicone BBQ glove he used as an oven mitt.

"Do you always cook like this for yourself?" she asked.

He laughed. "Not usually. But I have to admit, I like having a good breakfast. I'd much rather have real food in the morning than a protein drink or something like that." It occurred to him that he was getting used to sitting down for meals with her. He wasn't looking forward to going back to his lonely life.

"There's something we need to talk about," he said as he

dumped the muffins onto a plate and set them on the table next to a butter dish.

Renni, in the process of breaking a muffin in half and slathering it with butter, set it and the knife down and watched him, apprehension obvious in her clear green eyes.

"The Fibbies think we should send you to Denver so they can keep a close eye on you. Keep you safe."

"I can't leave my—"

"I know," he said quickly, holding up his hands in a conciliatory manner. "I have a solution. It would make me, and my bosses, more comfortable about you being here where we can keep watch over you."

"What's your solution?" she asked, gaze even more wary.

"There's a guy we work with at the station. Teaches self-defense classes. Boogey Mankiller." At her raised eyebrows, he added, "His real name is Boyd, but I didn't know that until I happened to see some paperwork at the office."

"Boogey Mankiller? You're kidding, right?"

"Nope. He's Cherokee. Mankiller is a family name. I asked him one day about his nickname, and he told me it has to do with a Cherokee ceremony he's involved in, and he prefers it to his legal name."

Renni's brow crinkled skeptically.

"We spent some time together in Afghanistan"—Brody blinked hard and looked away—"and talked about a lot of stuff, including where we were from. I guess he decided Rampart sounded nice because he moved here when he mustered out. Got back in touch. He teaches hand-to-hand combat and community outreach to a lot of western states' police and sheriff departments. He's a good guy. I think you'll like him."

He looked Renni straight in the eye. "I'll make you a deal. If you agree to have him give you self-defense classes, we can work out times you can drive and do things by yourself. But only some things, and not after dark. We don't know if this guy is watching you all the time or only occasionally."

"I don't need babysitters or guards," she said, eyes narrowed. "If he comes after me, I don't want anyone else to get hurt."

Buster stirred beside her, and Brody thought about how close they both came to being vaporized. "I'm sorry, but it's Boogey or Denver."

She chewed her lip. "If I agree, you'll take me to get my car? And I won't have to have a bodyguard all the time?"

He nodded but held up his index finger. "You can take your car on errands in town . . ." A second finger joined the first. " . . . during the day, to busy places, before dark. But . . ." A third finger. " . . . and this isn't negotiable, you have to take as many classes as he says you need. Miss curfew or skip classes and I'll have your car impounded."

"You can't do that!"

"Wanna bet? Deal or no deal?"

"You're a real bastard, Brody."

"So I've been told." He eyed her. "Well?"

"Deal."

—

Twenty minutes later, he stood beside Renni as she stared at what could easily have been a crater on the moon. There was very little debris around the old stone foundation; the fire department had collected most of it as part of their investigation. Every plant within thirty feet of the crater was gone. One whole side of a towering cottonwood was missing, and it would have to be cut down. The old orchard was far enough away to have escaped damage.

The garage was singed, windows broken, and pieces of siding and two-by-fours riddled the structure like porcupine quills. Renni unlocked and flipped up the garage door. Inside Brody saw her Spitz, with a little snub-nosed delivery van beside it. A small elliptical logo on the back of the van read Divco. The narrow space in front of the vehicles was occupied by a teardrop travel trailer. Both had matching paint and fancy Delacroix

Restoration logos along the sides. He was as surprised as Renni to find all three vehicles unscathed, except some broken glass on the seats of the Spitz.

He waited while she found boards and nails and covered the broken windows, not surprised when she refused his help. Temporary repairs complete, she backed out the Spitz and locked the garage. Brody followed her to the shop, smiling as Buster stood in the convertible's passenger seat, his paws on the dash and his chin resting on top of the windshield, tongue lolling in the breeze.

# Chapter Forty-Eight

As she jogged up the stairs to the lobby at 9 a.m., Renni was filled with a sudden unease. How would Maisie react if—when—she found out Renni sicced the cops on her cousin or whatever he was? *Surely Brody will be careful not to alert a suspect they're investigating, right?* She bit her lip and pushed through the door, making a beeline for her office.

"So, you got wheels again," Maisie said, stepping out from behind her desk and blocking Renni's escape.

"Yeah." Renni swerved around Maisie and tossed over her shoulder, "I'm free at last, free at last."

"When does the coach turn back into a pumpkin, Cinderella?"

Renni laughed, her mood lightening. "Before dark, but it's better than nothing."

She went in, sat quickly at her desk, and grabbed the phone. It was Monday, which meant Layton High School was open again. She dialed the school's number, and when an officious secretary answered, made up a story about putting together a reunion for a group of old friends.

"I'm trying to track down some photos to put up on the wall," she said, then rattled off names at random from the yearbook. Eventually, she was connected to a woman who had been a secretary at the school since the late '90s.

The secretary, Mavis Purchase, was a talker, reminiscing about the football team making it to state in '98, an unusual storm that flooded the school parking lot in '99, and heading into a commentary on the difficulties they ran into building the new gym the same year, before Renni managed to circle her back to the topic at hand. Mavis thought about it for a long moment before admitting any better photos, if there *were* better ones, would be located with the photographer, not the school.

After another thirty minutes of one-sided chatting, Renni made another call.

"Hello?" The scratchy voice warbled with age.

"Yes, hello. The Layton High School secretary gave me your number. I'm searching for originals of yearbook photos from 1998. Mrs. Purchase at the school thought you might still have them."

"Oh, dear. From 1998, you say? My, but that's a long time ago. I'm not sure we can find those, even if we do have them."

"It's very important, ma'am. Life or death." Renni hoped the woman wouldn't ask why it was so important. The old lady might not believe it, and Brody was unlikely to appreciate her discussing a murder case with an uninvolved party.

"I suppose if it's important, I can try. My son, Gerald? He does the photography now that my husband died. But he's on a big job over in Salt Lake. School just started. It's very hectic for us right now with football and the grade schools, and I don't think I can get down into the basement and go through the boxes by myself."

"When will Gerald be back?"

"What's today?"

"Monday," Renni said. *This isn't looking real promising.*

"He'll be home on Wednesday. I think we could check then. Would that be all right?"

*Guess it'll have to be.* "Sure, Mrs. . . . um—"

"Phipps. Emalie Phipps. Now, honey, you give me your phone number, and I'll write it down here."

Renni gave her the number, three times, and was still only half sure Mrs. Phipps had it right. Worst case, Renni could call back on Wednesday. She thanked the old woman and hung up.

She sat back in her chair. There was no telling if the photo would be worth anything anyway. The TV shows on crime scene investigation made it sound like they could do facial recognition on almost anyone or age a photo to see what they'd look like now, so there was always a chance it would help find the boy. But, again, there was no real proof Bill Davis was anyone but a kid whose paperwork got lost over the years.

Her cell rang. Brody's number. She thought about not answering but didn't want to find an APB out on herself. She picked up. "Yeah?"

"Hello to you too," he said. "Hope that's not the way you talk to clients, or you've got a lot more than an article to blame for lack of work." When she didn't reply, he continued, "I have your first class with Boogey scheduled at four today. His place is next to the hardware store on Freestone Avenue. Wear comfortable clothes. I told him you're going to be a little sore and banged up already, so he'll take it easy on you."

"Four? Today? Geez, thanks for the notice. What if I have appointments?"

"Cancel them or turn in your keys. I told you this wasn't negotiable."

"Ass." Renni clicked off. Realizing it was noon, she stood, stretched, and grabbed five beers from the fridge as she headed downstairs.

The space was empty. A murmur of voices drew her out the man's door, and she found Luke and Oscar outside spraying primer on the cleaned and sanded motorcycle frame. She held up the beers.

"Now there's a sight for sore eyes," Oscar said with a smile.

"Oh, and you too, babygirl."

She grinned and handed them each a bottle. Peering around, she asked, "Where's Bubber? And have you seen Maisie?"

The two men exchanged amused grins.

"Oh, they're around here somewhere," Luke said, smiling around a sip of beer. "Maisie was helping Bubber in the shop, I think."

Renni frowned. "Maisie? Helping in the shop?" The idea of her office manager getting her inch-long fingernails dirty, or risking breaking one, was ludicrous. Besides, she didn't know an Allen wrench from a torque wrench. "She never comes down here, and now she's here all the time. I guess she forgot she's supposed to be the office manager, not Bubber's assistant."

Her uncle snorted. "Well, if a shop assistant's supposed to hang all over the guy, asking stupid questions and wasting a lot of time, then you might oughtta change her job title."

"I didn't see them in the shop, but I'll check again. I'm thinking of ordering a pizza. You want?"

"I'm meeting Vicki at Aunt Bee's BBQ," Luke said with a shake of his head.

Oscar shrugged. "Fine with me. Find Bubber and that gal, and we can decide." He gave Luke a sidelong glance, the corners of his mouth quivering.

"Geez, the things I have to deal with. It's like herding kittens." She stomped into the shop. As she walked toward the back, Bubber stepped out from behind the staircase, stumbling to a stop when he spotted her.

"Oh hey, Ren," he shouted.

"You don't have to yell, Bubber, my hearing is fine now."

He chuckled self-consciously and fiddled with the buttons on his shirt, one of which was buttoned incorrectly. "What you doin' down here?" he asked.

She lifted an eyebrow. "Well, besides the fact this is my business and I quite often work down here, I came to ask if you and Oscar wanted pizza for lunch. Luke is meeting Vicki, and I can't find Maisie."

"I'm right here," Maisie called out, stepping from behind Bubber. "I needed to pee. That all right with you?"

Renni frowned at her defensive tone. "It's fine, but there's a perfectly good restroom upstairs. Why—"

"You telling me I can't decide where I want to pee?" Maisie demanded.

Renni held her hands up in surrender. "Nope, wouldn't think of it. So, you two want pizza or not?"

"None of them damn little fish things on mine," Maisie said as she clomped up the stairs.

"Sure, Ren. Can I have double pepperoni and extra cheese?' Bubber asked.

Renni chewed her lip as she went up the stairs behind Maisie. *Aw, crap. Something is definitely up with those two. Just what I need to go along with a serial killer.* She decided to take advantage of her newfound freedom and scheduled the order for pickup, then gathered her backpack and led Buster outside into the parking lot. "Come on, you mangy mutt. It's pizza day." The dog knew the p-word and happily jumped into the car, claiming the passenger seat, as usual.

# Chapter Forty-Nine

Renni shut the car's tiny trunk, stowing the pizza boxes safely out of Buster's reach. She shifted her pack under her arm and rummaged inside for the keys as she walked toward the door. "Hey, Busty . . ."

She screamed as two arms slithered around her chest and she was dragged backward through the open sliding door of a van. She sprawled across the floor. Buster snarled and barked ferociously before launching himself over the Spitz's door and landing beside her. Her attacker let go of her as the spaniel lunged, sinking his teeth into the man's wrist and tugging, shaking his head with a growl. Renni scooted backward until she came up against the far wall of the van.

"Whoa there, pup," her attacker said in a surprisingly gentle voice, reaching around Buster's chest to hold him as he squirmed to get another bite in. Once the dog realized Renni was no longer screaming, he quit wriggling and looked between the two humans.

Renni launched herself past the man, who knelt on the van floor next to the open doorway. She hit the ground and backed away, eyes searching frantically for someone who might be able to help her.

"Renni, calm down." His voice was soft, the words a request, not a demand.

She turned and stared at him. In the van's shadowy interior, only his eyes had definition. "Who are you?" She could barely force the words out. It seemed there was no air left in her lungs.

"A friend of Brody's."

"Brody? Why . . . What . . ." She frowned and rubbed her forehead, trying to sort out what was going on. She dropped her hand. "You're Boogey, aren't you?"

"I am." He released Buster and patted the dog on the butt as he jumped down and ran to Renni's side. "He's a good watchdog. The fact he barks is probably more important than his eagerness to bite."

"What the hell . . ."

Boogey slid to his feet and straightened in the sun. He towered over her, at least six and a half feet tall. She stepped back against her car. In the bright light, she realized he was a handsome man with a long face, high cheekbones and forehead, and blue-black hair cut in a military-style crew cut. His skin was a deep mahogany, his irises so black she couldn't see where the pupil started.

She was still trying to process what was happening when he asked, "What were you thinking as you came back to your car?"

"Thinking? I wasn't thinking anything. I mean . . . I guess maybe wondering if the pizza would still be hot when I got back."

"That's the problem. You're wandering along, not paying attention to what's around you. Bad things happen. Predators are always on the lookout for prey, but they don't want to work for it. They want the easy stuff. Women busy with their purses, talking on the phone, window shopping—because they're easy to take by surprise. Wham, bam, on the lam." He smiled, his tone friendly and upbeat.

Renni felt her blood pressure skyrocket. "Did Brody put you

up to this? Because if he did, I've about had it. He's trying to convince me I'm going to be attacked anytime I'm by myself. He's completely paranoid."

"No. He's not. He wants you to be able to protect yourself if this RMHK shows up, or preferably avoid the guy getting close to you in the first place. Brody knows bad shit happens to people every day, and how fast it happens. Most incidences can be avoided if people are prepared. If they have a plan. I'm here to help you make a plan. That's all."

Boogey pointed at the van. "Oldest trick in the book. Drive around a parking lot until you find a woman alone in a car. Follow her. If she parks in a space with an open one next to it, pull in. If she's slow getting out, maybe makes a call or rearranges her purse, you grab her when she climbs out. It only takes a second to open the door, grab her, knock her out, and drive off. Otherwise, you wait until she comes back. You grab her when she leaves the door open and gets her purse put away, checks her makeup in the mirror. Easy peasy."

"I get it. I'll pay attention to any vans parked next to me."

"It's not enough, Renni. I followed you from the shop. I was right behind you the whole way, in a tan van. Look, I get that thinking this guy wants to hurt you is hard to comprehend." He frowned and touched her lightly on the shoulder. "I know about your friend. You think she ever imagined anything like that would happen to her? Hell no. Brody wants you safe. That's all."

Renni dropped her head back on her neck and groaned. "Fine. So what am I supposed to do? Wait for you to randomly attack me and see if I can hit you or what?"

He laughed. "No. From now on we'll meet at my gym. I'll work with you on moves you can use in a lot of situations. We'll talk about some setups you want to be especially aware of." He grinned. "Like how to spot vehicles following you. Especially vans."

The corner of Renni's mouth turned up in a sly half smile. "Do I get to practice these 'moves' on you?"

"Oh yeah. I figure it's only fair." He pulled a card from his wallet. "This is my address. Meet me there at four. We'll start with a one-hour session. Once we see how it goes, and I'm comfortable you're healing well, we'll adjust as needed."

Renni nodded grudgingly. *I'll do this until they catch the guy, then I'm done with this shit.* "I'll be there." She gave him a hard stare. "No more jumping out at me, though, okay?"

"Four o'clock." He turned on his heel, went around the van, started it, and wheeled out of the parking lot before she realized he never agreed to her request.

"Great. Now I have to worry about the Boogey Man coming after me every time I turn around," she grumbled, opening the car door for Buster to climb in. "Good dog, Busty. You get your own piece of pizza. Hopefully, he'll have a mark to remind him what a vicious creature you are."

He gave her a sloppy doggie smile.

# Chapter Fifty

He scrunched down until he could barely peer over the dash of the old Nomad station wagon. He'd backed into the only empty space at the busy gym. It was at the end of the row, giving him clear line of sight to Delacroix Restorations across the road and down half a block. An enormous truck with a lift high enough for a kid to walk under occupied the space next to him, blocking the Nomad from anyone else's view.

With a pair of binoculars, it was like he was right there. He could see every detail of the upper lot, the driveway, lower lot, and the jumbo roll-up doors. It was a nice day, hot, and the doors to the shop were open. The shop guy—Luke—he recognized, but not the two old guys who seemed to be around a lot lately. They could be the ones from the silver car. Renni might have hired them, but if she had, she must be pretty hard up. They were a little long in the tooth for the hard work of restoring cars. He didn't much care why they were there—they were a problem, and he was going to have to deal with it. The old lady who worked in the office and drove the pink VW was there too. But she wasn't anything to worry about. Old ladies like her just went back and forth to work and probably had a dozen cats at home to stink up the place.

He had glimpsed the cop earlier when he dropped Renni off like he did most mornings. Having a cop hanging around screwed with things, even though he was probably only interested in coppin' a feel. The pun made him chuckle. Considering she'd moved in with the cop, it must not be too tough to talk her into it. Disappointing. And a problem. A big problem. Now he would have to figure out how to separate the two of them. But he'd come up with something. He wasn't worried.

He spotted a scrawny guy headed his way, a frown on his face.

"Shit." He sat upright in the seat.

The tweaker marched up to the driver's side window and stuck his face in. "What the hell are you doing drivin' my wheels, man? I didn't give you no permission to drive it. You's just s'posed to fix it up."

"Stan, you shithead, you know we talked about this. You gotta pay rent if the vehicle sits more than thirty days. It's been, what? Better'n two months? I'm doing you a favor by using this piece of crap to run errands instead of charging the rent. You wanna pay me rent instead? Fine. Fork over a hundred bucks." He held his hand out, palm up.

"What the fu . . . I ain't payin' you no hundred bucks rent. That car ain't worth more'n a grand. Get out and give me the keys. I'm taking it back." Stan reached for the door handle.

He grabbed Stan by the right ear and slammed his face against the door. As he held him there, he leaned down and said, "The car's mine until you either bring me the hundred bucks or pay the deposit to get the work done. That's the deal. You try to take it, I'll sue your ass. Besides, I know your mama's got more than two hundred bucks." He shoved Stan back and released him.

"Man, that ain't right." Stan rubbed his ear, tears welling.

He forced himself to relax and soften his voice, unclenching his fists. "I don't wanna be a bad guy here. But I don't do shit for free. The deal is, I won't use your car more than a day or two a week. Long as I use it, I won't charge you rent. You bring me the deposit, I'll do the work." He tilted his head and waited for a response.

"Deposit's five hundred, right?"

He nodded.

"So I bring you five hundred, you'll fix my car?"

"Yeah, but you don't get the car until you pay the other half. And once it's done, you don't bring me the rest, I'll sell it and keep the money you owe me. Fair is fair, man. Right?"

Stan scuffed the toe of his tennis shoe against the Nomad's front tire. "Yeah, I guess. I'll talk to Ma. Maybe she'll front me the deposit. I got a job lined up at the Kum and Go. I'll have some money soon for the second half." Stan shook his finger at him. "Don't you be getting my car all wore out drivin' it, you hear? I know how much mileage it has on it."

"You mean how much it had before the odometer quit," he said with a chuckle. "You get me the money, you'll get your car back, better than new. I guarantee it one hundred percent."

Stan smiled, his head bouncing like a bobblehead doll. "That'd be great. Cool. Okay. Bye." He waggled the fingers of one hand and shuffled off.

"Dumb shit," he said, leaning the seat back and picking up the binoculars. A moment later he tossed them into his lap and slid below the dash as a red car sped into the parking lot.

# Chapter Fifty-One

Renni worked on payroll and bookkeeping after lunch, still jittery from her introduction to Boogey. She wanted to be in the shop, but there wasn't enough going on to keep both her and Luke busy, and he needed the hours. The lack of new jobs was upsetting on its own, but work on the old cars was therapy, and she missed it when she wasn't building. It was the one place she could truly be herself. Just her skill against metal. It was what she was made for. Even with the funds from the resto-mod in the bank—and they'd stay there until the uncertainty of the serial killer was resolved—she still needed to have enough coming in for what was going out. She swallowed hard at the thought of losing it all.

It was a relief to shut down the computer at 3:00. She told Maisie she'd be gone the rest of the day and went down to the shop to check on the guys before heading out. Oscar and Bubber were cleaning up their workstation.

"Hey, Unc, where's Ed? I'm surprised we haven't seen him. He didn't leave already, did he?"

"Yeah, he flew back home for a day or two. He'll be back

pretty quick. Said not to be mad he didn't say bye."

"Maybe a little, but I'll forgive him." Spying Bubber, who worked very hard to avoid making eye contact with her, she sauntered across the room and sidled up to him. "So, did you ask her out?"

"What? Ask who out? What're you talking about?" Bubber's face was redder than a five-hour sunburn. He stumbled over to a toolbox and pulled out a drawer, pawing at air tools, none of which were hooked up to the compressor.

This was too good to pass up. Bubber had enjoyed giving her a hard time growing up, chasing off any guy who showed an iota of interest in her. He wasn't mean, but he never missed a chance to embarrass her. Now it was her turn, and she was going to make the most of it. She gave him a sweet smile.

"Oh, sorry. Guess I misunderstood." She sighed dramatically. "But when I think of poor Maisie sitting at home alone every night, it makes me sad. I bet she'd like you to call."

As Bubber's face flared even more, she turned to Oscar. "Hey, why don't you guys come for dinner tonight?"

Her uncle cocked his head. "Brody okay with it?"

"He told me to consider it my house, so I am. Six o'clock? Come hungry."

Bubber perked up, and Oscar nodded, saying, "We'll be there."

—

Renni dropped Buster off in Brody's backyard and checked her watch. She'd screwed around too long teasing Bubber and was running late. She needed to pick up some stretchy, comfortable clothes to wear. The only place close by that might have what she needed was the little retail shop at Bosco's Gym, so she headed there.

There was a parking space right in front of the gym, wonder of wonders, and she pulled in. It only took a few minutes to buy the clothes she needed and change in the dressing room. As she was climbing back into her car, she detected movement in her peripheral vision. She looked closer and saw Fruit Stand Man leaning against the building, staring at something in his hand. A camera, the same one he'd sported at the park.

He looked up, and their eyes met. Fruit Stand Man raised the camera toward her and snapped a picture, then ducked behind an immense black pickup that screamed "male overcompensation" and disappeared.

Renni sat in the car a moment, staring after him, debating if it was a coincidence. *It's a small town. I'm gonna see people now and then. And maybe he spends all his free time taking pictures. Get over it.* A glance at her watch reminded her she was out of time, and she put the incident out of her mind.

She wheeled into the strip mall on the dot of 4:00 and hustled into a nondescript storefront with the windows covered in sun-blocking film nearly impossible to see through. A seven-sided star between two curved, leafy branches, plus the address and a cell phone number, were painted on the door. No indication of what kind of business it was.

She pushed inside and found herself in a brightly lit lobby. Every solid wall surface was covered with beautiful murals done in soft tints like a watercolor painting. Beyond the lobby, the big floor space was covered with a thick, round, vinyl mat like she'd seen in school gyms for wrestling matches, except those had always been square. The mat was divided in quadrants with symbols in each section. The center held the same symbol as the front door. A sleek counter flanked a closed wooden door on the opposite wall, and in a sealed glass case above the counter, she noticed an intricately carved wooden mask with a grotesque expression.

"Welcome, Miss Delacroix."

She jumped and turned, not having heard the door open. Boogey walked toward her, his gait as smooth as a panther's, and held out his hand. She shook with him, her hand engulfed by his long fingers.

He jerked his chin toward the glass case she'd been staring at. "I see you've noticed my mask."

"It's very unusual," she said, not sure how to compliment something that was more scary than attractive.

"It's called a Booger Mask. It has been in my family for generations."

Renni remembered Brody telling her that Boogey's nickname had something to do with Cherokee ceremonies. "What does it, um, mean?" It seemed like a strange thing to have at a gym. But then, she had a feeling this wasn't an ordinary gym, and not just because of the mask and the round mat.

"It's worn in a ceremony that helps teach Cherokee children how to behave." He looked thoughtful as if trying to determine how best to help her understand. "The ceremony has been equated by some non-native academics to a European-influenced story parents tell their children about the Boogey Man coming if they don't behave, but that's not an accurate representation. Our ceremony has evolved over time to demonstrate the types of evil or unpleasant behaviors which other cultures brought to the Nation, such as drunkenness and lewd behavior. We—I am a dancer in the ceremony—act out these improper behaviors in a sort of parody. Other teacher participants explain and help the children understand why what we 'Booger Men' are doing is wrong and is not acceptable in our culture."

He smiled. "But the mask's story is not what you are here for." Turning away from the display case, he motioned toward the mat. "Now, shall we get started?"

At her nod, he led her to the center. "I hope I'm able to assist you," he said. His voice was deep, the kind of bass that sometimes belonged to the skinny guy in a barbershop quartet, and which was always a surprise. "Let's talk for a bit and go from there." His limber body collapsed onto the mat, folding smoothly into a mudra pose, but he immediately dropped his hands to his thighs.

It took Renni considerably longer to get down, and she

winced as she folded her right leg, her bruised hip giving a painful pull.

"You still suffer a great deal of pain?" he asked, his expression concerned.

"Not a ton, but I have a whopper of a bruise on my hip." She held up her left arm. "Hairline fracture of my wrist"—she jerked her chin at her harness—"and my right shoulder was dislocated. I have to wear the cast if I'm using my arm much, but the harness will be gone in a matter of days. My physical therapist says I need to keep mobile for my hip. Everything else is bruises."

He nodded. "Brody tells me a man who has killed several women might be targeting you because you've been named as having information which might help the police. No one knows what the man looks like, but either he's from around here or is familiar enough with the area to find your house and blow it up."

Having a stranger say it made everything a little more real, and a shiver went down her spine. "Yeah, I think that pretty well sums it up."

He nodded again. "What I propose first is to show you how to avoid having to defend yourself, as well as teach you things someone of your size can do to defend against someone larger and stronger when necessary, and ways to escape before you are completely incapacitated. These things must be practiced so they're second nature, and to allow your muscle memory to instantly recall the proper reaction should the need occur. To do that will require I play the part of an attacker. I don't believe in giving a false sense of security, so I will not 'go easy' on you. Do you understand what I mean?"

Renni blinked. "Sounds like you're saying you won't be pulling any punches and I better learn what you teach me quick or I might have a few more black and blue spots."

He smiled, showing perfect teeth. "That pretty much sums it up." He pointed at her shoulder. "I'm not going to do anything that will hurt you until you've recovered. Today, I'll show you some stretches to help with the healing, and which will prepare you for more strenuous workouts. Are you ready?" He stood in one fluid motion, and Renni wished he'd teach her how to do that but figured it probably wasn't in the lesson plan.

An hour later, Renni stumbled to her car, exhausted, but with less soreness than she had going in. The stretches Boogey showed her put her into contortions she didn't think her spine or hips could manage, but they did. He'd manipulated her right arm, increasing her range of motion significantly, but not causing even a twinge in the joint. Her calves and thighs felt like jelly, and her abs weren't much better.

"Wonder if I'll be able to get out of bed tomorrow," she grumbled, shaking her head at the fact that she'd agreed to be tortured every week for the next month. Madness, probably brought on by inadequate chocolate intake. But when the killer was caught, she could forget all about the classes and go back to a normal life. *Not that I had one before all this started.*

# Chapter Fifty-Two

Renni pulled into the lower parking area just as Luke was locking up. He gave her a questioning look, clearly not expecting to see her that late in the day. As she gingerly climbed out of the car, something in the field below the shop caught her eye. She stared harder. It was a person. A head stuck up above the grass like a gopher in a field. A flash, like binoculars or glasses.

"Luke," she called. Renni waved him out to her and asked him not to be obvious, but was someone in the field?

He pretended there was something on the windshield of the Spitz. "Yeah, I see him. Who is it?"

"I don't know, but I'm going to find out. Come on." She started toward the field. He had no choice but to catch up.

"Renni, you shouldn't go out there. What if it's *the guy?*"

"What do you want me to do, Luke? Call Brody and say, hey, I think there's a guy in my field?"

"Well, yeah."

"It might be somebody walking their dog. It would be terrible if a bunch of cops showed up and it was just some kid or something."

By then they were within about twenty yards of the person, who suddenly popped up out of the grass. It was a man with long, stringy hair. He stared toward them, then took off in the other direction. Luke, a star running back in college who stayed in shape despite his leg injury, pursued him. Even with his limp, he was fast and made a perfect thigh tackle. Renni arrived as Luke got to his feet, pulling the man up by his arm.

As soon as Renni saw his face up close, she said, "Wait, I know you. You work at the pet store."

"Yes, ma'am. I'm K . . . K . . . Kendrick," he stuttered. "It's nice you remember me." A blush spread from his neck to his forehead.

"What the hell are you doing here, kid?" Luke demanded.

"Watching birds." The boy held up the pair of binoculars looped around his neck, the lenses smeared with dirt and grass.

"Birds? What birds?" Luke said, gazing around at the empty sky.

"Um . . . I was . . . um . . . looking *for* birds." His shoulders drooped. "Okay. I wasn't really looking for birds. I just wanted to ask, you know, if you maybe had time to talk to me about, you know, our thing," Kendrick said, the blush deepening. "But I guess that was probably a bad idea, you know, not to call or anything."

"Your thing?" Luke turned to Renni, his eyebrows raised and an expectant look on his face.

Renni threw up her hands and headed back to the shop, Luke behind her with Kendrick in tow.

"What do we do with him?" Luke asked.

She shrugged. "Send him home, I guess."

"Brody's not gonna like that. I mean, this guy was right outside the shop spying on you."

"Hey, I wasn't spying. Not really . . ."

At the look Luke gave him, Kendrick stepped back and shut up.

"Oh crap," Renni said, a sinking feeling in her stomach. She pulled out her cell phone and called Brody, explaining what happened.

His response was loud enough to make Renni pull the phone from her ear, and his tone said he was furious. With that in mind, and knowing it wouldn't take him long to get there, she decided the better part of valor was to not be there when he arrived. She ran upstairs to retrieve Buster and then hurried out to her car. On her way through the shop, she passed a chastised Kendrick sitting on a low stack of tires while Luke frowned down at him menacingly.

Speeding down the street, Renni glanced in her rearview mirror. Red and blue lights flashed in the distance as she turned the corner toward Brody's house. Her escape promised only a brief reprieve, but at least she could have a little time before Brody laid into her about approaching the kid instead of calling 911.

A short time later, she heard him pull into the driveway and beat a hasty retreat to the patio, a fortifying G&T in hand.

It was clear Brody was still pissed as he stomped out the door and over to her, his back stiff. He assumed the same posture Luke had with Kendrick, hands on hips, staring down at her with a threatening glare. His eyes were hard, the skin at the corners tight.

Before he said anything, she held up her hands in surrender. "I get it. You're mad about today, but there wasn't any danger. Luke was with me. Besides, he's a kid."

"Oh, and you knew he was a kid from, what, a least a hundred yards away?" Brody snapped. "What if he had a gun, Renni? Luke said you saw a flash. Did it occur to you it could have been a rifle scope? Are you willing to risk Luke's life so you can be Miss Independent-And-I-Don't-Need-Anyone?"

"That's not fair!" To her annoyance, tears welled up in her eyes, more from frustration than anything else. "The guy hasn't ever shot anyone, has he?"

"We didn't know he liked to blow things up either, until he did it. Oh, and he tries to run people off the road too. I guess he's versatile."

"Oh." She bit her lip. "Shit. Right." She squeezed her eyes shut, then looked him in the eye and said, "You're right. I shouldn't have done it."

"You have to think about this stuff before you act, Renni."

"I know. I'm sorry. I promise I'll be more careful. It's just so hard to believe a killer could be out there watching me. That it could be someone I know."

"I understand. But until we catch him, you have to assume it could be anyone, even the most non-threatening person possible." He turned and went inside, and she heard the fridge open. He raised his voice and continued, "We're tracing the kid's movements and activities."

"You don't seriously think he could be the killer?"

He came back out with a beer and sat next to her on the chaise. "Renni, there have been killers who aren't even in their teens yet. These kinds of people usually appear normal, that's how they get away with what they do—"

The doorbell chimed. He looked at her, eyebrow raised.

"Oh man, I forgot." She winced and gave him an apologetic smile. "I invited Oscar and Bubber to dinner."

# Chapter Fifty-Three

She followed Brody down the hall. When he opened the door, they found three men standing in the late afternoon sun.

"Ed!" Renni squealed. "When did you get back?" She threw herself into his open arms.

"Just now. Oscar said you were doing dinner and invited me along. That okay?"

Renni slanted a glance at Brody. He gave a tiny shrug and said, "Sure. Glad to have you. Come on in."

She turned to her cousin. "Hey, Bubby, did you call her yet?"

"Call who?" Bubber asked, doing a poor job of feigning confusion.

"Your girlfriend, Maisie, of course."

"She ain't my girlfriend," Bubber snapped. He turned back to the car, then to Oscar. "You all go on in. I think I'll hang out in the car for a while. Maybe take a nap. I've had enough company for a while," he grumbled as he headed back down the walk.

"Wanna take my phone?" Renni called with a giggle.

He harrumphed loudly and refused to acknowledge her. With Buster prancing in circles around their ankles, the two old men followed her in and waited as Brody reset the alarm.

"Hope Bubber doesn't suddenly change his mind. I'd hate to have a bunch of cops raid your house," she said, trying to keep a straight face.

Oscar chuckled. "Serve the dimwit right, though." He peered down the hall toward the kitchen. "Got anything to drink around here?"

"Let's find out."

They trooped along behind Brody. Opening the fridge, he handed Oscar and Ed each a bottle of Oskar Blues Pale Ale, took one for himself, and looked inquiringly at Renni. "You want a refill?"

"I'll get a Diet Coke, thanks."

Drinks in hand, they followed Oscar out to the patio.

"What was all that about Bubber and Maisie?" Brody asked.

Renni shrugged. "I'm a little creeped out about it, not that I know, or want to know, what *it* is, but I owe him for years of giving me a hard time. I have to take advantage of it when I can."

Ed saluted Brody with his beer and scrutinized him up and down. "You the one she calls Dudley Do-Right?" He tipped the bottle up and took a long slug of beer.

Brody choked as his own beer went down wrong. He grimaced. "I guess that would be me. And on that special note, I'll fetch a couple more beers," he said. "Or would you prefer something else? I'll be having something a little stronger," he added under his breath.

Heat rose from Renni's neck to her forehead, and she gave Ed an exasperated stink eye. His attempt to look angelic came off more like a geriatric imp.

"Maybe I'll have a gin and tonic after all." She wanted to add, *Make it a double,* but she wasn't going to give Ed the satisfaction.

Ed jerked his chin at his nearly empty bottle. "I like these Oskar Blues. Not only are they kinda named after old Oscar here, they're pretty damn good."

Brody headed inside, and Renni followed him to the mudroom. "I'm so sorry. I swear Ed has Asperger's or Tourette's, whatever it is when they say crazy things."

She wasn't sure, but she thought Brody might have said "Must be contagious" as he opened the fridge door. He handed her the beers and pointed her back out to the patio. "I'll bring your drink out."

Mortified, she took his none-too-subtle hint and went back outside to join her great-uncle and favorite client. She sat next to Oscar on an ottoman, affectionately nudging him with her shoulder.

"How you think this deal is goin'?" he asked.

Renni didn't bother pretending she didn't understand the question. "It's okay, I guess. But I don't want to be here for months. Me and Buster need our own place."

"Here's the thing. You can't have your own place as long as the nutcase is out there. Eventually, he might get lucky. 'Sides, we're workin' on your house deal."

She squinted at the two codgers, suspicious. "Exactly what are you working on?"

"Now don't get your panties all in a wad. Me 'n Ed called a few friends. They know some other friends. I think we can get your house rebuilt so's you can't hardly tell it's new. That be okay with you?" Oscar said.

"What do you mean? My house was over a hundred years old."

"Yup. But so are a lot of other places, and they're torn down to make way for something else. And some people are like you— they don't think old stuff should be thrown away. They keep ahold of it, like your old cars." He grinned. "We're just gonna do a resto-mod on your house. It'll have all the newfangled stuff to meet code, but otherwise, it'll be like the old one. Hell, you sent me enough pictures when you bought it I don't think there's even one little square inch I ain't seen." He laughed.

Renni knew he was right. She'd been so excited to have her

very own house that she'd taken picture after picture and sent them all to him. She didn't have anyone else to send them to.

Ed jumped into the conversation. "First off, we need to get some plans drawn. I got a friend, he builds old-lookin' houses down in New Orleans. Did a lot of 'em after Katrina. He said he can find me some plans to pretty much match your place, and what needs changin' he can do. Once we get the plans all set, it's just a matter of getting the right finish materials."

Exasperated, she shook her head. "I give up on you guys. The fire's barely out, and you're all ready to start building a house we don't have plans or a permit for, and for which I haven't gotten an insurance settlement yet."

Ed waved a hand. "Details."

"Pretty damn important ones," Renni pointed out. She sat back and squinted at them. "And until I talk to my insurance adjuster and find out how much the settlement will be, please don't spend any money."

"Don't you worry about money," Ed said, but Renni was already shaking her head.

"I'll pay for a house I can afford. When I know how much I have to work with, I'll know how much house I can have." Renni fixed him with a hard stare. "There'll be no more discussion, or as Oscar is so fond of saying, *end of story*." She eyed them both as they exchanged a glance. There was some scheme in the works, but not much she could do about it until they laid their cards on the table. Renni shook her head. "What would I do without you two, Unc?"

"Oh, I 'spec you'd wither up and die, Renni, honey."

They were still laughing when Brody came back out carrying a tray loaded with her drink, one for him, and a bowl of chips, followed by another figure armed with his own beer.

"Why y'all leave me out there in the hot car for so long?" Bubber whined. The sight of thinning hair plastered to his head and large sweat rings around his armpits and belly made Renni regret teasing him earlier.

Oscar, clearly not sympathetic, answered, "'Cause you're a dimwit who wanted to sit in the car, that's why. Besides, it ain't been but a half hour or so."

Bubber plopped into a chair and attacked his beer, slurping down half of it without a pause. When he came up for a breath, he said, "Nice place you got here," and saluted Brody with his bottle. "Must have cost you a pretty penny."

"Bubber!" Renni chastised, looking to Oscar for help. He gave her a *what do you want me to do about it* shrug.

"It belonged to my mother. After she died, I leased it out for a few years, until I decided I wanted to come back here to live."

"So you're from here, are you?" Ed asked.

"Pretty much. Born in California, but we moved to Colorado when I was a kid. My dad died when I was three. My mom remarried, and she and I moved to Rampart when I was eight. I lived here until I left for college. By the time I graduated, Mom was gone."

A shadow passed over Brody's face when he talked about his mother remarrying, and Renni noted he never said what happened to his stepfather.

Oscar drained his beer and abruptly stood. "Well, we gots to be moving along. Come on, you two."

"What about dinner?" Renni asked.

He waved her off. "The dimwit wants to try some Lobster place, Green or Red or something. We'll come for dinner some other time when he don't smell quite so bad."

The three men left, Bubber plucking at his damp shirt and grumbling, "It ain't that bad."

Brody followed to deal with the alarm. When he came back, he leaned against the doorjamb. "Steak or pork?"

# Chapter Fifty-Four

The two of them ate outside at the bar-height patio set and enjoyed the evening as the setting sun lit the horizon in a brilliant blaze of crimson glory. Renni closed her eyes in the dimming light, relishing the sounds of children playing tag, dogs barking, people calling to each other as they wandered the neighborhood. She missed the cacophony of creature noises that surrounded her more rural house, but hearing friends call out to each other made her smile.

She'd been nine when her parents were killed and she was sent to live with strangers. Men she'd never even known existed before then. Oscar and Bubber traveled constantly, hauling her with them from race track to race track, never staying long enough for her to enroll in a real school. Oscar was careful about ensuring she was educated, ordering homeschool books and curriculum, and making sure she kept up with her homework and got good grades. But she'd missed out on childhood friendships. Sleepovers. Discussions about boys and what to do about, or with, them. Hide and seek in the dark.

She'd never attended a school dance. Her first real date

wasn't until college. The few boys who'd thought about taking her out before then quickly changed their minds after meeting Oscar and Bubber, who thought it was a real hoot to sit in lawn chairs cleaning a variety of guns or sharpening knives when boys came by. Only now could Renni admit they'd probably done her a kindness, considering how her first, and only, college romance turned out once she told her potential beau about her "gift."

It was nice sitting with Brody. Having someone besides Buster to talk to. But she still missed her place. The squeaks and groans of the old wood settling. The noisy bugs and other creatures who lived outside the urban areas.

"How are you—" Brody started to ask.

Suddenly Buster, who had been lying calmly on the chaise lounge next to them, jumped up and ran down the steps to the lawn, making a beeline for the fence. Once there, he growled and lunged at the boards, something Renni had never seen or heard him do.

Frowning, she opened her mouth to call him back.

"Let him bark," Brody said. "If he thinks something's there, maybe it is. He's not hurting anything. Probably a stray cat, but we've seen coyotes here before. Maybe he's saving Mrs. Bevan's cat from being dinner."

Renni settled back, forehead creased with a thoughtful furrow. After several minutes, Buster turned and trotted back to the chaise, plopping down as if nothing had happened. Brody exchanged raised-eyebrow stares with her.

She shrugged and asked, "What were you saying before Buster so rudely interrupted?"

"How'd it go with Boogey? You're moving pretty easy, considering."

"Now that's one interesting guy. You told me you met in the military. What's his background?"

Brody shook his head. "You don't need to know."

"Oh, yeah. I forget I'm not supposed to ask questions just because someone's trying to kill me. Sorry," she said, laying on the sarcasm.

"Damn it, Renni, it's not because I don't want to tell you. He was SpecOps in Afghanistan, for Christ's sake." He took a deep breath. "His past isn't something he talks about. Or that you'd want to hear. You have to deal with enough nightmares as it is."

"Oh," she said, telling herself she needed to mellow out a bit.

"Hey, listen." Brody rubbed his chin. "I was wondering if you thought . . . if . . . Jeez, this is weird." He took a deep breath. "If we bring the van, the one from Silverton, here. And you touch it . . ."

Surprised, she stared at him for a moment. "Maybe. But the problem is, I don't feel something with every car." *Thank goodness for that.* She tried to imagine what it would be like to get a read on every vehicle she ever touched. She chewed on the inside of her lip. "It might work. What I get, it's pretty random. I don't know if or when it will happen. And if he didn't . . . you know . . . do something in the van, then I might not get anything useful anyway."

"I'll get it brought up as soon as possible. Just in case. We can hope, right?"

"Sure. Yeah." Renni sighed.

"Tired?" he asked.

"I'm okay. Stiff and sore still, but it's getting better. I'll take a hot bath, and that'll help."

"I've got just the thing for you." He walked to a large upholstered rectangular box off to the side of the patio. Unclipping two fasteners, he flipped the padded top up and revealed a hot tub. "Soak away, anytime you want."

Renni shook her head, despite a longing to sink into the hot water and soothing jets. "I don't have a swimsuit. I'll pick one up tomorrow."

Brody waved around the backyard. "Neighbors can't see anything. I'll stay inside. Wear a T-shirt over your underwear or something. If you're hurting, do it."

The thought of skinny dipping in the hot tub with Brody

popped into her mind. She tried to shove it into a dark space, but it seemed to linger, ready to crop up again if she let it. "I guess I could."

"You got it. I have paperwork to do, so I'll be working in the dining room. Towels are inside the door here." He motioned to some shelves in the mudroom that held piles of fluffy towels and headed inside.

Renni went upstairs and stripped to her panties, digging out an oversized black T-shirt with the giant red lips of a Rolling Stones album. She'd found it in a bargain bin for a buck after they left the hospital. It would cover her up and not become transparent when wet. She missed her personal T-shirt collection, accumulated over the last several years of Christmases and birthdays. It became a tradition between her, Oscar, and Bubber to find the most obnoxious or individual-appropriate T-shirts they could. She wouldn't be surprised if the two of them were already on the hunt to replace the ones that went up in smoke.

A few minutes later, she sank into the steaming cauldron, finding a comfortable underwater lounge with a soft cushion at her neck. It was late enough the children had gone inside and the mosquitoes had gone wherever it is they go when it gets too cool for them.

She was drifting, half-asleep, when a sound drew her attention. She sat up with a splash and peered around. The night was ebon gloom. Brody had turned off the yard light, leaving only the rope lights tucked under the hot tub skirting for illumination.

Was the rustling she heard cottonwood leaves in a faint breeze? A small animal rummaging in the shrubbery? Her eyes adjusted quickly and she peered out into the night, but there was nothing out of place. No shadow that didn't belong. Buster slumbered blissfully on the deck. Her heartbeat returned to normal.

The wrinkles on her fingers told her she'd been soaking a

long time. Renni stood, black shirt sticking to her like flypaper, and stepped over the side onto a narrow set of steps. Her towel lay over the back of one of the chairs, and she leaned for it, wrapping it around her torso and using the dangling ends to dry her legs and feet. She flipped the hot tub's top down and fastened the buckles, then trudged through the pitch-black first floor up to her bedroom.

—

From the dark dining room, Brody watched her pad up the stairs, listening for the final squeak before he walked on bare feet to the back door. He checked the tub cover to ensure it was secure, but a vision of Renni standing up, rivulets of water streaming down her pale form, the black fabric creating a silhouette of her perfect body, was all he could see. The cool air puckered her nipples inside the thin cotton. Her narrow waist and flat belly contrasted with full breasts and a taut behind. The fabric stopped short of her hips, revealing trim and muscular thighs and calves as she stepped over the side.

He'd come back to check on her when she stayed out in the hot tub longer than expected—at least that's what he told himself—and she'd heard the faint sound of his hip brushing the counter. The fact that she was aware of her surroundings boded well for her safety, but he would have liked to watch a bit longer, instead of slinking back through the house to the dining room so she wouldn't see him spying on her. She'd been a seductive water sprite, head tipped back, eyes closed, arms waving back and forth in a slow, hypnotic movement, her expression more relaxed than he'd ever seen.

He hoped she got a swimsuit soon because he hated playing voyeur. Of course, if she wasn't comfortable sharing the tub with him, he'd have to be content with that role. Or man up and stay away from her like a good cop should.

He went back inside, aware he'd stepped over a line that couldn't be un-stepped. As he went up the stairs, he reminded himself to set his alarm clock for an hour earlier than usual. He wanted to check whatever Buster had barked at before he headed to the station.

# Chapter Fifty-Five

Brody was already awake and in the process of dressing when his alarm went off. He crept downstairs, staying to the outside of the treads to keep them from squeaking, and stuffed his phone in his hip pocket as he slipped out the door.

He paced along the back side of his fence, which put him in Old Lady Prichard's yard. She was a semi-invalid who rarely ventured outside, and never without her walker. Using the light over his patio as a guide, he honed in on the place that had attracted Buster's interest. Sure enough, there were several footprints in the flower bed edging the fence. One, in particular, was clear, the tread showing in the moist dirt, too large to be from his elderly neighbor.

He pulled out his phone and snapped several photos, then called CSI Rivera at home and asked her to get the van and meet him ASAP. She grumbled, but it was clear she was as excited as he was to have a potential RMHK clue. She was on-site in less than twenty minutes, Pete sitting beside her. They cast the shoe print and two others with decent detail. He left them canvassing the area, went to Mrs. Prichard's door, and rang the bell. It was early, before seven, but she was an early riser and lights shone in several windows.

He waited for her to come to the door as the clump, clump, clump of her walker's legs hitting the hardwood floor came nearer. The door opened an inch, and a beady, bright blue eye stared out at him.

"Yes? Oh, it's you, Matthew." She unhooked the safety chain and opened the door, speaking to him through the screen door. "What are you doing ringing my bell this early in the morning? Don't you know us old ladies need our beauty sleep?" She cackled gleefully.

He smiled at her mischievous attitude. "Sorry, Mrs. Prichard. I wanted to tell you there might be a Peeping Tom in the area. It would be a good idea if you made sure your windows and doors are all locked and don't open the door to anyone you don't recognize."

"Oh, my. A Peeping Tom, you say? Here? Well, land sakes, you'd think he could find something more interesting to peep at than an old lady, but I guess it takes all kinds."

Brody laughed out loud. He'd known the woman most of his life. She'd been great fun when he was younger and obviously hadn't changed much with age—mentally, at least. "You'll be careful? And call 911 if you see anything suspicious, right?"

"Suspicious. Hmmm. Would that include a pretty young thing soaking in your hot tub all by her lonesome?"

Heat flowed up his face. He'd forgotten Mrs. Prichard's upstairs bedroom overlooked his yard. She'd had a power lift chair installed on her staircase several years ago, right before he moved away, so she still used the upper level.

"No, ma'am. That would not be suspicious, just plain dumb luck."

That set off another bout of cackling. "I'll be sure to keep a lookout, except maybe towards the hot tub. Thanks for the warning, my dear. Tell that pretty young thing hello for me." She shut the door and the latch clicked, followed by clumping as she went further into the house.

He started home, musing that the night visitor couldn't have been Kendrick unless he was released from lockup, which was unlikely in that short a period of time. Kevin was still in the wind, but from what they'd dug up on him after the meeting, he didn't seem to fit the profile. Profiles weren't perfect, though.

As he came around the driveway, he saw something he'd missed in the early morning light. The right rear tire of his SUV was flat. He went over and bent down, checking for a slash mark. The tire was pristine. Could be coincidence. But, like most cops, Brody didn't believe in them.

# Chapter Fifty-Six

Renni opened her eyes to a room filled with muted sunlight and realized she'd slept later than usual. She let Buster out to the landing, assuming Brody would let him into the backyard and took a quick shower.

Clad in jeans, tank top, and work boots, she hurried downstairs. As she hit the floor at the bottom, it occurred to her she was, in fact, able to hurry. Her stiffness was markedly reduced from the day before. Hot tubbing, or Boogey, appeared to agree with her.

She found Brody in the kitchen, but instead of a full breakfast, he handed her a pair of Pop-Tarts and a fruit smoothie in a travel mug.

"I need to get going," he explained. "I have some stuff to take care of at the office. I'm going to ride the Harley today, and I'd like to follow you to the shop, so can we head out now?"

"Why do you want to follow me? Has something happened?"

"No. I just . . . Since you're ready and I'm ready . . . No big deal."

"Yeah, sure. Fine. I should probably get in early anyway. Ed and Oscar are bringing by some house plans for me to review, and that'll suck hours out of my day." She turned away and bit her lip, wondered if he was keeping something from her again. *How many* things he was keeping from her. She called Buster and hurried out the door before he said anything else.

—

The lobby door banged open, setting off the chime. She recognized several voices, all of them talking at full volume.

"Hey," Renni shouted, stepping out of her office. Ed, Oscar, and Bubber stumbled to a halt and eyed her like a bunch of third-graders in the principal's office. "I'm trying to run a business here. Maisie needs to be able to hear the phone ring and what not." She waved them toward the breakroom. Bubber veered off toward Maisie's desk and Renni shook her head, figuring he'd manage to waste the rest of his, and Maisie's, morning once he got started gabbing.

She, Oscar, and Ed settled into the breakroom together, where Oscar rolled out the set of plans he had tucked under his arm. Over the next couple of hours, and two carafes of coffee, the three of them reviewed the house plans. Renni voiced her opinion and asked questions, and notes were made. Eventually, she checked her watch and realized she needed to get moving if she wanted anything to eat before her 1:00 p.m. appointment with Boogey. Oscar and Ed grabbed beers from her fridge and left, telling her they needed to meet with "some people" about "some things."

She shook her head over what those "people and things" might be as she changed into her workout clothes. A quick trip through Speedy's drive-in for a whole wheat chicken and avocado wrap and Diet Coke, which she consumed in the Spitz under the shade of a tall catalpa tree in Boogey's parking lot, and she was ready for another session.

Boogey waited inside the door, a gentle, Zen-like expression on his face. She knew it was deceiving.

She was not disappointed.

They spent the first half of the two-hour session on stretches and tai-chi-type moves. Then Boogey asked her to empty her purse on the mat. Curious, she complied.

"I want you to pick out anything you can use as a weapon and put it over here." He motioned to a spot by her knee.

She checked the contents. Her wallet with credit cards and a little cash. A tube of lip gloss. Keys. A small flashlight. Pack of gum. Packet of Kleenex. Purse-size aerosol perfume. A pen and spiral notebook. A large paperclip holding notes she'd meant to put into the computer at least a week ago.

Renni put her keys aside and shrugged.

He reached over and added the flashlight, lip gloss, pen, notebook, and perfume to the pile. "Now, tell me what you could do with these things."

For the next half hour, they discussed ways she could use the items to fight an attacker. He showed her how to wrap her hand around the flashlight or lip gloss to make a solid fist with much more stopping power than a normal woman's hand. The perfume became a blinding spray. The pen, an object to be stabbed into eyes, ears, or throat. The paperclip and the metal spiral off the notebook could be straightened and used to poke out an eye, puncture an eardrum, or scrape deep into the skin. The keys, the only thing in the pile she'd always heard made a good weapon, ended up being only a small part of her arsenal. Boogey suggested she get more pens, ones with sturdy shafts, invest in pepper spray, and practice triggering the car alarm on her key fob.

The last thirty minutes entailed Boogey asking her what she'd do in specific scenarios and putting her through the actions and reactions. What if someone jumped out of the alley next to her? What if she was at a stoplight and someone approached her in the convertible? If she was at the gas station and someone reached into her car and grabbed her purse? Each time she answered, he'd ask her why she chose that option and they'd discuss other choices.

"Your homework is to make a conscious effort over the next few days to notice how many different times you expose yourself to a potential attack which could be averted if you took steps to be more aware of your surroundings," Boogey said as he walked her to the door.

She climbed into her car, thinking how interesting it was that most of her initial responses to Boogey's scenarios were based on assuming the best of people. He presented solutions that allowed her to react to the situations without thinking everyone was out to get her, showing her how critical self-awareness was. When she thought of all the times she'd gotten into her car, got her sunglasses out, put her purse away, and started the car, all before shutting her door, it made her realize how much easier she made it for someone who might want to harm her.

Just as after the earlier session at Boogey's, instead of being sore, her muscles were loose. Tired, but loose. "It's only the calm before the storm," she told herself, knowing when he deemed her healed, the real education would start. Which, feeling as good as she did, would likely be soon.

She went over the things he'd told her as she drove to the shop, noticing women standing beside their cars or wandering across parking lots with phones to their ears, oblivious to what happened around them. No wonder creeps like the RMHK thrived. Victims, especially women, seemed to be handing themselves over on a platter.

Back at the shop, she checked on Luke and found him installing the Caddy's chrome work. "Need some help?"

"No, I've got it. There are only a few more pieces left."

Miffed, and feeling more than slightly put out at being so easily dismissed, she went over to where Oscar and Bubber huddled over the old BMW R71 WWII-era motorcycle frame.

"What are you two up to?" she asked.

"Bubber wants a sidecar," Oscar said, standing with arms crossed, a barely suppressed smile on his face. Bubber stared at his feet.

"Oh, he does, does he? And does he realize the owner of said motorcycle might not want a sidecar?"

"You own it, Renni. You can do whatever you want. Don't you think it would be better with a sidecar? It'd be real cool," Bubber pleaded.

The BMW, bought from a guy at a swap meet, was a good deal, but there hadn't been time to do anything with it since client jobs were her priority. "Maybe, but I don't want to spend my cash right now. Maybe after we finish Ed's Caddy."

"I'll pay for it, Renni. We'll do all the work ourselves. Me 'n Pop. You won't have to do anything," Bubber said, stepping over to Oscar and prodding him in the ribs with his elbow. The old man nodded.

Renni eyed the two grinning white-haired men. It would keep them out of trouble. Bubber especially tended to get into mischief if he didn't have something to keep him occupied. They were going to be at the shop all day as it was. If they didn't have anything else to do, they'd drink her beer, watch the breakroom TV all day, and in Bubber's case, distract Maisie.

"Okay. You can see if there are any sidecars out there to fit, but don't buy anything unless you ask me first. I plan to make money on it, not go into the hole so you two can fool around."

Leaving the two jabbering like teenage girls, she hooked the Caddy's engine up to the Dyno to check the horsepower and tune before they installed it. She loved the sound. The grumbling roar of a perfectly tuned engine. Other girls liked shopping, or getting a pedicure, or dressing up for a party. But to Renni, that was a waste of time. Why pay for pretty nails when she'd just ruin them the next time she worked in the shop? And as for shopping, when and where would she get a chance to show off anything fancy, since she never went anywhere but work? No, taking an old wreck of a car, building new parts, repairing old ones, putting it back together better than it ever was—that was what floated her boat. If she put together a playlist of her favorite music, it would include the classic rock Bubber blasted from a boombox during their circle track years and recordings of all the different engines she'd built. She'd be able to identify every single one, of both kinds, within seconds.

By the time she was finally satisfied with the engine's performance, Maisie had gone home and Oscar was putting away tools.

"Where's Bubber?" she asked.

Her uncle rolled his eyes dramatically. "He was moonin' after that crazy redhead upstairs instead of paying attention to what he was supposed to be doin'. I told him to get on out of here before he broke something. You can give me a ride home."

Luke came over, wiping his hands on a shop rag. "I'm done with the chrome. The wheels and tires are ready to go on anytime."

She nodded. "That's great. The engine is ready too. We can start on that tomorrow. We need to find out if we're going to get the trailer back from the cops by early next week or if we'll have to rent one again."

"I'll text Brody," Luke said. "They ought to be finished with it since all we did was bring the truck here on it."

"Since when do logic and bureaucracy have anything in common?"

He laughed. "You're right. Anyway, the car will be ready."

"Once it's done, we'll have a breather." She sighed. "Probably a long breather, if we don't get anything else in." She observed the Twins. The Packard Coupes belonged to a couple who seemed excited about having them restored to match, but they hadn't replied to her emails and phone messages for almost a month. "I still haven't gotten deposits on the Twins and the Caddy is pretty much done, so we're in a holding pattern. Damn, Luke, what are we going to do?"

# Chapter Fifty-Seven

Karen sat in the kitchen eating cinnamon raisin toast and drinking a cup of Earl Grey. Her brother hadn't come in from the barn. She knew he was out there. Just like she knew he'd been gone for a day and a half without explanation.

She washed her plate and cup. When her brother came in, she could tell he was upset by the set of his jaw. "You want me to fix you some breakfast?"

"No. I don't want any damn breakfast."

At her stricken expression, he came over and gave her a hug, making sure he was on her good side like he always did. He couldn't bear to touch the other side. The bad side.

"Sorry, K-1. I didn't mean to yell at you. And it's your birthday, too."

She'd forgotten it was their birthday. The family never celebrated birthdays, or any other holidays, for that matter. Daddy said it was a waste of money. But her brother kept track of dates really well. Like when there was going to be a full moon or no moon. The first day of winter. He made notes all over the kitchen calendar. His annual vacation was outlined in bold red.

He took her arm and led her into the living room, encouraging her to sit in her chair. "I got you something." He reached behind the sofa and handed her a brightly wrapped box.

She smiled up at him, glad his bad mood was gone. "Gee, thanks. But I didn't get you anything. I'm sorry. It's just been so long since we did anything for our birthday."

"Well, it's time we started celebrating again. And don't worry about me, I picked out my own present this year."

"What'd you get?" she asked.

He gave her a smug smile. "It's a secret. Now go on. Open it."

She shook the box gently. "I wonder what it is?"

"Open it and find out, silly," he said, kneeling beside her chair, his arm around her shoulder.

Karen carefully unwrapped it, slipping her fingers under the tape to keep from tearing the paper. When the wrapping finally came loose, she folded it into a neat packet, enjoying the excitement and wanting to stretch it out. The box, labeled as a Camp-A-Lot heater, was resealed with new packing tape. She picked one end of the tape free and pulled it up, taking the top layer of the cardboard box with it, and lifted the flaps.

When she peered inside, she hesitated, chewing her lip.

"Well?" he asked, impatience in his voice.

"Oh, wow. These are great," she gushed, trying to sound enthusiastic.

"You don't like them, do you?" he snapped. "They're your size. I made sure of it. They're the color you said you wanted." His voice got louder. "I searched all over the Internet to find them. I wasted a lot of time on it."

Karen eyed him, her smile shaky. "But that was a long time ago, back when we were in school. I'm too old to skate. I'd fall and hurt myself."

He grabbed the box out of her hands and hurtled it across the room. It burst open on impact, and the bright turquoise rollerblades with light-up wheels clattered onto the floor. He began to pace. "I've done everything for you. Taken care of you. Given you everything you wanted. Pop didn't do that. He didn't care about you or anyone else but himself, but you were always happy with any little thing he gave you." Each time her brother said "he," his voice rose in volume. "You're the same as the rest. You take and take and then throw me away."

"That's not true! You know it isn't. Mom and me, we did everything we could to make Daddy realize what a great kid you were."

"Oh, you tried real hard, all right, until he got the least bit mad at you. You were the one he loved. Ma too. I was just . . . there. The only person who ever treated me good was Old Man Davis."

"The man in Utah?" she asked. "But he was going to throw you away, remember? He was going to Florida. Then he died."

"Yeah. But at least he treated me like I was his son right up until then. Taught me how to work on stuff. How to drive a car and tractors. Told everyone I was 'his boy Bill' and helped me get a driver's license. Said he always wanted a son, but not a wife." He kicked one of the skates and sent it skittering onto the kitchen linoleum. "But you're right, I wasn't family, not really. He turned on me, like you warned me he would. After all the work I did, all the money I made for him. Sold the business right out from under me. Cut me out. He should have given it to me. But no, he was greedy. He wanted to take the money and move to Florida. Thought I'd be happy to get a few bucks and an old truck. After all that work."

He stood, staring at the photograph of himself in his football jersey. "I did right by him, though. When he got sick, I made sure he didn't suffer. I just took what he owed me."

"That's where those coffee cans of money came from?" Karen asked in a whisper.

"Yeah. He didn't think I knew about them, but I watched him. It was tough to keep away those nosey people who came looking for him while I fixed me up a truck from all those junkers sitting in the field, but I was careful. It took a while, but when I was ready, I just up and drove away with those coffee cans sitting on the floorboards."

"What happened to Mr. Davis?" Karen asked. "You never said."

"Davis? He got sick, and then he died. He didn't suffer. I made sure. And I put clean clothes on him and laid him out proper on his bed." He whirled around and kicked the other skate, but it rebounded and hit him in the shin. He swore, kicking the skate hard enough to send it skittering into the kitchen, and snapped, "Why do you care about him, anyway? You're supposed to care about me. About your brother. Your twin."

She jumped up, her palms out toward him. "I do care. You know I do. Without each other we're not whole, remember? Remember when you told me that?"

Karen reached out and stroked his arm as he started to pace, clenching and unclenching his fists. He stopped pacing and stared at her. She made sure only her good side was visible.

"Yeah. It's true." Lips turned up slightly, he nodded. He was beginning to calm down.

"How about we celebrate our birthday with ice cream for breakfast? With chocolate sauce and cherry preserves. We can watch movies all day if we want. I bet there's something good on," she said.

He smiled at her. A genuine smile that almost made her forget how he'd acted only minutes ago.

But not quite. As she padded into the kitchen, she thought how much he was acting like Daddy with *his* temper tantrums. He was starting to put on a lot of weight too, which even made him look like Daddy. She suspected he did a lot of drinking out in the barn. He didn't seem to see the similarities, though. Somehow, he thought he still looked just like he did in the picture on the wall. The perfect brother with his imperfect sister. Someday, when the time was right, he was going to find out the truth.

# Chapter Fifty-Eight

Brody called the service department to send a tow to retrieve his car, instructing them to check the tire carefully for signs of tampering. Then he followed Renni to the shop on his Harley, before heading to the station.

Liv called to him from an open window on the second floor. "Brody, get your ass up here!"

The lab was already humming when he entered, and Liv waved him over. She pulled images up on an overhead screen. There were several shoe prints. One by one she overlaid them, confirming they were exact matches right down to a hole where part of the tread was missing.

"So, what am I seeing?" The shoe prints were from the fence, but there was more to it, or Liv wouldn't be so excited.

She used a laser pointer. "This full and these two partials are from your place. These . . ." She circled four others. " . . . are from two of the burial sites."

Brody sat heavily on the corner of the desk, a little weak in the knees. *Smoking gun at last!* "You're sure they're a match?"

"Hell yes, I'm sure. But I sent everything to the Fibbies to double-check. The chances of the exact same imperfections and dings on different pairs of shoes, let alone the same shoe size and comparative weight of the perp . . . In my mind, there's no way it's not the same person. No effin' way."

Before he realized what he was doing, he gave her a hug and a peck on the cheek. "Um, sorry. I . . . It's just . . ."

She giggled. "Don't worry. HR won't hear about it. You should have been here about fifteen minutes ago. I was dancing around the office singing 'We Are the Champions.'" She put her hand on his shoulder. "We all feel the same way, Bro. We have to catch the guy, and we all want a hand in doing it."

"Thanks, Liv." He hurried down to the task force office.

As usual, it was empty, but his email was full. Several more coroners had responded, two of them confirming bites and bodies available for exhumation, the others making promises to check. The FBI had obtained warrants on the first two bodies and expected to have them in their lab later that day.

AIC Tanner strutted in about an hour later, a tall Starbucks cup in his hand. "Hey, Brody, anything new?"

Biting back a comment that showing up in the office occasionally made it easier to keep up on things, Brody gave a quick recap of the footprint information.

Tanner pursed his lips and nodded. "That's pretty significant. Confirms the perp either lives here or knows his way around. Good work." He took a sip of his Starbucks and then sat down, leaning back and putting his feet on the desk, crossing his legs at the ankle. "My people found something that apparently slipped past everyone." He paused for effect.

"Oh?" Brody wasn't going to let the man bait him.

"Yeah." He sipped again. Paused. Sipped.

Brody counted to ten and forced his fists to unclench.

"Each of the bodies was missing a shoe. It's one of those little things that gets missed a lot by investigators with, um, limited experience because it's not that unusual during an abduction for someone to lose a shoe. But every woman was missing one and during cold weather. Some of them were even wearing boots. We're looking into it. I'll keep you posted." He stood and sauntered out.

Brody released an explosive breath. "Keep me posted, my ass. The only reason you told me was to one-up our find, you jerk," he said, after first checking to make sure the AIC was gone. *Damn Tanner showed up just to rub my face in it because they found something new. And now he knows about the shoe prints. He's probably on the phone right now taking credit for it with the task force. Too bad he didn't stick around long enough for me to tell him about Kevin. Maybe there's still a chance us hicks will crack this case.* He smiled grimly. *Besides, I've got the ace in the hole, and I won't let them get their hands on her.*

Then he realized he'd made Renni a pawn in a game of one-upmanship and shook his head. He needed to get his ego and his testosterone under control. The only thing that mattered was catching the bastard, and it *didn't* matter who did it. He turned back to the computer.

# Chapter Fifty-Nine

Brody kicked the Harley to life and headed home in the twilight, wondering how much trouble Renni had gotten into today. She wasn't much for sticking to the rules. Now she had her wheels back, who knew what she'd be up to?

He was pleasantly surprised to find the little red sports car parked off to the side of the driveway. He pushed a button on his key fob to open the garage.

With some shifting, he rearranged the space so the Jeep and bike fit on one side, leaving the other side for Renni's car. Brody didn't like the idea of the Spitz sitting out all night where someone, specifically a certain someone, could get to it. He went into the house, moving to the mudroom and gazing out the screen door. Sure enough, Renni and Buster were in the backyard playing chase in the grass.

"Renni," he hollered, "if you'll let me have your key, I'll move the Spitfire into the garage."

She stepped up on the patio and eyed him up and down. "Not sure you'd fit." She dug keys out of the pocket of her tight, cut-off jean shorts and came inside. "Show me where you want it."

*Damn, she's stubborn.* He followed her down the hall, but he found himself admiring the wriggle of her hips in those tight shorts and forgave her. Brody watched her tuck the little car away for the night and then tossed her the spare opener from the Jeep.

"Thanks," she said. "I'll put it in my backpack."

He followed her inside, enjoying the view again, and stopped off to grab beers on the way to the patio. He paused, eying the fridge shelves. A six-pack of Diet Coke, a hefty bag of dark chocolate Kisses, yogurt, cheese, a package of preservative-free beef brisket hot dogs, and several other items that weren't there before occupied the shelves. In the freezer, he found potstickers, frozen berries, ice cream, and other things he didn't recognize stuffed between his packages of frozen steak and pseudo-healthy TV dinners.

From outside, Renni said, "I picked up a few things on my way home. Hope you don't mind."

What could he say? Besides, he'd been hankering for ice cream. "No problem." He took the beers and went out to watch Buster chase the tennis ball Renni threw.

"Does he ever get tired of fetching?" Brody asked after more than thirty minutes.

"Yeah. When he does, he'll sit on the ball so I can't get it. He thinks he's doing it for me and not the other way around."

Sure enough, a few minutes later he dropped the ball in the grass and sat on it like he was trying to hatch it. Renni gave Brody an *I told you so* look as she sipped the last of her beer. A bowl of mixed veggies sat next to her elbow. He reached over and grabbed a sugar snap pea, unsure of how she'd react to his encroachment. He was surprised when she moved the bowl closer to him.

"Anything out of the ordinary happen at work today?" he asked, taking a sip of beer and munching on a carrot.

She told him about meeting to review house plans. "I can't

wait to get back into my own house, Brody. My new and improved old house. I'll have a real laundry room, lights that work, and no furnace that has to have coal shoveled all the time and then leaves a pile of coal clinkers I have to spread in the driveway to get rid of. Oscar says he already filed the permits, and now that I have the insurance check, we can start right away." She smiled as they headed into the house to start dinner.

Brody stood at the refrigerator, the door open, staring inside. He thought of what his house would be like when she wasn't there anymore.

"Is there something going on with the case, Brody? You seem distracted."

He grabbed another beer and slammed the door hard enough to rattle jars inside. "Just thinking about all the paperwork I need to do after dinner." He snatched up the platter of marinating chicken and took it outside to the patio, slapping the meat on the grill. He took out his frustration on the chicken breasts, viciously prodding them around the grill while using his beer to put out occasional flare-ups.

Renni came out with a salad, dressing, plates, and silverware on a tray. She continued to chatter on about her house throughout dinner, not noticing his lack of response. An occasional grunt or nod now and again satisfied her. As soon as they finished, he grabbed the dirty dishes and stuck them haphazardly in the dishwasher before heading into the dining room to boot up his computer. She stayed outside playing with Buster, probably to avoid his bad mood.

A while later, the screen door slammed and she came in, the spaniel at her heels.

"Guess I'll call it a night unless you're planning on hot tubbing," she said, her tone hesitant.

"Not tonight. I have a lot of work to do." He didn't turn around.

Her light steps and the click of Buster's nails went up the wooden stairs, and he waited for the tell-tale squeak of the last tread before slumping back in his chair, pinching the bridge of his nose. He was being rude, but he couldn't take any more about how happy Renni was going to be when she left. When she had her own place again. Was on her own again.

He'd spent the years since high school bouncing from three tours as a Marine MP in the Middle East to training at the police academy by day and working on his Criminology degree by night, which didn't leave him much time for any kind of relationship. Then he'd started at the Rampart Police Department. Since then, it seemed like every time he scheduled a date, he canceled due to a call out. Until Renni came to stay with him, he hadn't realized how nice it was to come home to someone. To have a quiet conversation over a drink or dinner. To have someone to enjoy the sounds of night birds and stare at the stars with. The fact that she was the perfect package—brains, body, and beauty—was a plus, along with being funny and interesting and . . . He shook his head.

He didn't want to give all that up. Didn't want to admit maybe all he was to her was a bodyguard and the only reason she was in his house was because it was a safe place. With a deep sigh, he logged out of the file he'd been working on. But before he could shut the computer down, it dinged. He wouldn't be getting any sleep for a while anyway, so he opened the email and read it. Moments later, he was sending a message to AIC Tanner, flagged urgent.

# Chapter Sixty

He was furious with himself. He'd been working for days to devise a perfect plan, but every time he thought he had it, his critical review pointed out a flaw. A fatal flaw.

He paced in the barn, in the room he'd built to exactly match Pop's shop. Before it, and Pop, ceased to exist. He'd figured if Pop deserved a workshop to screw around with all those wasted efforts, then there was no reason *he* shouldn't have something at least as good, damn it! There was plenty of life insurance money to pay for it. The old son of a bitch thought he was so valuable he'd bought a half-million-dollar policy on himself. Just another way he demonstrated what a narcissist he was. It was a good thing the policy was there, though, because after he died it would have been tough for Karen to get by until she found the job doing transcription.

Pop was always saying how much smarter he was than anyone else. He bitched at Ma because she spent a few bucks to get those photos framed, then turned around and spent thousands sending off for patents. He never got one, not once. He always claimed somebody at the patent office was stealing his ideas.

It was the old man's overwhelming need to prove he could win any argument that caused everything. Ruined everything. If Pop hadn't heard a guy talking to a professor about his son being bitten by a brown recluse, Karen would still be perfect, like him.

The professor made a stink about how it was impossible because those spiders didn't live in Colorado. Pop had to prove the university man wrong. Then when the bastard actually found one of the spiders, it made him a whole lot worse. He paraded through the house, holding the jar with the spider in it. Bragging about how he was so much smarter than those hoity-toity people with their fancy degrees. How he was going to be famous. Then he drank himself into a stupor out in the barn.

He shook his head. "I can't believe I still tried to make the old man proud of me. What a joke. Did I honestly think he'd ever say something like 'Son, I'm sure glad you're my boy.' How could I be so stupid?"

When Karen came home from cheerleading practice, he'd taken the jar from its place of honor in the middle of the kitchen table to show her Pop was right all along. He tossed it up and down, making her screech with horror when he held it up in front of her and shook it to make the spider wiggle its legs. But the ceiling in her bedroom was too low. One toss a little too high. The jar hit the ceiling and shattered, dropping the spider onto Karen's face. He could still hear her scream as she slapped at her cheek. Neither of them realized it bit her, not then.

That was when he left. *Pop would have beat me to a pulp when he discovered I lost the spider somewhere in Karen's room. Stupid idiot should never have put it in a glass jar. Shouldn't have left it sitting on the table while he got drunk. If he was so smart, he should have known better.*

He paced the small workshop, pounding his fist into the palm of his other hand over and over. *I'm smarter than the old man. I'll prove it when I get rid of Renni. Then I can keep making my annual trips, right under the cops' noses.*

# Chapter Sixty-One

Brody was up with the sun. He wrote a brief note, reminding Renni to make sure she kept in touch with him when the others weren't with her. He left it by the coffee machine, then texted Luke to come by and follow her to the shop. Minutes later, he raced up the Interstate on-ramp, turning on the rooftop and grille lights as he sped west. At the far end of the valley, he pulled onto a dirt parking area already populated by several law enforcement vehicles, one of them an FBI Cadaver Dog transport.

Last night's email from Liv said she'd found traces of gilsonite in the Marmon, a hydrocarbon refined in a small facility at the west end of the valley several decades earlier. It wasn't a common element anywhere they'd found a victim so far, leading them to believe there could be another body still undiscovered.

The AIC was lining everyone out when Brody stepped up to the group. Tanner gave him a nod of acknowledgment and continued. "We'll have one team on each side of the Interstate. If you find anything unusual—a depression, disturbed soil, anything like that—call out. Pay attention, and don't crowd the dogs and their handlers. Let them work."

Brody participated in the search, staying several yards to the north as the dogs tracked back and forth, noses to the ground. It was well into the afternoon, some of the officers beginning to rumble about calling for pizza delivery when a dog on the far side of the Interstate started yipping and whining. Brody hurried across the four lanes, eliciting a loud blast from the air horn of a passing semi, and climbed over the sagging wire fence. The dog was about fifty yards away, staring intently at an area where large cottonwood branches littered the ground. Brody held back while techs carefully approached, circling the area, placing evidence markers, and taking photos. They spiraled in closer, only moving branches and leaf debris once they marked, measured, and photographed their original locations.

It took nearly two hours before they were able to get close enough to discover a depression in the soil, but only a few minutes more to brush away enough dirt to see a body. A woman's body. And wisps of blonde hair.

# Chapter Sixty-Two

When Renni came out of her room, she saw Brody's open door. A moment later, she was reading his note in the kitchen.

"I'm sick and tired of babysitters," she grumbled. She was being unreasonable, but she'd never been much of a team player. As a kid growing up around the circle tracks, she was the only girl anywhere in the pits. The drivers and crews ignored her, as did the few boys who accompanied their fathers. She'd learned to find things to do by herself unless Oscar or Bubber needed either an engine or a car body put back together—then she was right in the middle of it with them.

In the early years, she'd sat on a beat-up three-legged stool, learning the names of tools and passing whatever was needed to hands sticking out from under the car's chassis or hood. She learned quickly, and it wasn't long before Oscar invited her to join him, letting her stand on the same stool so she could lean under the hood. He made a miniature creeper so she could slide under the cars with him.

As time went by, she learned how to use the tools in the

voluminous red toolboxes to rebuild an engine or transmission in a matter of hours, along with tools to repair and restore car bodies, including an English wheel and dollies, and later the intricacies of fiberglass bodywork. Those years were the beginning of her love affair with car restoration. When she got accepted to the Pennsylvania College of Technology's renowned Classic Car Restoration Program, she was already miles ahead of the other students.

After stopping at Hole in the Wall Bakery for a dozen glazed doughnuts, she pulled in at Seth and Amy's produce stand and got a one-pound container of strawberries, then ran into the market for a quart of cream. She'd treat the crew to breakfast.

Even after all her stops, she arrived before any of the others. She prepared a bowl of sliced strawberries and left it on the breakroom table with the doughnuts. As soon as coffee was brewing, she went into her office and booted up the computer to check the day's schedule. There was an email from Maisie letting her know they'd gotten a deposit for the Twins. Renni did a double fist pump. Money in the bank, and better yet, work on the books. Getting their schedule set up would be her focus for the day. She went to cancel her 2:00 p.m. appointment with Boogey, before thinking better of it. She wanted a whole day in the shop, but she didn't trust Brody not to make good on his threat to take her car away.

As she made sure she'd remembered to stuff her yoga clothes in her bag, Fruit Stand Man flashed into her head. Seeing him at the gym and by the river. The way he stared at her. And he had long hair.

Renni chewed her lip. First Kevin. Then the kid from the pet store. If she called Brody, would he think she was the whack job who cried Wolfman every time she turned around?

Then she remembered how mad he'd been when she didn't call him before going into the field after Kendrick. Wincing, she dialed his number. Straight to voicemail. She left a message explaining about the stranger and how he acted. Even to herself,

Renni sounded like a looney. She fretted that she should have waited to talk to him in person as she put the child-proof gate up on her office to keep Buster contained and hurried down to the shop.

The next hours were heaven as she happily started the Twins' checklists, jotting notes on the job sheets regarding what parts were reusable and what would need fabricated or replaced. She'd sic Maisie on the replacement parts. If her office manager didn't have most of it located within a month through her spiderweb of classic part contacts, Renni would eat a gasket.

Luke would be happy with the amount of woodwork he'd need to do on the frames. He was a master carpenter and loved fabricating replacement frames and trim pieces from the stash of exotic and hard wood in a shed out back. Woodworking wasn't one of her best skills, and until she hired Luke, Renni had purchased restoration kits from Jim Rodman's Autowood Restorations. A friendly man with a flowing Santa Claus beard, Jim was still a speed dial on her phone for when the shop was too busy to do it themselves.

As she always did when working on cars, Renni became absorbed in her task and lost track of time, responding with a vague wave to Luke's hello as he passed through the shop on his way to the Caddy. She was scrunched on the floorboard, looking under the dash of one of the Twins to check out wiring, when her phone vibrated in her hip pocket. She jerked and banged her forehead on the steering wheel.

She turned off the phone alarm and headed up to the office. It was 1:00, her self-imposed deadline to call Mrs. Phipps, the widowed wife of the Layton High School photographer, if she hadn't yet heard from her or her son. Renni dialed the number written in her notes. Mrs. Phipps answered and went to fetch her son.

"Hello, Miss Delacroix, this is Gerald Phipps. Mother explained what you need, and I think I've found it."

"That's great, Mr. Phipps. You found a larger print of Bill

Davis?"

"No, but I found the original negative. I'll be able to enlarge it. It will be ready by the end of the day. If you'll give me your address, I'll get it in the mail today or first thing in the morning."

"Can you scan and email it?"

There was a moment of silence. "I'm afraid I can't. We're a small company, and I work from the house, which is an hour's drive from town. My computer is on the fritz, and the repairman can't get to it until at least the day after tomorrow, but if you'd like me to wait . . ."

"Oh, no, that's fine. If you'd please send it by overnight mail, I'll reimburse you for the cost."

Silence again.

"I can give you my credit card information now, and you can charge the cost of the new print, postage, and your time and mileage."

"I suppose we could do that."

She gave him the address and her card number. He said he'd include a receipt for the charges in the package, adding she should expect it no later than Friday.

—

"Are you ready?" Boogey asked, greeting her with another of his deceptively sweet smiles.

Two hours later, she flopped into the seat of her car, her sweat-soaked T-shirt sticking to her back. It took a few minutes before she could even muster the strength to put her hands on the wheel.

After Boogey checked her injuries, he'd decided she was fit enough for a tad more aggressive lessons. Her neck was raw and her back muscles like Jell-O from the day's agenda of avoiding and escaping chokeholds. She'd been slammed against the padded wall and the padded floor and lifted off the ground, with an obi belt from Boogey's karate gi looped around her neck. He taught her to ignore the black cloud creeping in from her peripheral vision and focus on using her hands, arms, elbows, and cast for leverage to break his holds. She aimed the heel of her palm, fingernails, fists, and thumbs at his eyes and throat. Grabbed his ears and pulled the bridge of his nose down on the top of her head, which now sported several painful goose eggs.

She leaned forward, resting her forehead on the steering wheel, groaning, and inserted the key. "I hope to hell Boogey feels as bad as I do," she said, then was instantly struck by a twinge of guilt. He'd taken several pretty hard hits during their session, some of which drew blood, all for the sake of helping her.

After checking the gauge, she wheeled the Spitz into the Maverick gas station to fill up, treating herself to a King-sized dark chocolate Hershey bar and fountain soda. The chocolate melted in her mouth. She felt like she'd been on bread and water for days without her chocolate fix.

As Renni pulled into her shop's parking lot, she realized she'd forgotten to mention the Layton High School yearbook photo to Brody. She rolled her eyes. Okay, maybe not precisely "forgot." *So I'm waiting until I see what I've got before I show him. Nothing wrong with not wanting to get him all excited when it might not be anything.* But she admitted to herself she didn't entirely trust he wasn't still using her. She'd proven more than once what a poor judge of character she was. Not only could she not figure out who might be hunting her, but there'd been a few times she'd thought Brody was interested in her as . . . well, something besides a suspect.

Luke came over, and together they reviewed the list of remaining items to be completed on the Caddy. The new interior was installed, the buckskin-colored leather a perfect foil for the glossy crimson paint. Luke's polished woodwork set it all off to perfection. The chrome trim shone like polished sterling.

"Let's take it out this afternoon for a quick road test," she said. Luke nodded and turned to a double-decker red tool chest. With a self-satisfied smile at the nearly complete Caddy, Renni wiped her hands on a shop cloth and clomped up the stairs.

# Chapter Sixty-Three

Brody really wanted a shower after spending the morning in the hot sun, dust-dry dirt, and leaves swirling thickly in the air from all the searchers traipsing around. Instead, he headed for the fruit stand to check out Renni's phone tip. The owner, Selma, was hesitant to talk to him until Brody said, "You're not in any trouble, and the guy probably isn't who we're looking for. We're just trying to cross him off the list." He gave her the brief description Renni had included in her call.

"Yeah. I hired a guy to help out at the fruit stand. He said his name was Dude, and he was looking for a short-term job for the fall before he headed south for the winter. I needed some help at the stand, and I, um . . ." She squinted up at Brody. "I paid him cash. Am I gonna be in trouble for that?"

He shook his head. "Not my jurisdiction. I won't pass that along to anyone. What else can you tell me about this Dude guy?"

"I think he's a mechanic. I met him at Fuzzy's at closing time, oh, I don't know, a few months ago maybe, when my car wouldn't start. He noticed me in the parking lot because his van and my car were the only ones left by then. He said the problem was something to do with the starter, then dug around in his van for tools and parts and had it going in no time."

Brody tamped down on his excitement. "Describe the van."

"It was a beat-up old VW Vanagon with a cloth sunroof, hitched to a funky hand-made trailer. There was a toolbox where the passenger seat used to be, another one in the back, and all kinds of parts and tools hanging on the walls. It was tan. Or maybe blue?" She rolled her eyes and shifted her jaw as she thought about it. "Heck, I don't remember. Anyway, Dude lives out of the trailer. Well, except after he moved in with me. I let him park the van and trailer out in the old barn behind the house. But I ain't seen him since he quit comin' to work a week ago. I been checkin' all the bars around here lookin' for him, but he ain't been around." She wrinkled her nose and grimaced sheepishly. "We kinda fought about him messin' with a chick at Fuzzy's and he left. By the time I got home, all his stuff was gone."

When Brody asked if she could remember what the license plate looked like or where it might have been from, all Selma could say was "old and rusty, and maybe whiteish."

Brody pressed her for as much info as he could get, but besides discovering the two of them drank like fishes and the guy was pretty great in bed, he was no closer to identifying the man known as Dude. The promising lead fizzled to a dead end.

He called the CSIs in. They inspected the fruit stand inch by inch, searching for fingerprints and potential DNA, but between all the customers and Selma's poor sanitation habits, it was a nearly impossible job. They did it all again at Selma's house. There they discovered a lone dirty sock under the bed and several fingerprints, some of which were smeared in what might have been attempts to wipe them off. That in itself was a red flag to Brody. It appeared Dude was trying to stay off the radar.

Brody left Liv and Pete to their job and drove to Fuzzy's Distillery, where he spent a considerable amount of time talking to the employees. The two bartenders thought they vaguely remembered him. The waitresses, however, remembered Dude quite well.

"For an old guy, he was pretty cool. Lots of funny jokes, and polite, you know? Most guys just want to get their hands on me," said a petite brunette who introduced herself as Steph. "I mean, he was old enough to be my granddad and all, but fun to hang out with."

The blonde beside her nodded. "Said he was a champion surfer, and he was pretty buff, you know, for an old guy." Both women laughed.

"After that, we called him Surfer Dude," Steph said.

The bartender overheard her. "Oh, yeah. I remember now. He heard you say that and said to call him 'Dude.'"

"None of you ever heard a real name? How about credit card receipts?"

The bartender shook his head. "Paid cash. Hardly ever needed to, though. He was pretty popular and lots of people bought him drinks. The boss really liked him. Even asked him if he wanted a job, you know, as a bouncer or just to keep people happy, something like that, but the guy said he didn't like to be tied down to any job or place."

A sketch artist on loan from the CBI made the rounds and eventually provided a face Selma and the bar staff agreed was accurate. Brody sent him back to the station to scan it and put it out on the network. As soon as it came up on his tablet, he started doing the footwork that was the basis of most investigations.

Nearly every local bar's staff recognized Dude, and all had pretty much the same to say about him. He was popular. Never caused any problems. But what was surprising was that Brody didn't find anyone in retail shops or restaurants that recognized Dude's sketch.

In the end, none of the people he interviewed provided information to move the investigation forward. He returned to the station to check on fingerprints and DNA. IAFIS didn't have anything on his prints, and the DNA processing was incomplete. Brody left a note for Liv to send the fingerprints to Interpol, then added a reminder to check Californian, Hawaiian, and Australian police departments in case the guy *was* a surfer.

It was after midnight when he got home, and Renni's door was closed. He set his alarm and was out as soon as his head hit the pillow.

# Chapter Sixty-Four

Renni woke early again, more exhausted than when she went to bed. Her sleep had been disturbed by nightmares. Flashes of light and dark, like a ferocious storm. No pictures. Feelings of fear. Pain. Cold. The crackle of lightning. Smells of ozone and sweat. Over the years there'd been a lot of bad things in her dreams, but this time . . . the Rocky Mountain High thing . . . it was more than bad. She just wanted—needed—it to stop.

Too out of sorts to go into the office early, she made a cup of tea and sat out on the patio until she heard Brody moving about.

He came outside phone in one hand, coffee in the other. "Hey," he said as he sat beside her. "We have some info on Mister PO-man Kevin. We won't have to ruin Maisie's day after all. Apparently, he spent the weekend in question in San Diego at Comic-Con."

"What's that?"

"Damned if I know. Wait, they're sending me an image." He studied his phone and started laughing. "Oh, hell no." He held the photo up for her.

Kevin stood in the middle of a group of costumed adults.

He wore a flesh-colored muscle suit of some kind that made it appear he had a massive six-pack and bulging biceps, gloves with metallic-looking blades coming out of the knuckles, and a wig.

"Is he supposed to be . . . Wolverine?" Renni leaned in closer. "I think they're all X-Men."

Brody scrutinized the picture and shook his head. "If you say so." He laughed harder, and she joined in.

The phone dinged again and they sobered. Brody read down the screen. "We've confirmed Kevin was out of state the entire weekend. He didn't return until yesterday. Apparently, after he stopped at your place and you didn't fall into his arms over him buying out the flower shop, he decided to head to the convention at the last minute. Maybe find a girl who was more, um, exciting?"

Renni giggled. "I'm so glad it wasn't him. I didn't want to have to tell Maisie she was related to a killer."

"You and me both," Brody said with a wry grin. "We'll probably clear the kid today too. We're checking a few more things, but he's had alibis for most of the murders, plus he would have been too young to drive or probably even see over the steering wheel when the first woman disappeared. We're checking the night your house blew up. Should have something later today." He shook his head at her expression. "No, I never thought he was the guy, but we have to check it out. 'Dude' . . ." Renni frowned, confused. " . . . your fruit stand guy . . . is in the wind, but I've got people looking into him."

"He's probably just some poor schmuck, going along taking pictures of random things, minding his own business, until I freak out and sic the cops on him," Renni said, blowing out a depressed breath.

"Hey, don't do that. Someone *is* after you. That's a fact. If the guy's clean, we'll move on and no harm done. He won't even know we were looking."

Renni nodded. Brody stuck his phone in his pocket and

headed inside. She followed, but she couldn't shake the feeling she'd repeatedly sent everyone on wild goose chases. Anxious to be on her way to the shop, she opted for a couple Pop-Tarts again, much to Brody's chagrin, and hurried outside to the car.

She waved to him as she happily munched her gooey pastry and sped off. *I'm glad Kevin's in the clear, and I hope Kendrick is too.* But that meant she wasn't. Not yet.

# Chapter Sixty-Five

He sat in the Nomad next to a defunct restaurant kitty-corner from Delacroix Restorations. The car was hidden from the road by an unruly hedge of evergreens. He'd been there since dawn. The floorboard held a quart milk jug half full of urine, and a pile of Gatorade bottles and plastic wrappers from doughnuts, Doritos, and Cheetos. His butt ached, but he wasn't about to give up now.

When a truck boasting signage that said A-1 Security pulled up at the auto shop, it gave him a moment of concern. A man clambered out and went inside. He came back out a half-hour later and left. Not enough time to have installed anything in the building yet, but it confirmed tonight would have to be the night.

Dusk fell. One by one, people exited the building and drove off. The old lady got in a car with one of the old guys after she locked up. A Rampart police cruiser passed by around 8 p.m., but the brake lights didn't even flicker. After that, it was dead quiet. No cars, not even any barking dogs. He struggled to stay awake, catching himself nodding off a couple times.

The cruiser came around again at midnight and he roused

himself, scrubbing his hands over his face. As soon as the taillights were out of sight, he eased the Nomad, headlights off, across the street and down to the lower parking area. He backed the car tight against the side of the building where it couldn't be seen from the road. After putting on a black baseball cap and some leather driving gloves, he turned up the collar on his dark work shirt and climbed out of the car.

The lower man door and overheads were all keypad-protected and beyond his ability. He slunk up toward the front door, lugging a small duffel bag. A pair of headlights swept down the road, and he threw himself flat in the landscaping, hoping the small shrubs would hide him from any casual glances. Once the car passed by, he ran to the front door and crouched, pulling a battery-operated drill with a large bit from the bag. After checking there weren't any late-night walkers or cars in the vicinity, he stood and quickly drilled the door's lock out.

He headed straight for Renni's office, duffel in tow. Setting the LED flashlight on the floor to keep the light focused, he immediately set to work.

He was twisting off the last pair of wires when he thought he heard voices. He crept over to the windows overlooking the shop and peered down. The expansive space was dark and still. Shaking his head at unaccustomed jitters, he finished up and gathered his tools, shoving them into the duffel. He nudged the bits and pieces of plastic, stripped wire ends, and other detritus under the desk with his boot, then adjusted the trashcan to hide the bomb.

He was halfway across the lobby when a door opened and a voice said, "What the hell are you doing here?"

He whirled and saw the old lady who worked for Renni standing in the stair doorway. There was just enough light from outside the glass front door to illuminate her pale face, but her body was a dark blob.

"Miss Delacroix asked me to check her, um, air conditioning system," he improvised, turning and moving toward the stairs, a smile on his face. "I been real busy, and this was the first chance I got."

"What's wrong with the air conditioning? She didn't say anything to me," the old lady snapped, fumbling to catch a length of fabric wrapped around her like a cape as it slipped off one shoulder. She squinted at him. "Who are you?"

Completely losing it, he ran the last few steps toward her and shoved, sending her head over heels down the metal steps. He turned and ran for the front door, sprinting down to the Nomad and leaving rubber on the pavement as he peeled out.

Back at his shop, he ditched the car behind several others and threw a cover over it for good measure. Ten minutes later, he strolled into the living room, relaxed and calm.

"Hey, sis, whatcha watchin'?"

# Chapter Sixty-Six

Renni snapped awake when the door opened, and she saw Brody, fully clothed, silhouetted in the hall light. She turned to read the alarm clock and saw it was nearly two in the morning.

"Renni, you need to get dressed. There's been an accident at the shop. Maisie's hurt."

"Maisie?" Renni struggled out of bed, balled fists rubbing sleep out of her eyes. Brody made a strange sound, and she glanced up as he disappeared into the hallway. She blushed in the dark as she realized her thin, tight T-shirt had ridden up her belly almost to her breasts and the tiny bikini panties left little to the imagination. Dressing quickly, she hurried down the stairs, a lethargic Buster on her heels. "Brody?"

He handed her a travel cup and waved her down the hall, talking as he went. "I don't have any details. Bubber called 911, and because everyone knows the location of your shop thanks to the extra patrols, the dispatcher called me after sending the ambulance—"

He bumped into her back when she stopped to look over her shoulder, asking, "What was Maisie doing at the shop?"

He shook his head. "That's all I know right now."

He tripped over Buster and shooed the spaniel back down the hall. "Stay!"

The dog stopped, gave Brody a glare, and turned and bounded up the stairs with a snort. When Brody glanced at her, Renni shrugged.

"He doesn't like the s-word."

"So I gathered."

It was only a few minutes to the shop. There were several Rampart police cruisers, lights flashing, parked in both the upper and lower lots. It seemed the whole force had been called in. Brody eased his Explorer to the side of the drive near an ambulance. A gurney was pushed up near the rear of the vehicle, and several people, including two wearing jackets labeled EMT, were clustered around it.

Renni outran Brody and skidded to a stop next to the crowd. "Maisie?" She shoved her way between bodies, stopping beside Maisie's pale face. Her eyes were open but slightly unfocused. The woman gave her a crooked smile, appearing every one of her sixty-something years.

"I'm 'kay, Ren. Don't chew worry. Go check on Bub . . . Bub'r. I nev'r seen a body s' het—" Maisie's eyelids fluttered and her slurred words petered off.

Renni looked at the EMT in dismay.

"Don't worry," he said. "It's normal for her to be a little out of it after that kind of fall. She's likely concussed. We need to get her into the ambulance now." The EMTs shouldered her aside gently and loaded the gurney into the ambulance. Moments later, it headed out, siren wailing.

Renni turned and rushed toward the overhead doors, Brody at her heels. One was open, and in the blaze of lights inside, she saw Bubber talking to a uniformed cop. Before they reached the building, however, the screech of tires and blaring of a horn caught their attention. They turned as Oscar's rental car scattered a group of officers. It continued toward them, braking a scant five feet away. Oscar was out of the car and at their side before the startled police officers could regroup.

"Get him inside," Brody whispered. "I'll smooth over his dramatic entrance."

She smiled her thanks and grabbed Oscar by the sleeve, pulling him into the shop. Bubber spied them and hurried over.

"Is Maisie all right? They wouldn't let me talk to her," he said peevishly.

"She's a little out of it, but I'm sure she'll be just fine, Bub. I think they just want to make sure." Renni peered around the shop. "What happened? What were you doing here in the middle of the night?"

Bubber looked down, stubbing his shoe repeatedly against the concrete, and shrugged, not meeting her eye.

Oscar leaned in, index finger prodding his son's chest. "Answer her, you idgit."

Grimacing as he looked up, Bubber took a deep breath and said, "We had dinner, saw a late movie. Stopped at a bar for a drink or two. Decided to . . . um, so . . . we sorta, um, like each other, but her place is pretty far away and I didn't want to take her to the hotel, so . . ."

Renni closed her eyes, then said in a honeyed tone, "So you two came here?" Her voice rose several octaves. "To my shop?" Then, in a veritable shout, "Are you kidding me?"

Oscar started chortling. "Not the best choice for a little nooky, I have to agree."

She shot him an exasperated look and turned to her cousin, praying he'd only relay details related to Maisie's trip to the hospital. "You and Maisie came here. Then what happened?"

"Well, um, I kinda fixed up this little place under the stairs and we was, um, gettin' ready to, um . . ." He licked his lips and rubbed both hands over his face.

"Okay. I get the picture. But how did Maisie get hurt?"

"She went up to get some whipped cream from the fridge."

Renni choked, and Oscar roared with laughter until she

elbowed him in the ribs. "You're not helping, Unc." She turned back to Bubber. "She went upstairs and . . ."

Bubber sighed. "I heard her yell, then come crashing and banging down the stairs. I ran out and found her and the packing blanket she wore all tangled up in the railing 'bout halfway down."

"Packing blanket? Why was she wearing a packing bla—" She stopped and held up a hand. "Never mind. I don't want to know." Renni's stomach flipped over at the thoughts flying around her head. Oscar was still grinning, letting out a snort of laughter now and then.

Brody strode up and pulled Renni aside, his expression grim. "I need you to come upstairs with me."

She followed him, having a hard time keeping visions of Bubber and Maisie, sans clothes, from flashing into her head. Clomping up the stairs, she realized the packing blanket tangling in the railing likely saved Maisie from getting much more seriously hurt, possibly killed.

A crowd of officers filled the lobby, including one wearing heavily padded equipment with helmet and face shield. She stared at Brody. "Who are all these people?"

He nodded at a young policeman talking to one of the same detectives who had interviewed her in the office a few days earlier. "When Officer Zink talked to Maisie, she wasn't making a whole lotta sense, but he thinks she saw her assailant come out of your office."

"What? Assailant? You mean someone else was in here, besides Bubber and Maisie?"

Brody put his hand on her shoulder. "Yes. Now settle down and listen to me, this is really important. After the EMTs got here, Zink looked around. He realized your chair was several feet away from the desk. Made him curious, so he looked closer and saw wire ends and plastic insulation in his flashlight beam." Brody caught the young officer's eye and gave him a nod and a smile. "Kid's pretty sharp. He knew about your house and called the BS boys right away."

"BS? Oh, bomb squad." As the meaning of that sunk in, her jaw dropped and she felt her heart thump hard in her chest. "Shit! There was another bomb? When you woke me up and said Maisie was hurt, I just thought she fell. But you're saying someone pushed her and there's a bomb?" She raised a shaky hand to her throat.

Brody inhaled deeply. "Yep. There was a trigger under the chair mat. Once you stepped on it . . ." He didn't finish the sentence. "We won't know for sure if it's the same person until the CSIs find a connection in the materials, but it's pretty much a given."

The suited detective motioned him over.

"Give me a minute, then I'll take you to the hospital," Brody said.

"No, you do your thing. I'll go with Oscar and Bubber. Call me when—if—you find out anything, please?"

"Do what I can." He squeezed her shoulder.

—

The three of them drove to the hospital, but even after circling the lot a couple times to find parking, they still spent almost an hour in the waiting room before a doctor came out to speak with them. He told them Maisie had a moderate concussion and a lot of bumps and bruises but miraculously hadn't broken anything. They were finishing up some tests before they released her. He recommended a couple days of bed rest.

She was wheeled out a few hours later looking as regal as a queen on her throne, except for the fact that her eyes couldn't seem to stay focused. "The doc says I can go home, but only if there's someone to keep a close eye on me." Maisie slowly batted her eyelashes up at Bubber. "A real close eye."

She looked half-drunk, and Renni figured they had her on some pretty strong painkillers. Bubber threw his shoulders back. "You got the best one for that job right here, Maisie, honey."

Renni and Oscar exchanged head shakes as they watched the more-than-middle-age duo make goo-goo eyes at each other.

—

The sun peeked over the flat-topped mountain to the east as Renni and Oscar walked back to the car after settling the patient and her lovestruck orderly into Maisie's sprawling ranch-style house.

"You want to go to Brody's?" Oscar asked.

"No. The shop. I want to find out if they've confirmed it was the same bomber who blew up my house."

There were fewer police vehicles in the lots, but Renni spotted Brody's SUV still parked where he'd left it earlier. An officer stopped them at the edge of the sidewalk until he radioed in and received approval for them to pass behind the yellow tape. A man and a woman, both in suits, lounged in the leather club chairs, sipping coffee from cups that more than likely came from the shop's breakroom. They barely glanced up from their discussion when Renni and Oscar walked in.

Brody, standing in the doorway to her office, gave a little jerk of his head and turned into the breakroom. They followed him in and he shut the door.

"Well?" she demanded.

He took a deep breath. "We think it's the same guy. The wires match those found at your house."

Oscar's fuzzy caterpillar eyebrows nearly hit his hairline. "They found wires in that mess?"

Brody smiled. "The FBI arson guys are pretty good. They know what to look for. They've figured out how the explosion was set off, and even found most of the parts for the ignition source in the rubble. A camp heater."

"What now?" Renni asked.

"What do you mean?"

"I mean, are you any closer to figuring out who this is? Are there any fingerprints? He's going after other people, Brody.

You have to do something before he kills someone else." Renni was near tears. First Lauren. Almost Ed and Oscar. Now Maisie. They had to find the person who was doing this. She couldn't be the cause of anyone else's death.

He squeezed her shoulder. "I know this is hard. We're doing everything we can, but this guy is too careful to leave fingerprints. I interviewed Maisie at the hospital while they were running tests. She was pretty loopy, rambling about nothing being wrong with the cooler, and talking to me like she thought I was your cousin." Brody's face flushed, and Renni bit her lip as she imagined what Maisie might have said to trigger his embarrassment. Shaking it off, he continued, "And then, clear as a bell, she said, 'He had a pet spider. Imagine that. It was crawling right there, on his arm.' I don't know if she really saw something, or was hallucinating, or what, but it could be important."

"A spider? That don't make sense," Oscar said.

"We're thinking—hoping—she saw a tattoo, not a real spider. As soon as she's up to it, we'll try to get some details we can enter into the database. In the meantime, we'll be checking local tattoo shops. It's one more piece of the puzzle. Now, go on home. I'll be there as soon as I can."

Renni sighed. "The shop's a crime scene again?"

"Yep. Sorry."

This time Brody actually sounded sorry.

# Chapter Sixty-Seven

He sat glued to the TV, waiting for the news to come on. When the familiar banner headline flashed onscreen, he saw a dozen police cruisers and black SUVs scattered around Delacroix Restorations instead of fire trucks. The reporter, this time a guy who was maybe all of twenty, stumbled his way through a script.

"Rampart police responded in the early hours of the morning to a reported break-in at a local body shop. They found one victim with non-life-threatening injuries who was transported to the hospital via ambulance. Due to undisclosed items found at the scene, the bomb squad was called in. No further information is available at this time, but we will keep on top of this breaking story."

Swearing, he threw the remote at the TV. It exploded, pieces of plastic shrapnel flying in all directions as Karen screamed and covered her face with her hands. He ignored her wailing and stomped out of the house, headed for the barn. It was time to be more hands-on with his efforts toward Renni. He couldn't sit back and wait for an explosion or car accident to do the job. He needed her out of the way, and soon. No way was he allowing some . . . girl to mess up his plans. It wasn't happening. He was done screwing around.

He went into the barn workshop, slamming and locking the door. After pacing across the room and back several times, arms flailing as he shouted and raged, he jerked out the chair, turned on the lamp, and grabbed a legal tablet and pen. It took him several slow, measured breaths to calm down before he scooted up close to the desk. He covered the paper with doodles of exploding bombs as he thought through the problem.

No one knew his identity yet. Otherwise, the police would be beating down his door. Still, his window of opportunity was closing fast. If he didn't get Renni out of the way soon, he would eventually make a mistake that would lead them to him.

He began listing the steps he'd need to take, numbering them as to order. First, he'd separate Renni from her guards. Get her alone. Vulnerable. Where he could do what needed to be done. It wasn't the right time for the ritual, but Renni didn't fit anyway. She was blonde, but not tall. She was pretty, but not in the perfect, creamy-skinned way Karen and the others were.

Renni would never be found. The others needed to be discovered, to show their families what they should have appreciated when they had it. To know the pain he'd suffered through all these years. *She* needed to go away.

With a shake of his head, he focused on eliminating Renni, putting the ritual out of his mind. He kept writing, walking himself carefully through the necessary steps. When he'd included everything he could think of, he rewrote the whole thing without the scratch-throughs and erasures. The plan needed to be perfect. Neat. Like him. And it needed him, in person, to make sure it was finished.

The sun had set by the time his plan was fully fleshed out. He gathered up his equipment and materials, leaving some in the shop and putting others in his pickup. Once everything was where he would need it, he gathered up the diagrams, notes, timelines, and checked-off list of materials and put them in a folder labeled *The Final Plan*.

# Chapter Sixty-Eight

Renni was too keyed up to sit still, even though she was exhausted after being up all night and wished she could go into the shop. Buster sensed her anxiety and hung right next to her knee as she puttered around the house, pulling linens off of beds and starting a load of laundry, cleaning the kitchen, even weeding some of Brody's flower beds. When the doorbell rang, she ran down the hall, barely remembering to check the peephole before unlocking the door.

It was Luke. She let him in, and despite it being mid-morning, fetched a couple beers and led him out to the backyard. Once she assured him Maisie wasn't seriously injured and would be back in fine fettle within a few days, they turned to discussing the bomb.

"How the hell did he get into your office?" Luke demanded.

"Broke in the front door. Brody said it would have taken less than a minute to do. Christ, Luke, I almost got Maisie, and maybe even Bubber, killed."

"You didn't do anything. And if they hadn't been there, it's likely you, and half the shop, wouldn't be here right now."

Renni got up and paced the length of the deck. "There's no way of knowing who'll get hurt next. It could have been you, or Oscar, or Ed. Any of you. I can't take this much longer."

Luke reached out and grabbed her arm. "It's not your fault, Ren. Whoever this guy is, he knows more about us than we do about him. But we're getting closer. It's only a matter of time. Oh, and Ed Benson called. He said a new security system'll be installed at the shop tomorrow. A really good one."

They talked for a while longer, but it soon became clear they were rehashing the same information. Luke told her he'd be at the shop when the security guys got there and left after eliciting a promise that she'd call if she heard anything new.

—

Brody stopped by a bit shy of noon, exhaustion written all over his face. Renni held off asking any questions until he sat in the shade out back with a tall iced tea and a plate of elk summer sausage and smoked gouda at his elbow.

"Brody?"

He took a sip and set the glass down, leaning forward with his elbows on his knees. "I don't have a lot to tell you. Both bombs were made with the same wire. The triggers were different, but both were fabricated from materials, and with instructions, easily found on the Internet. There aren't any fingerprints. I talked to Bubber. An old Nomad was parked by the overheads, but they assumed it was a restoration project someone dropped off and didn't pay a lot of attention. Seems there were other things on their mind." He smiled. When she didn't reciprocate, he sobered and continued. "Based on burnout tracks, we figure it was the bomber's car and he left in a hurry. We've got an APB on it. It's a pretty distinctive vehicle. CBI is pulling highway camera footage to see where they came from and went to. We'll find it."

"And if you don't? How long before another woman dies? Or Luke or Oscar or—"

"Don't go there, Ren. It doesn't help."

"So we keep doing . . . what? I hide out. You spend all your free time babysitting me. My friends have to keep checking over their shoulders. And when my house is done, I'm supposed to let it sit there, empty?"

When he didn't answer, heading toward the front door instead, she called, "Have they released the shop yet?"

"Yeah. You're good to go," he said over his shoulder.

So she did.

The office was a shambles. Styrofoam cups lay like snowballs on the table, and black fingerprint powder painted most surfaces in her office, as well as the doors. Remnants of doughnuts and pizza were scattered across the surface of the breakroom table. Coffee grounds spilled across the counter by the coffee maker, more dumped in the sink. It would take hours to clean it all up. With a sigh, she grabbed supplies from a cabinet by the restrooms and got started.

As she walked past the door down to the shop, she thought about the spider tattoo. It made her think about her own tattoo, but only for an instant. After all, hers was something entirely different.

The sun was falling toward the western horizon by the time Renni finished, and she was wrung out, physically and mentally, as she steered the Spitz toward Brody's. Buster, who'd spent quite a bit of time following her around and getting in the way, curled up in a ball on the passenger seat, one beady brown eye opening every few minutes, as if to reassure himself she was still there.

She left the car in the garage and trudged to the front door, Buster plodding along at her heels. Mind hazy with exhaustion, Renni had entered the first two digits of the security code when she realized there was a shoebox leaning against the door. Gray duct tape wound around it from all directions. A handwritten note that said "Reni" was taped to the top with packing tape.

She paused, head tilted, and considered the package. The

writing wasn't familiar, and there was no return address. It didn't have the familiar smile logo or any barcodes, and no printed label, so it hadn't been delivered by UPS, FedEx, or the post office. Renni instinctively leaned down and reached for it, but jerked her hand back as if it were fire. Glancing toward the drive, she could see Brody's car wasn't there. After a moment of indecision, she pulled out her phone and tapped in Brody's number.

"What's up?"

"Um, I'm not sure it's anything, but there's a package by your door. It's addressed to me, but the name is spelled wrong. I—"

"Don't touch it. Get at least two blocks away. Now!" The phone went dead.

She called to Buster, who was nosing around the lawn and jogged to a cross street several houses down.

A pack of boisterous kids, some on bikes, others on skateboards or scooters, rolled down the street away from Brody's. Fragrant smoke from a backyard barbeque wafted to her and, based on the time, she figured they were probably all heading home to dinner. The sounds of laughter, music, and conversation fluttered on the wind, and Renni began to panic. If the package was a bomb, and from Brody's response that seemed likely, people could be hurt. Children, parents, friends. Whole families. What had she brought to this quiet neighborhood? Would she be the cause of an unimaginable catastrophe?

Sirens wailed in the distance. Within minutes, a fleet of patrol cars, fire engines, and ambulances was pulling up behind her. One of the first figures to emerge was Brody. He motioned her to come toward him, further from the house. She gave Buster the command to "heel" and hurried toward the line of emergency vehicles.

Several other officers huddled around Brody, parting to make way for her. Half a dozen uniforms fanned out and went to houses along the street.

"Tell us exactly what you saw," Brody demanded.

Renni gave as complete a description as possible, then watched as one of the officers split off, headed for a dull tan vehicle with a blunt, military appearance similar to a Humvee. A man and woman met him, both dressed in black from head to toe and wearing bulky vests and helmets. The two black suits went to the back of the truck and unloaded a tracked robot-like piece of equipment while the other man donned buff-colored stiff pants and jacket, a vest, helmet, and gloves. The three of them followed the little robot down the street for about fifty feet before the robot continued forward alone, the woman controlling it with a remote in her hands. The robot turned up a driveway, then down the sidewalk to Brody's walkway, and slowly maneuvered up the step to Brody's stoop. It halted just short of the box propped against the door, but something attached to it continued to move.

Families hustled out of their homes and into the street. Directed by the police officers, they pooled in groups behind the emergency vehicles and waited to see what was going to happen. A man in a suit put a bullhorn to his mouth, and his voice echoed as he said, "Please turn off all cell phones immediately. Anyone with an active cell phone will be arrested."

Renni pulled her phone from her pocket and switched it off. Others in the crowd did the same. Brody stepped up beside her and she glanced over at him, eyebrows raised.

"The BS guys are going to check it out. The sniffer has several sensors that analyze for chemicals and toxic materials. If there are explosives in the box or trace on the wrappings, it should pick them up. It can also detect electrical fields. We've got a cell signal blocker on just in case, too."

She looked around her at the frightened faces of the crowd and the intense faces of the officers. *This is all happening because of me. I put all these people at risk. If something happens . . ."*Put me on a bus for Denver tonight, Brody. It's not safe for anyone else if I'm around. All this is happening because of me."

He frowned, but before he could reply, a familiar voice called out, "Hey, Ren, whatcha doin'? What's happening?"

She turned to see Oscar and Bubber behind a yellow tape barrier and hurried over to them. Oscar nodded at his son and said, "Maisie's got a police scanner at her place. Numb-nuts here heard Brody's address and fetched me. What's goin' on?"

Before she could explain, the bomb squad truck backed a large boxy green trailer into the middle of the street and the three of them turned to watch. As soon as it was positioned, a ramp was lowered from the rear. The truck was unhitched and driven back to the barricade. The robot slowly picked up the package and trundled down the drive toward the street.

"What're they doing with your present?" Bubber asked, frowning.

Renni whirled around. "My present?"

"Yeah. I got you some things. Wrapped 'em and everything, then forgot the dang thing this morning. I couldn't go get it 'cause I was watchin' Maisie, so I called the hotel and one of the guys said he'd drop it off on his way back from lunch."

Oscar heaved a sigh. "I have a feeling Brody ain't gonna like this."

"That's the understatement of the year," Renni muttered to herself, running over to Brody. He turned and waved her back, an impatient expression on his face.

"No, wait," she said, "you need to know this."

She explained what Bubber told her. Brody ran over to the bomb squad trio and they held an animated discussion, punctuated by frequent glances in her, and Bubber's, direction. The robot stopped at the foot of the trailer's ramp, and Brody and the others went to the heavy-duty armored vehicle and surveyed something at the back.

A moment later, Brody came toward them, waving. "You and Bubber come with me."

Renni waved Bubber over, and Oscar followed—uninvited—

but no one stopped him. The glower on Brody's face was enough to silence even Bubber. They followed him around to the back of the truck where a laptop sat. Its screen showed video from the robot.

"Is that your package, Bubber?" Brody asked.

"Yep. I wrapped it myself."

"What's in it?" the female bomb disposal tech asked.

Bubber looked back and forth between Renni and Brody, uncertainty clear in his face. "It's some T-shirts." He nodded to Renni. "You know, to replace the ones blowed up at your place. I ordered a whole bunch from a website with all kinds of 'em." His shoulders slumped, and he gave her a sad-eyed look like a basset hound caught with the Thanksgiving turkey. "I didn't mean to cause a ruckus, Ren. I thought it would be fun."

"Did you put it here?" Brody asked.

"No. I forgot it. I called the hotel and they said one of the maintenance crew was fixin' to head out to lunch and could drop it off for me. I gave him the address and Renni's name." Bubber eyed the screen. "He spelled your name wrong."

She let out a snort. "I don't think that's the real problem here, Bubby."

"Is the wrapping on the package yours?" Brody asked.

"Yep, except her name," Bubber said with an affirmative nod.

Shaking his head in disgust, the senior bomb squad officer waved the three of them back behind the barricade while he and Brody returned to huddle with the bomb techs again. The robot started up the ramp and put the box inside, then dutifully came back to the squad vehicle. The trailer ramp and a set of thick metal doors closed remotely. Visors down, the pair of bomb disposal techs connected a hose from the closest fire truck to the side of the trailer and a nearby hydrant. Once the fireman wrenched open the spigot, the trailer rattled and shook. The bomb squad watched their computer screen, and after a few minutes, signaled the fireman to cut the water. They unhooked the hose. The trailer opened and several hundred gallons of water spilled out and ran into the gutters.

"Why'd they do that? Your shirts are gonna be all wet now," Bubber grumbled.

"Water will kill most electronics," Brody said, overhearing them as he approached. "Even if there isn't anything but shirts in the box, the BS guys wanted to make sure. Plus with all the work they'd already gone through, it was a good chance to run a drill."

The police officers talked with the huddles of area residents, who began to disperse back to their homes. One of the bomb techs walked over and dumped an armful of soaking wet T-shirts into Brody's hands, shook his head, and turned away, already beginning to strip off his armor. Renni noted the man's shirt was soaked through with sweat.

Brody turned to Bubber, shoved the wet bundle at him, and said, "You three go on back to the house. Stay put. I'll be there as soon as we get this all sorted out."

"Am I in trouble?" Bubber asked.

"No. It's a hell of a lot better to be safe than sorry. Other than a burned steak or two on the barbeque and some kids with great stories to tell at school, no harm done."

"Bet you're gonna be real popular around here with the neighbors, Brody," Oscar piped up.

Renni gave him a dirty look. "It's not his fault. If I wasn't here, this—"

"Oh, quit being such a martyr, babygirl. This ain't your fault. It's the nitwit's. And speaking of the nitwit, I'd better get him back to his babysitting job."

Renni knew he was trying to make her feel better, but it wasn't working. None of this would have happened if she'd let Brody send her to Denver when he first mentioned it. Who knew what would happen next? She sighed and traipsed back to the house, not sure which was higher on her list—bed or a tall cold G&T.

# Chapter Sixty-Nine

He checked his watch and realized he'd spent more time than he should have engrossed in news reports about yesterday's bomb scare by the cop's house. Were the cops trying to lure him out somehow? It didn't matter. He wasn't connected—it wouldn't affect his plans. If he waited much longer, though, the cop would be getting off work. With a determined nod, he grabbed his phone and typed in six digits. His finger hesitated before poking the seventh one. *No turning back.* He finished dialing.

—

Renni sighed and put down the trade magazine she was too unfocused to read, pulling her phone out of her pocket to answer it. "Renni Delacroix here."

"Miss Delacroix, it's Klete Cavanaugh. Sorry to bother you on a weekend, but I could use your help, and I know you usually work on Saturday."

"What can I do for you, Mr. Cavanaugh?"

"A guy brought a pickup in here a while back. A '57 Chevy

Cameo. I did a lot of prep work on it without a deposit because he was an old friend. I even ordered the custom-mixed paint, which isn't returnable. I had just put it in the booth when he called and said he's not going to have the money to pay me. He offered to sell it to me for a thousand bucks. I've got that much, but I'd need to know I could sell it for four or five grand to cover my costs and make a decent profit. My sister has a lot of medical issues, and I was counting on that job covering 'em. It's short notice, but any chance you could come today to check it out? Make sure I'm not throwing good money after bad? I'm supposed to go pick up a car in Rangely this afternoon, and my friend says he'll have to sell to another guy if I don't get back to him right away."

Renni hesitated. The security crew was still finishing up work on the lower overhead doors, and she'd retreated upstairs to stay out of their way. Not getting anything done was making her antsy, and very grumpy, especially when there wasn't usually anyone around to disturb her work on the weekends. There wasn't any reason she couldn't forward the shop's phone to her cell and lock up.

She glanced at her watch and was amazed to see how late it was. She switched the screen on her phone to messages, expecting a half-dozen angry ones from Brody, but there weren't any. *Maybe he's found out something that means I don't need babysitting anymore?* Whatever the reason, she was glad he hadn't called the cavalry on her, because Cavanaugh was someone she wanted to keep happy. He'd done an amazing paint job on the resto-mod—probably got them at least an extra forty grand—and Ed's Cadillac looked like dynamite on wheels. Plus she'd have more work for him with the Twins. No-brainer.

"Sure, I can take a peek. Price can vary depending on the condition of the interior and the engine and drive train. Give me thirty minutes to close up and get there."

"Great. I'll be watching for you."

—

When she wheeled into the lot, Klete stood outside the door to his tiny cinder block office. The small building was dwarfed by the large metal shop tacked on to one end. He stepped over and opened her door for her.

"Thanks a lot, Miss Delacroix. I'll try not to take up too much of your time." He pointed to the shop's overhead door. "It's right here." He hurried to open the office door.

Renni told Buster to stay in the car and went inside. She was always amazed at the immaculate condition of his office. Most automotive painters inhaled so many chemicals over the years that they operated on about half their original brain cells, but Klete was different. It was one of the reasons she liked him. He was always on time, and his paint and paperwork were faultless. It was a pleasure to work with him.

Before she could open the door to the paint booth, he reached around to do it for her. The cuff of his long-sleeved T-shirt pulled up. At the same time she realized the booth contained a ten-year-old Chevy Silverado, not a classic, she saw the spider tattoo on the back of his wrist. Before her brain could process the information, unbearable pain seared her body.

—

He stared down at her twitching form, then at his watch to start the countdown. Once she quit moving, he picked her up and threw her over his shoulder. A clatter caused him to look down. Her cellphone had shattered into pieces on the concrete. Making a mental note to clean it up as soon as he could, he continued into the paint booth and around to the front of the truck. He laid her on a prearranged drop cloth, then rolled her up in the paint-stained fabric like a cigar. *Bet she don't weigh more'n a buck soaking wet.* He hefted the roll up. In seconds, he had her stashed on the floorboards of the truck. He ran the booth's overhead up and backed the Chevy out.

The dog in her car jumped from the passenger seat to the driver's seat and started barking to beat the band. Klete went back into the office, made sure the paint booth door was secure, then called to the dog, "Come on, Buddy. Here, Buddy, or whatever your name is." He kept his voice light and friendly, patting his knee. The dog jumped out of the car and trotted inside, following his nose to the paint booth door. Klete slipped outside and slammed the office door shut, quickly locking it. The dog immediately started barking, and his head bounced in and out of view through the glass upper half of the door.

"Damn dog'll probably make a mess in there," he groused, angry that he hadn't taken the dog into consideration when drawing up his plan. He shrugged it off. No big deal. It was inconsequential in the grand scheme of things. "I'll take care of the mutt tomorrow."

Then he remembered her phone. He started to unlock the front door, but after a glance at his watch decided he needed to make better use of his limited time before Renni was conscious.

He drove her car into the booth, ignoring the scrabble of the dog's claws against the door to the office. After locking the overhead, he drove the Chevy out to the street. He stopped only long enough to shut the gate, fastening two padlocks on the large chain like usual. No one passing by would find anything out of the ordinary.

The sun had set by the time he drove the truck down the long drive and parked along the left side of his barn. He hefted Renni's body and slipped through a small door cut into the weathered red siding, out of sight of the house. After carrying Renni inside the workshop and laying her on the floor, he went back and locked the entry door. It wouldn't do for Karen to get a wild hair to barge in. She wasn't allowed in the barn, but she'd been acting a little strange lately.

Renni started to wriggle feebly, so he grabbed the edge of the fabric and tugged until she rolled out. Before she could do more than moan and turn her head toward him, he gave her another shock, extending it to five seconds since the earlier three-second stun didn't seem to do her any permanent damage. While she was out, he zip-tied her hands behind her back and then her ankles, and used a clean bandana to gag her. When she was safely trussed, he propped her up against the side of his desk so he could see her face and waited for her to wake up.

He was beginning to worry he might have stunned her too long when her eyes started twitching. It took several more minutes before she was fully conscious and aware.

He cocked his head. Strange. She was tiny compared to the other women he'd had in this same predicament, but they were all scared. Crying and moaning. Renni didn't seem afraid—she was *pissed*. Her eyes shot daggers instead of raining tears.

He knelt beside her outstretched legs. "You shoulda let it go, Miss Delacroix. I didn't wanna have to do this, but you just had to get in the middle of it." He reached up and stroked her cheek. She jerked away from his hand. "They don't suffer. That's important. And I make sure they get found real quick too." He sighed. "Wish I could do that for you, but I can't. The cops won't find you. Not even the guy you been shacked up with. It ain't proper, you know? Disappointed me to find out you were like that."

Klete tilted his head and shrugged. "You aren't right for the ritual, so I'm using a different spider. It'll be like the others, but it'll hurt more. I think you deserve it for all the trouble you put me through, don't you?" He patted her leg and stood. "I'll be back with one of my little friends so we can get it over with. If you want to pray or something, now's a good time to get it done."

# Chapter Seventy

Renni watched as Klete went across the room and through another door, disappearing into the black interior of the building. She had no idea where she was. How far she'd been taken. While he talked to her, she'd been flexing her arms behind her back, testing the restraints in case there was enough play to pull a hand free. There wasn't. She kept at it, pausing frequently to listen for sounds of his return.

Silence.

She didn't have the luxury of waiting for a rescue that likely wouldn't come. It was up to her to escape before Klete could do whatever he had planned, and based on her dreams and his parting comments, she had a pretty fair idea what that was.

She scanned the workshop. Long tables against the walls were made with two-by-four timbers. Pegboards lined the walls above, and spray-painted silhouettes showed where specific hand tools normally hung. Unfortunately, the pegboard didn't have any sharp instruments handy, but she hoped they might be laying on the tabletop above her sightline.

Renni tried to lever herself up by pushing with her feet and wriggling up the side of the desk, but the floor was gritty, and her feet slipped out from under her. She hit hard, banging the side of her face and head on the concrete floor. Cursing, she started to roll onto her back to try again.

Something metallic glinted on the floor under the workbench. Instead of making another ill-fated attempt to stand, she rolled blindly toward the shiny object until her shoulder smacked against a table. She shifted around until she could peer into the darkness underneath. Barely visible under a thick layer of dust was a circular saw blade with varying size teeth. By pressing her back against the table leg, she was able to stretch her bound hands far enough to pull the blade out. Renni maneuvered it upright and wedged it between a set of adjoining table legs. Rather than waste time getting her hands free, she worked at cutting the zip tie on her ankles, remembering Boogey's lesson that if she could run, she could escape. Having only the use of her hands would put her at a disadvantage if Klete returned.

Her breath wheezed in and out her nose as she balanced on her butt in a gut-clenching half sit-up. She raked the plastic over the sharp teeth, increasing the tiny slit with each scrape.

The blade flipped loose and rolled between her legs. She scrambled to get it back in place, unable to resist flicking her eyes to the doorway. Empty. But for how much longer? Sweat trickled down her face as she frantically sawed at the plastic.

Two more scrapes and she was free. She kicked to her feet and ran for the door Klete left by. It began to open toward her when she was still three feet away, but she continued at full speed, turning her good shoulder to the door as she crashed into it.

It swung for a foot before connecting solidly, knocking the breath out of her. Klete yelped as the door smashed into him and then slammed shut. She spun and fumbled for the deadbolt, flipping it over a fraction of a second before the doorknob rattled. She ran for the other door, sucking in air. It also had a deadbolt, and she scrabbled behind her back to open it. The locked room might provide temporary safety, but she needed to move. Put distance between herself and the killer. The lever clicked over, and she slipped through into deep shadow.

She snorted air into her lungs like a racehorse, relieved to find it was fresh air, and nearly plowed into the truck from Klete's paint booth, swerving around its fender at the last second. From inside the barn came the crash of wood on wood. She sprinted hard down the dirt drive toward lights.

# Chapter Seventy-One

Brody spent the afternoon updating the RMHK files, adding information on the break-in at Renni's, the bomb materials, and everything he knew regarding the body they'd found off the Interstate by the old Gilsonite plant. The victim hadn't yet been identified, but he wondered if Renni would recognize the face from her visions. The task force briefing took more than two hours and included both the newly discovered victim and the bomb at the shop. The FBI had sent over a half-dozen more agents from various offices, and the task force room, already full to overflowing, was expanded by two more offices and a conference room.

His email dinged, and he opened the file. It was from Maisie's home computer. He read the message, his heart beating faster with every word.

*Detective Brody, Elmo picked up the shop mail for me yesterday, but with all the excitement, forgot about it until today. There was an overnight package from a photographer in Utah. The note with it says it's a larger version of one in the Layton High School yearbook of 1998. It's of a Bill Davis, who may or may not be related to Jon Davis, the last registered owner of the Marmons that made up Renni's truck. I don't know how important it is, but it looks like Renni has been trying to find information about this Bill Davis for the better part of a week. I've been trying to call her, but she doesn't answer. Anyway, I've attached a scan of the photo. Hope this helps.*

*Maze*


Maisie might have been down, but she wasn't out. The attachment showed a high schooler with wavy light-colored hair. It hung past his chin on both sides of his face. He wasn't smiling, but he would probably be considered a handsome kid.

Brody shook his head. Why hadn't Renni told him what she was doing? Was he holding a picture of the RMHK or some kid she dated in school? And why did Maisie mention "*Marmons that made up Renni's truck*" like there was more than one? Law enforcement knew Jon Davis had been the last known person to register the truck, but he'd been dead for years. Renni had some explaining to do, and he needed to have the CSIs look into potential other VINs in the truck.

He dialed Renni's number, but it went straight to voicemail. He texted Oscar and Luke next. They each responded that they hadn't seen her—both had tried to call her, but neither got through. Oscar was headed to the shop to check on her and had sent his friend Ed to Brody's place.

Brody called a tech over and showed him the picture. They discussed whether it was clear enough to get a viable result from running it through age progression software.

"I can try, Detective. It might be a little vague, but if anyone is familiar with him, the photo will probably be good enough for them to be able to tell, unless he's got a beard or something like that," the tech said. "We can fool around with that too."

"Run it." Brody took a deep breath as adrenaline coursed through his veins. Maybe they were finally on the verge of a breakthrough. His phone chimed. Oscar. "What'd you find?"

"Security guys said they heard her leave a while ago, probably at least an hour or so."

"Damn it!" Brody shouted, just managing to stop himself from throwing his phone.

"Simmer down. Phone battery coulda died and she don't realize it." Oscar's reasonable conclusion didn't match the concern in his voice. The call disconnected.

While he waited impatiently at the tech's shoulder for the photo to be manipulated, Brody put in a request for Renni's phone to be pinged, knowing that if her battery really was dead, they'd get no results on its location. After about ten minutes, the tech sat back, shaking his head.

"This is the best we're gonna get, I'm afraid."

The photo on the monitor was hazy, like an overdone glamour shot. Brody asked the tech to send it to his own computer, the local LEOs, and the FBI. He then sent it to Renni, her staff, and Oscar.

He was on his computer checking out the Layton High School website when his phone chimed. It was Luke.

"Brody, I think I know him. It might be the guy who paints for us. His name is Klete Cavanaugh. His shop's off Mesa Avenue between 5th and 6th. I'm going there now."

"On my way. Wait across the street until I get there. I mean it. Under no circumstances do you approach the shop, you hear? Wait for me."

He gave the potential suspect's name and business address to the tech officer, and asked for a background check, rap sheet, property records search, and to contact the AIC and tell him what they'd found. Grabbing his keys, Brody ran for his patrol car.

It was only a few blocks to Cavanaugh's business, Sion and Son Painting. Luke was already there, pacing the sidewalk across the street from a ten-foot-tall chain link fence with razor wire curls at the top. There were no signs of human activity, but Brody heard a dog barking inside. It was a familiar bark.

Luke frowned. "Is that . . . Buster?"

"I was thinking the same thing." Pivoting on his heel, Brody ran to the black and white and threw up the rear cargo door. He yanked out a canvas carryall, rummaging until he found a set of bolt cutters. He jogged to the gate, Luke beside him. "I want you to stay here at the gate, Luke. Keep quiet, and run like hell if this goes south. Got it?"

"You shouldn't go in there alone, Bro."

"I'll call for backup, but most of the patrols are tracking down information on the bombing or down past Fruita at a crime scene. No one will get here soon enough." Brody turned away and cut the chain, then handed the cutters to Luke, giving him a hard stare. "Stay put. I can go in under probable cause, but I don't want you in the middle of this." He radioed in as he peered across the parking area, bare for forty feet or so. On the far side were several cars parked tightly together, but they wouldn't provide cover.

He slipped through the gate and ran as silently as he could toward the building, then crouched and crept along the front. The office was solid cinder block with one small barred window and a half-glass entrance door on the front. It was attached to a sizable metal building with an extra-tall overhead door. As he crept closer, the barking grew louder, and he saw Buster's head in the glass for a fraction of a second.

He turned the door handle, but it was locked, and the movement only served to ramp up Buster's agitation. It took less than a minute to circle the building, verifying no other doors or windows. When he came back out front, he hollered toward the fence, "Get the pry bar out of my car." Less than a minute passed before Luke ran up, a yard-long iron bar in hand.

Brody took a quick peek through the window and saw a small neat space with no hiding places. It was vacant except for the frantic spaniel. Brody pointed to the overhead door. "See if you can pry it off the rollers. I'll cover you."

Luke was determined, and the flimsy aluminum door gave way with minimal effort.

"Son of a bitch," Brody cursed at the sight of Renni's car in the otherwise-empty booth. He used the passthrough interior door to get into the office. He struggled to keep thoughts of Renni being abducted by the RMHK from interfering with his investigation and keep Buster from knocking him down.

"Take the dog and put him in your car," Brody said.

Luke called Buster and headed toward the street, shouting over his shoulder, "You shouldn't be here by yourself, Bro."

Brody ignored him and grimly surveyed the office. He needed to find an address. Another vehicle. A man.

There was an old file cabinet along one wall, and he opened it, flipping rapidly through well-organized files. He hit pay dirt in the third drawer. The folder was labeled "utility bills." It contained two sections, one for Sion and Son Painting and another for a residential address. The residential bill was in the name of Opal Woodward. Why would Cavanaugh pay the bills for a property belonging to someone else? Was Opal family? A girlfriend?

He made a note of the address and ran to his car, using his shoulder mic to call for CSIs and to verify if Cavanaugh owned the property, and if not, who did.

Luke hurried over. "Did you find something?"

"No sign of Renni. There'll be detectives and CSIs here shortly. Tell them what happened and where Buster was. They'll take it from there." He paused. "You ever hear of a woman named Opal Woodward?"

Luke shook his head.

"Okay, go home as soon as they'll let you. I'll call if we find anything."

Brody plugged the address for the Woodward property into his unit's GPS, called again for backup with the new address, and sped west. The properties in this part of town were mostly old farms and orchards set along the railroad tracks, with an occasional mercury vapor light to pierce the deepening twilight. He followed the computer voice over a humped railroad crossing and turned off his lights as he coasted down a long driveway. He stopped in deep shadows under a grove of cottonwoods. The drive continued in a relatively straight line for what looked like a quarter mile, ending next to an old two-story farmhouse and outbuildings. A large newer-vintage barn was set back two hundred feet beyond the house.

He searched for signs of life. Thin drapes covered windows with the glow of lights behind them. There was no sign of movement inside. In the shadows of the barn, he could just make out a pickup parked beside it.

Impatient, Brody slipped out of his car and moved toward the house, expecting backup any minute. An overgrown fence line provided some cover, and he eased carefully toward the house, scanning his full field of vision.

Movement to the left drew his attention and he swiveled toward the barn, gun up and ready.

# Chapter Seventy-Two

Renni sprinted full tilt for a hundred yards before she heard the door behind her slam against the barn. *If I can just keep ahead of him . . .* A shot rang out, and a puff of dust erupted a foot to the right and ten feet ahead of her.

*Shit. That changes the odds I'm getting out of this alive.* She juked left and right as she headed for the old farmhouse, hoping to get around a corner. Her heaving lungs, the beating of her heart, and the thud of her footsteps seemed loud enough to drown out a freight train. A door at the side of the house opened. A shadowy figure stepped out the door onto the stoop, and Renni stumbled in confusion. It was a woman. She waved frantically.

"Over here. This way!"

Renni veered sharply as another shot rang out. A white-hot streak burned across her left hip. Another twenty steps and she'd be inside.

She only got four.

It was a strange sensation. Pain, yes, but more like she imagined a trout would feel when someone set the hook. A sudden uncontrolled jerk forward.

Renni landed face first in the dirt, sliding and tumbling for several feet until she came to rest on her back. The gag had been roughly scraped off her mouth, and she sucked in deep breaths between pained groans. She blinked dust out of her eyes and fought to focus on Klete as her ears rang and her head throbbed in cadence with the gunshot wound. He raised the barrels of two guns, confusing her—until she realized she was seeing double. But there was still one gun, and it was pointed directly at her face.

"Klete!" screamed the woman in the house. "You know you won't get away with this!"

The gun shifted higher, away from Renni. "Why not, Karen? I've gotten away with a whole lotta shit. What do you care, as long as I take care of you? Every fuckin' day I take care of you. Just like Ma and Pop took care of you every day before they died. You just go back in the house and fix us a couple bowls of ice cream. I'll take care of this and be in shortly." He looked back down at Renni, the gun held loosely in his hand but definitely pointed in her direction.

Suddenly he stiffened and raised the gun, aiming at the woman he'd called Karen. Fury sharp in his voice, he said, "I should have expected this. You always thought you were smarter than me. Just like Pop. You never cared about me. You don't deserve to be my sister."

It was there. In his voice. Renni knew it was coming. She bit her lip against the pain, jackknifed at the waist, and kicked her feet toward her head. She spun on her side and stuck one foot between his knees. Using every ounce of strength she could muster, she scissored her legs as she rolled onto her stomach, hoping to knock his legs out from under him. Even before the gun cracked, it was clear her effort was too weak. Too late.

The shot seemed to echo from a long distance. She felt detached from what happened as a shadow soared over and enveloped her in darkness, stealing her breath away, a roaring in her ears getting louder as the sound of the shot faded.

Was she dead? But the pain of gravel digging into her cheek and chin, and dust filtering into her nose as she breathed, told her she was still alive. She twisted her head, moaning as sharp stones shredded her cheek. There was a weight on her back and head, pinning her to the ground, compressing her chest. Each time she exhaled, it became harder to draw in a breath. A pair of tennis shoes came into her field of vision, which was shrinking like looking down a train tunnel. The shoes stopped a few feet away. She heard a wailing in the distance. *Brody?*

A hand reached down and picked up the gun Klete had dropped when he fell. As blackness closed in, leaving only a pinpoint of light, Renni heard a whisper.

"Thanks. Oh, and sorry."

She closed her eyes, filled with relief the woman was all right. Before she could stop herself, a deep breath sighed past her lips, further restricting her ability to breathe. She gasped, trying to pull in tiny wisps of air, but succeeded only in filling her lungs with fine dust. There was a sudden loud blast, and the weight on her back and head amplified. Even the dust left her lungs. It was the end of all consciousness.

# Chapter Seventy-Three

She stared at the cup of green Jell-O in her hand. Renni didn't like green Jell-O. Had never liked it. Cherry or strawberry or peach—they were fine. But being served the green goo repeatedly since she'd awoken in the hospital room was beyond enough. The sight of that particular color made her . . . rebellious. The temptation to catapult the quivering blob across the room was overpowering.

She positioned her spoon, gauged the distance to the sink next to the door, and let fly. Her aim was impeccable and would have been dead on . . . if Brody hadn't stepped into the line of fire.

He was followed in close order by Maisie, Bubber, Oscar, Ed, Luke, and Vicki with Buster on his leash. The attack caused a minor melee as Brody stumbled to a halt and the others tripped over each other trying not to run into him. The sight of a large glob of green sliding from his forehead to his cheek, then the wet "plop" as it hit his immaculate uniform shirt, rendered them all speechless. But only for a moment.

It took several minutes and a buxom charge nurse shushing

them to get everyone to settle down. By then, Brody had washed his face and shirt with a paper towel at the sink. He turned and walked purposefully toward her, his face blank. Renni bit her lip to keep from laughing as she craned her neck to see what he was up to. She was propped on her right side by pillow bolsters to keep pressure off her left hip and buttock. Thick bandages crisscrossed her side. They covered a deep grazing slash across her hip and the hole on her left butt cheek, which had contained a .22 slug. She was careful to move as little as possible to avoid the sharp streak of pain from pulled stitches.

Brody stopped next to the bed, studying her as he shook his head. He reached out, plucked the half-empty cup of Jell-O and plastic spoon from her motionless hand, and ate every bit, never taking his eyes off her.

Oscar was the first to get his laughter under control enough to speak. "I think we need to get you out of here, girl. If you're up to shenanigans like that, you don't need no more mollycoddling."

"*Please* get me out of here," she begged, throwing her arm over her forehead like an overplayed actor. "This place is killing me."

"We'll ask the doctor. If he says yes, we'll have you out of here faster'n a greased pig."

They rounded up chairs from the hallway and pulled the ones in the room closer to the bed, facing her. It appeared they were expecting a performance. Bubber lifted Buster onto the bed, and the dog immediately curled up next to Renni's feet, his big whiskey-colored eyes glued to her face. Once everyone else settled, Brody took his place at the side of the bed next to the headboard so she could see him without straining her neck.

"I'd ask if you're up to hearing what's been happening, but that's obviously a moot point," he said with a mock frown.

She grinned and shrugged, then winced. "Come on, spill. What's going on? Nobody will tell me anything."

"That's because Brody refused to talk to any of us until he could tell you too," Luke grumbled. Oscar harrumphed, motioning for Brody to get on with it.

"If it hadn't been for Maisie finding the package from Utah, more than likely we'd all be gathered somewhere else, and for a whole different reason." Brody gave Renni a chastising glower.

She ignored his censure. "Oh, the photo. It came?"

"Yes, and if you'd told me what you were up to with it, we might have got our hands on it faster," he said.

"Knowing what I went through to get it, I'm not sure I agree. Was it Klete?"

"Whyn't you let the boy talk," Oscar cut in, "so we all know what's goin' on?"

Renni bit her lip and glanced at Brody, whose eyes crinkled at the edges, but his mouth stayed carefully neutral.

"Yes, Unc."

"We discovered your disappearance about the same time I got Maisie's email. One of the techs took the photo and enhanced it, using software to age the face and get the hair out of his eyes. I sent it to this bunch . . ." He gazed around the room. " . . . as well as law enforcement."

"Klete called and asked me to come look at a truck, and it was getting late anyway." Renni saw disapproval on the ring of faces. "I know I should have called someone, but I'd seen Klete a few days earlier when I dropped off the paint chips. I mean, you know, we've been working with him for a couple of years. It didn't even occur to me he might be the one . . ."

Luke piped up. "It was my fault he knew you were in Santa Fe." He grimaced and shook his head. "When he told me he needed to change the paint chips, I said you weren't there, and I must have told him where you were going. I honestly don't even remember. I was really worried that telling him to go ahead with the color change might be a mistake. Maybe ruin Ed's car." He hung his head. "I'm so sorry, Ren."

"Oh, Luke."

Before Renni could say any more, Oscar cleared his throat loudly and Brody took up the saga.

"Luke identified Cavanaugh, and Buster confirmed we were at the right location." At Renni's frown, he explained, "He was locked in the paint shop office, but we could hear him barking clear out on the street." Brody reached over and scrubbed his knuckles under the spaniel's ear, earning a lick. He continued, "I found an address in his files and headed there while the CSIs started on the office. The farmhouse belonged to Cavanaugh's mother, under her maiden name. The utility company never got a request to change it after she married or when she died."

"What about the paint shop? It said Sion and Son, and I know it was a new business. It opened after my shop did."

"The CBI profiler says the word Sion is related to the Mormon religion. Maybe something to do with Jon Davis. Or maybe Cavanaugh just liked the name. We'll probably never know."

"All this is interestin,' but how 'bout we get to the meat and potatoes of this thing?" Ed grumbled, clearly at the end of his patience.

Brody laughed and gave an assenting nod. "I arrived at the farmhouse just after dark and parked at the edge of the tree line, about a half-mile away. There was a yard light on a tall pole, and it cast a lot of shadows around the buildings. I didn't see anyone for several minutes. All of a sudden, you came barreling out from behind the shadow of the barn and into the light. You were pelting down the driveway, hands behind your back. I was about to call out to you when the side door of the house opened, and a woman came out."

"Is she okay? She tried to help me, get me to the house. I remember . . ." Renni frowned. "She told me to come toward her. And then Klete was there. I thought he was going to shoot me. But then he shot her—wait . . . He said something about their parents and that she didn't deserve to be his sister, I think. Everything gets fuzzy after that."

Brody blew out a hard breath. "Fuzzy isn't the half of it. This is where things get interesting. The light was near enough to the house to show a woman on the steps. Cavanaugh came charging around the barn after you. You were zigging and zagging all over, and she was yelling. I ran down the fence line toward you, shouting that I was police and to drop his weapon, but with everything going on, nobody seemed to hear me. He fired, and I saw you go cartwheeling through the dirt . . ." His voice cracked. Maisie patted him on the back, and he took a deep breath. "As I aimed at him, I saw the woman raise a gun. Cavanaugh saw it too, and he took his gun off you and pointed it at her. By then, several police cars were coming down the road behind me with their sirens blaring. I wasn't sure who was about to get shot— you, him, or her. You pulled your ninja move right when they fired at each other. She hit him, right between the eyes, and he fell on top of you. He only winged her."

"So she's going to be all right?"

"She was well enough to run over, pick up his gun, and aim it at you."

Renni gasped. "But why?"

Oscar cleared his throat loudly.

Brody dipped his head to the old man and continued. "I didn't have any choice but to shoot her before she shot you. I aimed as low as I dared without taking a chance of missing. Once they got her stabilized at the hospital, she confessed that she was going to shoot you with his gun, then claim he did it and she killed him in self-defense." He raised his eyes and studied the dials and blinking lights on the wall above Renni's head.

"So, she's alive?"

"Yeah, but not in great shape."

"Why would she shoot her own brother?" Renni asked softly.

Brody heaved a deep sigh. "Liv and Pete, the CSIs, were the ones who solved that mystery. They searched the farmhouse and found some scrape marks on the floor in Karen's room. Seems the dresser was moved repeatedly. They found a bunch of spiral notebooks taped to the back. The books went back more than twenty years, to when she was in grade school. Not even Klete realized how much alike they really were."

"What do you mean?" Renni asked, brow furrowed.

"Klete and Karen were twins. Klovis Cavanaugh, their father, died in an explosion about fifteen years ago. It was ruled an accident because he was a heavy smoker and known to drink. There was an older model portable propane heater in the barn. It didn't have an auto-shutoff. The fire chief decided it fell over and caused a gas leak, and Klovis lit a cigarette and ignited the gas. Ruled it an accident. Not long after he died, Mrs. Cavanaugh died in her sleep at a nursing home. Karen wrote, in great detail, how she killed them both."

The group exchanged incredulous stares.

Renni was the first to speak. "You mean she was a murderer too? But why did she kill her parents? Did she know what her brother was doing? Why—"

Brody held up his hands to halt her questions. "She hated her old man for the way he treated everyone and his part in her disfigurement."

Renni opened her mouth, but then shut it as Oscar growled, "Let him tell the damn story, girl."

"She manipulated her father into getting a large life insurance policy about six months before he died by telling him she read an article about how a person needs to put a value on their intelligence and earning power." Brody shrugged. "Apparently, he was a bit of a narcissist. Seems it runs in the family. She knew just how to play him. She and her mother were the beneficiaries since Klete had run away to Utah by then and she never expected him to come back. Karen thought her mother was weak and a waste of space—her words, not mine—and didn't want to have to spend any of the money taking care of her. She smothered her mother, but due to her medical conditions, they ruled her death as natural causes. After Klete came back, Karen didn't know for sure what he was up to, but the journals show she at least had a good idea what he did when he went on his *annual vacations*," he said, making air quotes.

After a deep breath, he continued, "According to the journals, it was her brother's fault the spider bit her, causing severe scarring on her face. She hated him and was furious when he came back. But then she realized he could do things for her she couldn't do herself, so she tolerated him. However, when the articles about you being a psychic came out in the paper, her computer records show several searches on poisons. She's a medical transcriptionist, so if you didn't know the background, she could probably have passed it off as research for her work. We think she was making plans to get rid of her brother to keep him from bringing the police close to her."

Renni squirmed to get into a more comfortable position, and Vicki adjusted the pillows at her back.

"What will happen to her?" Oscar asked.

"There's a good chance she'll be permanently paralyzed. A paraplegic. She gave a full confession in exchange for a guarantee she won't end up in general population. She wants to spend the rest of her life in solitary confinement. Most likely, she'll end up in an institution for the criminally insane."

Bubber slapped his hand on his thigh. "Ho-ly shee-it. Here I thought this town was some quiet little backwater, and it turns out to be Weirdsville on steroids."

"It gets a bit weirder . . ."

Everyone's eyes swiveled back to Brody.

"The barn contained the most damning evidence of all. In the back of the building, we discovered a room full of terrariums. Inside each was a spider. Most were brown recluses, but there were several other poisonous species. The CSIs almost had a heart attack when they were processing Cavanaugh's clothes and an enormous black widow crawled out of his pocket," Brody said with a laugh. "They found a broken glass vial too."

Renni shivered.

"Cold, honey?" Maisie asked as she pulled up a blanket folded at the foot of the hospital bed.

Brody noted the expression on Renni's face. "What is it?"

She swallowed, remembering Klete's expression when he told her she'd disappear for good after he made her suffer. "The spider was for me. He wanted to punish me for causing him problems."

Oscar swore long and loud, and Bubber jumped to his feet, hands fisted.

Brody nodded. "According to an entomologist the FBI contacted, most people don't even feel it when a recluse bites, but a black widow is pretty painful."

"Damn," Bubber said. "I wish I could go back and shoot that som-a-bitch again. He deserves it, and a hell of a lot more." Renni smiled her thanks at him, and Maisie slipped her arm around his waist and hugged him.

"And then there were the shoes," Brody said, catching everyone's attention again.

"Shoes?" Luke asked.

"Shoes inside the terrariums. Like for spider houses. All the victims were missing a shoe. Cavanaugh kept them as trophies."

Ed blew out a long breath. "No way this can get any stranger."

Everyone gaped at Brody, waiting for him to toss out some other incredible tidbit.

"That's pretty much it. We found files in Klete's workshop with names, dates, where he picked the women up, and where he left them. That'll help us find the missing victims. Based on the evidence in the barn, there are several more than we were aware of. We'll find them, and give their families closure."

He turned to Renni. "Oh, and your fruit stand guy? He really *is* a champion surfer and a pretty good photographer too. We found thousands of photos in his van once we finally tracked him down in Green River, Utah. He had several of you tacked up on his visor. Guess you made an impression." Brody grinned at her. "We matched his DNA to a file in Hawaii from a bar fight years ago. His real name is Bennett Wilson. He jumped bail to keep from going to jail after the fight and went a little off the reservation. He has some short-term memory problems from the fight and receives disability, and he does some mechanic work for cash. His parents keep track of him through an ATM card. When the money runs low, they add to it. He bums around, staying for a few days or maybe a few months, then turns up somewhere else. Never causes any trouble, so he's not on anyone's radar, and does what he can to keep it that way. He didn't know the statute of limitations expired on the fight charges a long time ago."

They discussed the strange details of the case for a while longer, until Oscar abruptly stood and started shooing everyone out except Brody.

When the room cleared, Brody turned to Renni, his face serious. "You know, you're a real pain in the ass."

She grinned and eyed her butt. "You have no idea."

The charge nurse chased him out an hour later, leaving Renni with a smile on her face and the memory of warm lips.

# Chapter Seventy-Four

**"I** have a bid of one hundred fifty thousand. Remember, folks, the proceeds from this sale are going to scholarships for the victims of violent crimes. It's a hell of a good cause. Can't we get a bit more?"

More paddles popped into the air and the bids continued, raising another twelve thousand. When all was said and done, the Marmon sold for a hundred and sixty-two thousand dollars. The owner, a certain Ed Benson, smiled from ear to ear as he handed over his check.

—

Two days later, a large group assembled in a dusty, oil-tinged parking lot. Renni, surrounded by her friends and family, Buster at her feet, stared up at a massive piece of equipment. Ed handed her a metal control box attached to a long, thick cord.

"Whenever you're ready, honey," he said.

She eyed him. "Are you sure? That's a hell of a lot of money to flush down the drain."

"I ain't gonna let them lunatic fellers who get off owning

stuff from serial killers get their hands on it. Do it."

Renni hit the green button, and the mammoth machine in front of her let out an ear-splitting groan as it closed down on the Marmon, crushing the beautifully restored truck into a colossal lump of metal, wood, and rubber.

She let out a sigh. Klete was dead, Karen in prison for life with no chance of parole. The RMHK victims were all returned to their families. The nightmares had stopped. And she and Brody? Well, they might be starting something.

Brody's phone chirped. He checked the screen and then glanced at Renni, a frown on his face. Before she could ask him if something was wrong, he turned away, phone to ear, and moved to the far side of the dirt lot. His back was stiff, and he nodded repeatedly at whatever he was being told. When he came back to the group several minutes later, he wouldn't meet her eye.

"Can one of you take Renni home? I need to deal with a situation."

She watched him hurry back to his Explorer. Something was going on. Renni had a bad feeling, and this time it had nothing to do with a car.

# Acknowledgements

Very Special Thanks to Wade Blevins with the Cherokee Nation for his insight into my Boogey character, the Booger Ceremony, the masks, and the history behind them. Also, to Cherokee Nation members Melvina Shotpouch, Travis Noland, Lisa Hanlon, and Kelly Jo Martin.

For technical assistance and expertise: Grand Junction Police Sgt. Pete Chapola and Sgt. Doug Norcross, Mesa County Sheriff Deputy Casey Dodson, Jeremiah Casselberry, Eldon Prax, Freddy Bishop, and Jim Carp.

Literary Wanderlust publisher Susan Brooks, and my editor Jennica Dotson – both of whom went above and beyond to make sure this book was the best it could be.

The "original" Ed Benson, for letting me use his name for one of my characters.

And last, but not least, all the dark chocolate I've known and loved while writing. May you rest in peace.

# About the Author

Terri Benson has been creating stories and characters since grade school. Her books always include mystery, history, and a touch of romance. Research is her "rabbit hole" because there's always something new (or old) to explore. She teaches classes on writing at a local Community College, writes humorous articles for magazines and newspapers, and blogs irregularly (that can be taken in more ways than one). She lives in Western Colorado where she writes while trying to keep her Brittany spaniel from batting her hands off the keyboard. When not writing, she works at a Business Incubator helping people start and grow their small businesses, and spends time in the outdoors with her husband and said spaniel. Website: https:// www.terribensonwriter.com/

# Books by Terri Benson

*The Angel and the Demon*
*An Unsinkable Love.*

www.ingramcontent.com/pod-product-compliance
Lightning Source LLC
Chambersburg PA
CBHW030400200726

48286CB00015B/1762